INSTAR

"I was like the beetle with his soft new shell—*instar* I believe it is called. And like the weary vulnerable beetle, I, too, had changed, had molted."

Instar

by RYDER BRADY

Doubleday & Company, Inc., Garden City, New York
1976

Designed by Laurence Alexander

Library of Congress Cataloging in Publication Data

Brady, Ryder.
Instar.

I. Title.
PZ4.B81216In [PS3552.R245] 813'.5'4
ISBN 0-385-11508-3
Library of Congress Catalog Card Number 75–30458

To Cindy, Ellie and Riff

part 1

BEGINNING

Cuttyhunk Island

September 21

Dearest Consuela,

This will bring you up to date.

Dear squid, buckets of viscous, rubbery squid greet me every time I flick on the forty watt bulb in the shed. They seem to stare at me with their membrane-covered, sightless eyes from the mucus of their bodies while I hone my knife and wait for the dawn traffic to begin. I've been cutting bait all summer, ever since Abner Coffin had a stroke and Mrs. Veeder asked me to help out during the season. Cutting bait is about all I can do, now, no strength left for fishing even if I wanted to, no aggressive spirit, no outside interest, everything drained.

Sorry I haven't written you since I left in March. The only writing I have done is in my notebooks—I always have one with me to scribble in while I wait for the florid fishermen to drive up in their tiered Chris-Craft. Philip is right about writing it out. It keeps me occupied, and forces me to think more clearly. The only trouble is that the effort of writing grows tougher every day, like every other thing I do.

I am, in a word, a mess. I'm glad neither of us can see me. Charlie didn't believe in mirrors, but I don't need one to tell me that my hair is long and matted, also much thinner than when I came. My fingers are chewed and red where I have nibbled them away to the quick. I have not shaved or bathed since I left the mainland, and I broke an incisor somewhere around April (my one fall off the "wagon"), which makes me sinister indeed whenever I speak or smile, which is fortunately almost not at all.

It is difficult for me to listen to anyone. Already I am so accustomed to my own company that I find all talk confusing and yes, deafening. Even your nice letters tire me out, like a stand-up cocktail party. That's not really fair, they do bring some comfort, and I am glad there have been no more accidents.

3

Charlie's little house has sheltered me from storms and cold. I fry my fish on his kerosene stove and sleep a little every night (when Waffles lets me) on Charlie's sagging bed. I shit in his toilet with the drippy overhead tank, feed Waffles from Charlie's pie plate, and try to read by the light of his lamp on sleepless nights. Waffles hates me to read, will do anything to keep me from it. Nor does he like me to sleep. I have just packed up my notebooks—you should get them in a few days. Please read them. It's the only way you can possibly understand *what* I have been going through the past year, if not *why*. I don't know *why* this has happened, and happened to me, I may never know, not even if it should stop. I wish I could change that "if" to "when," but I can't, not yet.

If the people (you, for instance), places and events I have written about seem distorted to you, it's because I've recorded them exactly as they seem to me, or, when I can remember, as they seemed to me at the time. You'll agree that I've become pretty distorted myself. I wrote mainly as a kind of therapy, and secondarily for you, Lucy, Omar and yes, if need be, for the children when they are much older.

The story is ugly. The violence, cruelty and perversions shocked me anew as I wrote them down, in fact, they were almost more terrible in retrospect than they had been at the time. Waffles allows me to write, I think because the writings have to do with him, the self-centered mutt.

I am beginning to wonder how long I can go on like this. I have found myself thinking of suicide, and then I remember my father. Just before he died, in a rare lucid moment, he said suicide was the only way out for the coward and the unbeliever. He mixed another martini as he spoke, and then held up his glass, a toast to his own plodding suicide. That is what my father's death was, suicide by alcohol. We both knew it, but I was too frightened then by death and by him to say anything. I wonder now if I had tried to get him to talk to me, could he have warned me or in some way prepared me for all this? Maybe not, maybe we must do it alone. Well, I am doing it, day by day. Just barely. I try to convince myself that I am neither a coward nor an unbeliever. If anything can pull me through it will be faith and a certain vigilance.

That's the trouble, I have begun to doubt my own stamina. Doubt is tantamount to putting Satan's foot in the door. How long can I fight this burgeoning desire to give up? As always I take each day as it comes, one by one by one.

I will stop writing here in my shed with the limp squid and my sharp knife, and wait for the dawn to spread over the Sound. There is a hurricane coming, so I hear. The other ice and bait sheds on the dock are closed tight, and most of the low-lying houses are already boarded up and empty. It makes no difference to me. Boarded up? Evacuated? How can I worry about the weather? My only precaution will be to put these notebooks on what may be the last plane.

Forgive me my long-windedness—it's the first real talking I've done for six months. I love you all dearly, please remember that. My great hope is that some day I will give you another notebook just like all these, but only one, and its title will be END.

Pray for me,
Hugh

5

Gosnold's Bay

The revolving door dumped me into the August heat and bleating traffic. Three-thirty. I unlocked the door of the Subaru and slid my briefcase in, glad to unclench my fingers from its sticky handle. The empty briefcase seemed alien to me without its usual complement of briefs, as alien as the excitement invading my customary dull respectability.

Hark the Herald Angels Shout, No More Days 'til School Gets Out, and here we go, down the blistering expressway. Never mind the fact that it is already prematurely burdened with other eager weekenders, it still points to salt water and Consuela. With any luck, I should be in Gosnold's Bay with her and the children in time for a swim and an early drink. I switched on the radio and heard the top ten with half an ear as I slalomed through the campers, convertibles and boats on trailers.

Why my schoolboy exuberance? After all, it's just another vacation, right? And I don't even like Gosnold's Bay especially. Like so many summer colonies it is expensive, prejudiced and irritatingly dull. Why are the rich so boring? There are, of course, a few exceptions, and Consuela is one. She has spent at least a part of every summer of her life in Gosnold's Bay and will not alter this tradition happily. And so year after year I acquiesce, and we return to stay with nasty Aunt Edith and bland Uncle O, for as short a stay as Consuela will allow.

Visiting Edith-the-Genteel will always be a problem. It's not just the superficial awkwardnesses she puts on me, the constant fear of dirty fingernails or unzipped flies, but the general evil-mindedness beneath her tiresome euphemisms. Her self-righteousness, bigotry and suspicion are carved from New Hampshire granite, and there's no altering them. I find all contact with Aunt Edith unpleasant, and prolonged contact enraging. Consuela claims my intolerance is excessive, and maybe

6

she's right. She also thinks I was against Aunt Edith from the start because of her fondness for and access to Uncle O's money. Uncle O lifted her out of the mill owner's high life of Nashua, N.H., when he married her. Edith wasted no time in learning the ropes of Boston Brahminism. And like Becky Sharp she is facile and quite deadly. Yes, Consuela may be right, Edith put me off instantly because she is rich. Consuela refers to the financial chip on my shoulder as The Great Hugh Murray Money Warp. Consuela is lucky not to have it, too.

Admittedly split on the subject of money, like everyone else, I blame it all on my parents. They were raised in what they thought would be a never ending affluence; I grew up in the rapid depletion of it. Eventually land poor, they one by one sold off our (my) treasures: first twenty acres of Maine waterfront so my brother Omar could go to Exeter, then the Concordia yawl so I could follow him, and finally, when Omar went to Harvard, they sold the house and remaining land in Vinalhaven, gave up the New York apartment and moved to my grandparents' house in the Berkshires. By this time, Pops was drinking so much that his law firm fired him, no more $40,000 a year. With time on his hands he dropped in and out of Ewell-Lowe more often and stayed longer, drying out. I had felt that they had sold my future.

Their financial cancer must have fostered my dread of being rich. As they were consumed by their losses, I am consumed by wanting a great security, and by a fear of having it and losing it. When I found out that Consuela had a whopping trust fund, half of me wanted to run. Consuela could not, does not understand.

She had never thought about money; it had always been there, until with marriage, she took me on and discovered a "have-not" in her midst. Still unruffled, she tried to make her money ours. I said no. She found this ridiculous, could not grasp my dread of being a kept man.

If I had been pulling down an adequate salary as a chic young lawyer perhaps we could have avoided a resolution. But I was hell-bent on pursuing my do-good inclinations and wanted to be a public defender instead. To make this possible and pleasant, Consuela bought, with a fraction of her inheritance, a nice house in Cambridge. Just like that.

I came home from law school one afternoon and Consuela told me she had bought a house on Raymond Street.

"Well, there's no room for a baby here." She waved her arms to describe the obvious and dingy limits of our Porter Square pad. "Since you're so peculiar about my money, consider it *my* house. Someday we'll sell it and move to a bigger one, I mean *I'll* sell it, and with the proceeds buy the next one." Which is exactly what she did four years and two babies later.

Not only did Consuela buy the farm but she decided to work it as well, raising cattle. I attributed this to some strain in her semi-Venezuelan blood. To raise cattle has never been my dream, but this is entirely Consuela's venture. She cannily sold our Cambridge house on a sky-high market and sank the profits with a bit more of her inheritance into Sweetwater Farm in Still River, a whistle-stop outpost of Harvard, Mass. After six years and two more babies, Consuela is turning her venture capital to profit.

She does have some help. Kip and Jenny, leftover flower children, live rent-free and macrobiotically in the small tenant house. In return they help work the farm, Jenny with the children and the house, and Kip in the barn and field. He, unlike me, knows how to sink a new fence post or cajole a cranky tractor, and he somehow keeps in his mind most of the various needs of our household.

Consuela also recruited an old cow-hand at the Topsfield Fair named Will. He rules over all, although his interests seem to be limited to cows and what they eat. He is tolerant of Consuela and the other novices, even, I suspect, glad to have their help from time to time. But his supremacy in the cow barn is unchallenged; those cows are Will's. And I suppose that farm is Consuela's, not ours. She says it's ours.

The Bourne Bridge loomed into view. I lighted a cigarette and began the slow crawl over the hump of the bridge. I was hot and impatient and yet my excitement continued to spread like the sweat stains on my shirt. I wanted to stamp the accelerator to the floor and go, but instead, I was stuck, wedged in the caterpillar of cars inching up and over. "Why do I feel so God damned happy, even exhilarated?" I wondered. "Well, I have been lonely, but is that it?"

Consuela and the children had left me two weeks earlier, and I had missed them more than I had thought I would when I stubbornly refused to join them for the weekend in the middle. At the time, the minuses of seeing Aunt Edith outweighed the pluses of seeing Consuela. Now I thought I had been wrong. Edith may drive me nuts, but she can't be all bad. I must give her some credit, albeit grudgingly, for having raised Consuela. I remembered Aunt Edith's slanted account of the tragedy. Uncle O had told the story better, but then, he is a better person.

Oliver Shaw (Uncle O) and his younger brother Justin (Consuela's father) were heirs at a young age to United Carib, a company that bought coffee, cocoa and sugar cheap in the Caribbean and sold it dear at home. Justin was sent to Venezuela to learn the business in 1936, a week after his graduation from Harvard. When he returned to Boston three years later, he had two new possessions: Elena, his dazzling bride, and Roman Catholicism.

Neither acquisition pleased his family and all the Shaws were conspicuously absent at the christening of Justin and Elena's daughter seven months later. Baptized Consuelo (after her South American grandmother) and Bradford Shaw (after her very North American great-grandfathers, right back to the *Mayflower*), her name did not seem to come easily from pursed lips at the Ritz.

"Really! It reminds me of Pancho Villa!" said one of Aunt Edith's friends, her pheasant feather trembling at the edge of her felt hat as they had lunch before Symphony. "Such a masculine-sounding name, Consuel*o*."

"You are right. Not just foreign, which is bad enough, but *mannish*. Well, *I* shall call her Consuel*a*!" announced Edith. "Although when joined with Bradford Shaw, either Consuela or Consuelo is an aberration!"

When Justin and Elena, agents of the "aberration," were

killed driving home from an excessive dinner party a year later, everyone said, said Edith, "It was to be expected."

In public, Aunt Edith's generous heart seemed to overflow, and she magnanimously agreed to take on "the child." This was not an overwhelming burden as Consuela came with a nanny and a sizable inheritance into an otherwise childless and well-heeled household. I think that Uncle O has been genuinely delighted and even grateful to have had Consuela as a daughter, which compensates in part for his wife's feelings of martyrdom. Poor Uncle O, he is a good man, but limp. I'm sorry he has none of his brother's legendary wits and bravado.

Not until I made the sharp right turn onto the dirt road which leads to the Shaws' driveway did I consciously remember that Aunt Edith and Uncle Oliver had left Gosnold's Bay to do their North Shore duty. How could I have forgotten? Edith's absence for a week had been Consuela's trump card in getting me to come at all. Even stringy Mabel, the help from Nova Scotia, had gone off to a cousin's, and the zealous sense of law and order which glistened in the polish of her kitchen would doubtless be smirched by now. So it really might be a homecoming after all. I let out a sigh of relief and slowed down as I saw the gray gables of the house pushing up through the scrub oak. Ahead of me lay the blue beginning of Gosnold's Bay.

Aunt Edith's beach with its dock and boathouse was the last of five identical sandy crescents collaring the sea just before the harbor entrance finally tamed it. I practiced the names of the owners: Shaw, Edith and Oliver, then Livingston, is it? George et ux., Giannelli, Val and I think Margaret, nice people, then some old lady, forget her name, and last, on the point, the Potters, Philip and Caroline, cream of the crop. The only two families worth remembering, the Giannellis and the Potters were at least handy to Aunt Edith's house.

The smell of little dead fish and rotting kelp, "salt air" to the Chamber of Commerce, blew in my window. It was an old, familiar smell, and nostalgic like the curious mingling odors of chalkdust and sweaty feet in schoolrooms. Unlike the school smell, which triggers the dread of unfinished homework, salt tang brings back old summers when I was young, and thoughts of Cousin Lucy. But I don't think of Lucy any more.

And as if to reprimand me for having done so, the smell of the sea was suddenly overpowered by the heady fragrance of landlocked melons from the back seat. I had picked those melons at eight in the morning from Consuela's garden in Still River. They were warm now, and getting bruised as I bumped down the road. Too bad; I had brought them all this way as a kind of present to Consuela. Or did I really bring them as a gentle reproach, a reminder to her of her true place at home with me?

I turned up the drive and tried to ignore the fading hydrangeas; they looked like clumps of used litmus paper. I twisted my head for a glimpse of the water. There was none. My excitement and hope all at once gave way to tiredness and rage. Rage at the stupidity of anyone living five hundred yards from the sea and willfully hiding it, and tiredness from having put my life in order, as lawyer and bill-paying citizen.

I turned off the ignition and the rabble spilled out of the house, barefoot and sunny, crowding out most of my crossness with their terrific energy and love. Behind them Consuela waited, smooth and brown. She stretched out her arms and gave me a good, hungry look. When I kissed her, I knew I was home.

"I missed you, love," I said, not bothering to brush her hair from my lips.

"I missed you. You look hot and frazzled. Why don't you go for a swim?" Consuela put her dry hand in my moist one and squeezed it, and the boys worried my trousers like puppies, talking very loud all together.

"Yeah, Pa, let's swim."

"I wanna come too."

"I can do a jackknife. You have to watch me."

"Stop it, all of you," ordered Consuela. "Pa's tired and he needs some peace. Now, go away. Go on, go."

"Peace? You have no idea how damn much peace I've had for the past two weeks. Let them come, it's O.K." The three

11

boys shrieked again and danced off to get their suits, shedding belts and shirts on the way. "Where's Rebecca?" I asked.

"Still at the beach."

"Why don't you come too? You're in your bathing suit anyway."

"Oh, sweetheart, I can't swim now." Consuela shook her damp hair. "I have to rinse off the salt, get dressed and feed the children. We're due at the Potters' at seven for dinner. You go. We can have a drink when you get back."

We walked into the gloaming of the house, protected from sunshine by the deep veranda. The living room is large, dark and uncomfortable, paneled in walnut and sparsely furnished with massive ironwood chairs and carved tables from the Philippines. The one sofa is horsehair. Not my idea of a summer cottage. Upstairs, the rooms are at least bright and some have a view of the Bay. The walls are whitewashed and the furniture again minimal, altogether too much like a convent for my taste.

I threw my bag on the bed and unpeeled my shirt. Then I saw Consuela standing in the doorway and I no longer wanted my swim, I wanted her. Just as I began to kiss her again Cam bolted through the door, his blond hair stiff with salt, his scrawny arms and legs tattooed with scratched mosquito bites.

"Oh, come on, Pa, hurry up. We're waiting for you."

"All right, Cam. Just let me say hello to your mother and get changed."

"Yeah, well, don't take all day, that's all." Cam had driven his wedge between Consuela and me most effectively. The moment had passed, and there was no use now in pursuing her, so I grabbed a towel instead.

I felt old and a little foolish walking gingerly down the path ringed by my bright young sons. I looked at my flesh. It reminded me of uncooked veal.

There on the sand lay Rebecca, basted with baby oil which highlighted the new curves of her body. A cacophony of hard rock pulsated from the radio under her long hair. She looked like her pretty mother. My Rebecca, just starting through the labyrinth of adolescence while I, her father, begin to dim. I

12

tried to push away these mystifying truths and blame it all on a hot Friday and a dry throat.

"Hello, Rebecca. Turn down that radio and let me give you a kiss."

"Hi, Pa. Guess what? I have a new friend named Polly Miller, who actually won a cosmic colored T-shirt from WRKO. She's really nice. You look hot. Can I turn on my radio now, please?"

I watched Justin and Ward thrash their way to the raft, where Cam waited. He stood arms akimbo on the diving board.

"I'm the King of the Castle. Come on, Pa."

I dove into the two boys' wake and surfaced, then rolled on my back and blew like a whale. I churned toward the raft, pleased that my muscles could still respond so well to my demand for power. We jackknifed, jumped and splashed and finally came to rest flat down on the raft, heads hanging overboard to watch a trio of pilot fish wink through the green water between the two pontoons.

Rebecca startled us as she popped her sleek seal's head out of the water.

"It's after six. You better go back or Mummy'll be furious." And with this warning she vanished feet last back into the sea as noiselessly as she had appeared.

We stood up reluctantly, wincing at the wind on our wet bellies. The boys moaned and groaned about jumping into the cold water.

"Race you in. Last one home empties the trash." They fell for my old trick, and I fell for theirs and was stupidly generous with the head starts. They were delighted when I lost, and I was momentarily taken aback by their savage enthusiasm. I had never been such a cutthroat; where had they gotten it from?

Consuela was sitting on a rock like a dark Psyche, drying her hair. The boys rushed past her, thumped up the porch and went inside. I slung my towel over the porch railing with theirs, another sodden flag to desecrate Aunt Edith's stark porch in her absence, and I looked back at Consuela. Oh, to take her now, right there on the grass behind the rock. Risky with the children running in and out, but for that, all the more tempting.

And think what Aunt Edith would say if she ever found out! It was really convenient that the telephone rang. Like Pavlov's dog, I hurried inside to answer it, proof that telephones were easier for me to answer than a rare, whimsical urge to screw in the afternoon.

"Why, hello, Aunt Edith. How's Prides?" She told me at length how Prides Crossing and her relatives were. Much the same, I decided.

"Well, it's good of you to call, Aunt Edith. Don't let me keep you, though." But I wasn't keeping her and she was not ready to hang up.

"Yes, dinner with the Potters tonight . . . so I assume Consuela found a baby-sitter. . . . No, I don't know who. Some local nymphet I suppose. Do you want me to find out which one?"

She did. I have a brief shouted conversation.

"Consuela says Francesca and Daisy Giannelli."

"Oh no!"

Then nothing except the sound of her outraged breathing. For me to say anything to her now would be the same as interrupting her, and I could see Edith preparing for one of her orations. She's like a pilot with a checklist before taking off: Adjust bra straps, tug skirt to cover knee cap, suck dental interstices for bits of lodged lunch, moisten lips. While I waited, I tried to stretch the telephone cord to the table with the gin on it but the cord was too short by several yards. Damn. Aunt Edith cleared her throat to signify that all systems were go.

"You there, Aunt Edith?"

"Don't rush me, Hugh. What I am about to tell you is most important. A *disgraceful* thing happened this morning just before we left for Prides."

Another pause.

"Oh really? What?" *Disgraceful* things are always happening to Aunt Edith. I looked at the gin.

"Well, I sent your Uncle O down to the beach to make sure the boys had returned the oars to the boathouse. Children need supervision, you know." Pause. "And so do some adults, it seems!"

But of course, Aunt Edith, the whole world is in need of *your* supervision, I know that. "Mmm?"

"Uncle O did not come right back although I had instructed him to. I must admit that Mabel and I accomplished a great deal while he was out from under our feet, you know how Oliver hangs over me."

I did not know how Oliver hung over Edith; indeed, I find it unlikely that anyone would hang over Edith. I wondered if I could put the receiver on the rug and make a dash for the gin. Would Edith detect that her words fell on the worn oriental instead of my ear?

"Well. After he was gone almost an hour, I went down to fetch him myself." There were no glasses or ice on the tray, just gin. Oh, come on, Edith, you old windbag, get to the point.

"Do you know what I found Oliver doing on the dock?" she asked me.

I suppressed a catalogue of frivolous replies—Uncle O entertaining a dozen Playboy Bunnies, maybe, or Uncle O dancing *La Spectre de la Rose* on the end of the dock? Uncle O jamming with the Rolling Stones?

"What did you find him doing, Aunt Edith?" and will you get to the point so I can get a drink?

"I discovered Oliver with all the children watching the most disgusting spectacle that I have ever seen in Gosnold's Bay!"

"No! Well, what was it?" How Edith loves suspense! While I yearn for gin, she rearranges her breath and for all I know over the phone, probably her underwear.

"They were watching those two Giannelli girls and some man, probably a seaman from the Coast Guard Base, doing dreadful things on the raft."

"Dreadful? What do you mean?"

"They were all *naked,* to begin with." Wow. "And not only that, they were *fondling* each other's *genitals!*"

I didn't point out that that was usually more fun than fondling your own.

"What did you do, Aunt Edith?" Join them?

"Well, I took Oliver-and-the-children home." She ran the words together. "I took them home directly. What could Oliver have been thinking of, to let those children watch?" I had a pretty good idea. "Those children will be scarred for life, mark my words. And I think you are making a very grave mistake if you let those amoral girls baby-sit tonight. I have forbidden the children and Oliver to stay at the beach if they are present. I knew from the beginning it was a mistake to let the Giannellis in to Gosnold's Bay, and now that I have proof, it's too late to do anything about it. But I won't have them corrupting Oliver and the children." Aunt Edith was on the warpath.

"Did you tell Consuela?" I asked her.

"Consuela, as usual, was playing tennis. You tell her."

I said I would and rang off. Edith's words echoed in my head as I sloshed more gin than tonic into a glass. "Fondling each other's genitals"—a peculiar combination of clinical and pulp vocabulary which made the words sound shockingly lewd coming from Aunt Edith's prissy mouth. Or was it because I could see her, smacking her lips as she told me? I continued to ruminate on her dirty mind while I showered, shaved and dressed. Consuela came up from the children's supper. I watched her slide into a dress.

"What else are we doing this weekend? Have you roped me into the Saturday clot of cocktail parties?" I asked, fumbling with the tiny hook at the back of her neck.

"No. I left tomorrow night open. Val Giannelli is arriving tonight. Maybe he and Margaret could come to dinner."

"Good idea. What else is happening?"

"Sunday is free, except for Mass. We might play some tennis if you want to." Consuela stopped and took a breath. "Also, I guess I should remind you, tomorrow is Race Day."

"Oh, shit."

"I know you hate it, but all the children are swimming. You've got to come, they're counting on you."

I didn't reply or even look at her, but just kept on buckling my Dr. Scholl sandal, silently cursing Race Day—the highspot of the summer in Gosnold's Bay. It is remembered and anticipated for twelve months. Brother is pitted against brother, neighbor against neighbor. Parents, flushed with pride or disappointment and certainly with warmish vodka, steer their children to the starting gun and possible victory. The children wait on the dock, shivering and tense, their sunburned faces so drained by nerves that not even their peeling noses are distinguishable. All for a blue satin ribbon stamped with gold letters.

"Dammit, Hugh. I know how you feel. But it's *harmless*."

And so Consuela opened up one of our annual disagreements.

"It isn't harmless, it's corrupt. It's also a waste of time and you know it. . . . I'll go. . . . Christ!"

"You make me sound like the common scold."

"Nit wit. Of course you're not a scold. And definitely not common." We laughed and I sat on the bed, watching her at her dressing table, putting on the final touches. "I just don't want to spend a week of my vacation, or for that matter any of my vacation, totally removed from you and the children listening to a lot of drivel. Why should I have to put up with all those rich mealymouths?"

"You don't, you don't." Consuela had on her soothing voice. "I trust you are not including the Potters? It's not a waste of time to see them, is it?"

"Of course not, you know that. They're only rich, not a bit mealymouthed." I thought of Philip and Caroline Potter then, and was grateful that they had been surrogate parents to Consuela.

Philip had been her father's closest friend from their freshman year at Harvard until Justin's death. They had shared many things besides college rooms and large allowances, perhaps the most important was their infectious enjoyment of life. Philip once told me about their escapades together, and about how both of them had been almost driven to use up their lives. Philip's words in fact had been "to eat the whole thing," an unattractive cliché but somehow applicable.

Philip and Justin had gone to Venezuela together, wooed Elena together, and when it was clear that Justin was the victor, Philip had returned to New York to bury his father and manage the family monies. On a trip to Scotland with his mother, Philip had met Caroline and married her.

She is extraordinary too. I think she has secretly pledged her life to the well-being of other people. Her ministrations and concern are so subtle as to seem almost unconscious, like a practiced Jesus Prayer. When I am with her I am only aware of her tenuous beauty and quiet acumen, while in retrospect I realize how truly comfortable she has made me.

"Well, let's go or we'll be late." Consuela gave her hair a last brush and we went down to the kitchen and the children.

The Giannelli girls had arrived, two solid blue-jeaned pillars topped with Andrea del Sarto heads, their passive Renaissance faces only barely visible within a tangle of dun-colored curls. Common pleasantries fell like stones on these two, a prickly reminder to me of how smug adolescents could be, and I gave up trying to talk with them and turned instead to the children. Sticky, gusty kisses were washed down with the last of my gin, while Consuela communicated emergency numbers and specific bedtimes to the unresponding Giannellis with an ease and grace I wish were mine.

We walked up the lawn and through the garish garden. Aunt Edith has the indoor gardener's love of artificial-looking waxy plants. In Chestnut Hill she raises african violets; in Gosnold's Bay it's tuberous begonias and dahlias, with a few giant marigolds thrown in, maybe for smell? I remembered my telephone conversation with her.

"You won't believe what Aunt Edith said to me on the phone," I said. "She called while you were drying your hair."

"Oh, is that who it was? Do I really want to hear what she said, Hugh?" I looked at Consuela and felt mildly sorry for her. I wondered if she was in fact affected by the tirades she listens to with such composure. Not only is Consuela my sounding board, but also the children's, Edith's and almost everyone's who needs her to listen. She's an excellent listener. When I finished relating Aunt Edith's lascivious gossip, I was surprised to see concern twist Consuela's eyebrows. She didn't find my story funny, in spite of my efforts to tell it that way.

"What's wrong?" I asked. "You're not taking this

seriously, are you?" Aunt Edith is so awful that she has had to become a joke whenever possible. I couldn't believe that Consuela would suddenly be hurt by yet another jab at dreadful Edith.

"I don't know. Poor Uncle O." Consuela looked downcast. "I bet he paid for his minute of pleasure, probably one of very few he's had since he married Edith. I hope he had fun as a bachelor, because I am sure he's never had any with his wife. I wonder if she's ever let him in her bed? I doubt it." Consuela came on strong and bitter.

"Don't be absurd, love. Even old Edith was young once. For all we know, she might have been a real sex pot."

"Aunt Edith?" Consuela was incredulous. "Listen, if she was a sex pot, it wasn't with Uncle O . . . she hates him . . . just like she hates all men." Consuela was groping and halting in a most uncharacteristic way.

"What are you saying? That she's a Lesbian?"

"I didn't say it, you did." She snapped at me. "But I guess that is more or less what I'm saying, yes. A repressed Lesbian." Consuela looked as if she wanted to spit after saying such an unfamiliar and to her clearly ugly word.

"Whatever makes you say that? She's just a bourgeois prude, that's all."

"So I used to think. But anyone that prudish must have some horrendous sex hang-up, don't you think?"

"What rot, Consuela. Edith may have 'hang-ups' as you call them, but she certainly isn't an archetypal bull-dyke."

"Well, she has castrated Uncle O, hasn't she?"

"O.K., O.K., but that doesn't mean she's a Les." I tried not to sound combative but did anyway. Consuela was getting very worked up but she wasn't giving me any reasons why, and I began to think that we should end the conversation.

"Dammit, she may not be obvious to you, but she is to me. She's done some weird and pretty nasty things." I could feel Consuela sucking me in again.

"Look, do you want to tell me about it or not?" I asked her.

"The question is, do you want to listen?" I wasn't at all

sure I did, but I had never seen Consuela like this before and thought I'd better hear her out.

"Yes, I want to hear."

"Well then, I'll try to tell you. I've wanted to for a long time, but I don't know how to begin." Consuela started and stopped, stopped and started.

"Go on. You haven't said anything yet."

"No. Well. It's hard, God dammit. It started the night before we were married. She came into my room in the middle of the night." Consuela was finally letting go and her words came whipping out, clipped and hard. "I was asleep. I remember I had taken a Miltown. When I heard her crying I half woke up. There she was, standing next to my bed in her nightgown, tears streaming down her wrinkly face. I was scared, thought something awful had happened. I sat up and took her arm. That was when she grabbed me. She pushed her pug-dog face right into mine and . . . oh, God, it was foul . . . she kissed me. Not a normal kiss. It was her tongue, probing around my mouth. Prod, prod. I felt like throwing up when her frantic hard little tongue was in there. It still makes me feel sick."

Consuela's renewed horror was as startling to me as her words. I tried to interject a few murmurings of comfort, but she kept on talking and drowned me out. She didn't need my help, just my ear.

"The worst part was that her mouth tasted like Lavoris. Do you see what that means? At three in the morning her mouth tasted like Lavoris! She had gotten out of bed and deliberately cleaned her mouth before coming into my room. Like a bride, scented and bathed. I find that truly perverted." She stopped abruptly and didn't meet my eyes.

"Why didn't you tell me this before?" I regretted the accusing tone of my question, but Consuela didn't seem to notice it.

"It didn't have anything to do with you. And I felt too guilty. Maybe Aunt Edith was only being affectionate, not perverted. My dirty mind, not hers."

Consuela turned her face away and I let her silence hold us, not certain whether I should fill it up with empty words, sensing that she hadn't quite finished. Then she started again.

20

"But I still feel she violated me. I felt it every time she watched Rebecca as a baby in the tub or on the changing table. She used to slaver over that baby; she never looked at the boys with anything but disgust. Does that sound absurd? Who's crazy, Aunt Edith or me?" Consuela's customary composure still held, but only by a thread.

"Don't be silly, you're all right. I just wish you'd said something sooner." Now it was my turn to look away, chastened by how little effort I had made to really know this creature with whom I share bed and body. "Haven't you told anyone?"

"I tried talking to a priest. Drove all the way to Boston to the Paulist Fathers."

"Boston? Why didn't you just go to Father Healy?"

"Well, he's deaf, for one thing. And besides, he would have recognized my voice." Consuela was embarrassed.

"Haven't you heard of the anonymity of the confessional?"

"Listen, I didn't want to go to Father Healy, O.K.?" Annoyance crept into her voice and I retreated. "The Paulist father wasn't any good, either. He didn't have any idea what was bothering me. He just gave me a summary absolution and sent me out. Fat lot of good it did, I felt guilty before I left the church. And still do."

"Why didn't you tell me?"

Consuela shrugged. "I guess I thought I could cope by myself."

"Well, that was dumb. You shouldn't have bottled it up. No wonder you feel guilty." I tried to shift my position in this discussion. "Look, Lesbianism isn't so terrible. Everyone ought to deal with homosexuality some time. It's when you don't that everything gets messy."

"You sound like a lawyer, distant and fair." Consuela seemed to reproach me. "Don't you see that Aunt Edith *isn't* dealing with it? And so her poison spreads, and I begin to think she's evil."

"Now you're going too far. She's a stupid woman, but not evil, Consuela. Full of self-deceit, yes, but that threatens only herself." The sun was sinking and I was thirsty.

"But it's the same thing; self-deceit *is* an evil." No music in Consuela's voice now, even her face had taken on a new sharpness which I didn't like, and my pity and concern turned to edgy impatience.

"Jesus Christ! If bitchy old Edith wants to lie to herself, let her. Why in God's name should *we* worry? If she started feeling up Rebecca, well, then it would be different. But you really can't believe she'd do that! I don't give a shit about her repressed urges, and I don't want to talk about them any more." I regretted my patronizing tone even while the words were still coming out of my mouth. Consuela dropped her composure and control for the first time since I had known her, and she pounced.

"You selfish bastard, how can you say that? Aunt Edith brought me up. I may not like her but I do care what happens to her. I guess you don't. I wonder if you've ever really cared about anyone, or anything for that matter, that didn't directly affect you!" Consuela was suddenly inexplicably open. She uncovered a bitterness that I had never suspected, and I felt unsure of her and of myself. I tried to hide my doubts with anger.

"What are you saying? Of course I care about other people. Why the hell else would I be a public defender? For the money? The glory?"

"Maybe to prove your nobility? To earn your own salvation? You're pretty concerned with that, aren't you? Hugh Murray's immortal soul! What about Aunt Edith's? She has a soul too, you know. Do you care about hers?"

"Consuela, stop it!"

"Well, do you?" she interrupted. "You complain about *me* and *my* 'comfortable mediocrity,' while *you* pretend to strive for a Christ-like excellence. And you don't give one good God damn about anyone else. So what if Edith is drowning, or whatever, I suppose that's *her* problem?"

I was perilously close to being beaten at my own game. Clever Consuela! Vicious Consuela?

"Will you shut up? For a minute?" I tried to recoup my losses. "I tried to help you. You forget, this whole thing started out as your problem, not Aunt Edith's. Then you turn everything around and launch a theological attack on *me!* Get a hold on yourself. Get some proportion."

Consuela didn't answer me. She just walked faster, ahead of me. I saw her square her shoulders and knew without seeing her face that she had closed herself up again. And I was relieved that I wouldn't have to deal with her stripped down like that. With my relief came also an ugly realization that I didn't like her bare honesty. It had made me feel weak and ineffectual. Consuela's superb self-control in a way controlled me. I had respected her intelligence and sure-footedness all along, but I certainly hadn't been aware of the power which lay behind them. I had been cheated, or, looking at it another way, had gotten more than I had bargained for. There wasn't time to sort it out, and I hurried to catch up with her.

"It's Friday night. My vacation is just beginning—and badly." I took her hand. "I adore you, Consuela. I'm sorry if I was awful but I'm worn. Come on, let's take the shortcut. It's quarter past seven and we both need a drink."

She apologized for her outburst and in reply I helped her over the Potters' stone wall. We skirted the blackberry bramble and cut through the clothesyard to the kitchen door.

Peaches were poaching on the back of the stove, and the kitchen smelled of cloves and ginger cookies. Consuela looked up at me as I pushed open the swinging door into the pantry and we stood in the doorway for a second, both of us back together again and on solid, friendly soil.

Philip Potter's laugh sounded from the top floor and bounced off the stone wall of the tower which held the spiral stairs. We followed his laugh up to the third floor, where Caroline and Philip and the martinis were waiting for us in the "big room."

The Potters' house always reminds me of Noah's Ark resting on Mount Ararat. It stands high and unprotected on the knoll at the very end of Gosnold's Neck, almost entirely surrounded by water. Built by Philip's grandfather a hundred years ago, the house has withstood hurricanes and winter storms despite its vulnerable position. Inside there is a womblike safety, especially on the top floor. The "big room" is just that; a huge rectangle straight up from each of the four cornerstones, with a bulge on one side for the tower. Two great stone fireplaces stand at either end, and the long walls are lined with casement windows opening on two narrow porches. The thick ceiling beams arch like the inverted ribs of a boat. Embraced in this sure shelter, the Potters expend their considerable talents to make it comfortable and comforting to others.

Philip and Caroline control their leisure time and fiercely defend their privacy. They do not run with the pack from investment offices in Boston or New York to the endless cocktail party circuit of Gosnold's Bay. Philip's father had been a successful broker and sachem of Gosnold's Bay society. In fact, leader of the pack. But Philip was aloof. The pack likes followers, not individuals, and was naturally delighted to spit back at Philip and mock him when he abandoned bluechip stocks at the age of thirty-one to enter Columbia Medical School.

Philip and Caroline had one son, Ward, for whom our youngest is named. Ward Potter was a normal, robust baby until he was found dead in his crib. Philip was numbed by the casual shrug of "just another crib death—cause unknown" from the pediatrician and decided to become a doctor. He carries his black bag throughout Manhattan on house calls, and when he comes to Gosnold's Bay to rest, the pack shows no respect. He is called night and day to their beds, and having restored their bodies as best he can, they in return go on making him the butt of their shallow humor. It irks me, but he is more tolerant.

"Hugh! Consuela! How happy Philip and I are that you both could come!" Caroline rustled out of her chair and came to us, formal yet warm.

"Caroline, I'm sorry we're late. I hope we haven't kept you waiting?"

Consuela's charm and confidence, born, I suspect, of an untroubled life of beauty, brains and financial stability, filled me again with admiration. And, I suppose, with envy.

Still churning from her grotesque revelations of the real

Aunt Edith, I tried to change gears. Philip, to my rescue, shook hands as if he meant it and handed me a martini.

"Well, Hugh. You look as if you needed this vacation. How is the public defending going? You restoring burglars to their friends and their relations?"

"Off and on. I'm now working with the juvenile court, too. It gets pretty tough when you manage two acquittals for some promising kid and then he turns up a few months later on a third offense. I begin to feel it isn't people I'm defending, but society I'm bucking, and not very effectively."

"You're right, of course. Our civilization seems to be unhealthy to the point of decay. I had an interesting thought over the backgammon board last night. Backgammon, tennis and so forth are essentially blood sports, very popular in an excessively bloodless period. We slay no dragons, Hugh; the Winchester does not stand by the kitchen door against Indian attack. We wheedle and finagle on paper and phone, an anemic substitute for actual confrontation. Men are violent creatures, eager to display their courage and prove their honor. Almost impossible today, so we make our own situations, form gangs for neighborhood supremacy, steal cars for kicks, trip out on drugs. Or we play more refined games, like backgammon, and drink our whiskey often and neat."

Philip had retained his collegiate gusto and revitalized it to keep step with his own dedicated march. Typically, he introduced a new element to my dreary muddle, my futile sortings out of today's mess, tomorrow's despair.

Riding on the crest of my second martini, I found my thoughts zeroing in with a fine accuracy, and my spirits rose again. Dinner was announced and we circled down the stairs to the dining room to meet our trembling hummocks of consommé. Caroline inquired after my young clients with a dual sympathy for them and me. She noticed right away my exhaustion and frustration, and again I was amazed by her intuition.

"Hugh, why don't you and Consuela take the *Melande* next week and cruise? Philip is returning to New York on Monday for the week so we shan't be using her. You should have a change." Caroline looked down the table for confirmation. "Philip, don't you agree?"

"A splendid idea! Yes, take the boat and enjoy yourselves. The cabin key hangs in the telephone closet. Consuela, you remember where it is. Just come and take it." Consuela watched me, waiting for my ready acceptance.

"Thank you, Caroline, Philip. A kinder offer was never made. And I appreciate your recognition of the 'damp, drizzly November in my soul.'"

Philip liked that.

"Yes, Hugh. Melville knew what it was all about. Good! So you'll take her." My turn to look at Consuela. She nodded and spoke.

"We'd love to take her, Philip, but I'm afraid you're suggesting it because you know that our charter fell through for next week. It's just like you two to save our vacation."

"Don't be silly, Consuela. An unused boat speaks ill of her owners, something we certainly don't want," answered Philip as he fussed with his zucchini.

Conversation turned and turned again, until we rose, nourished several ways, and repaired to the little sitting room downstairs for coffee, enjoying the effortless intimacy which should follow true bread-breaking. The ladies dozed over their Cointreau, while Philip and I breathed in great sniffs of Remy-Martin, then rolled it slowly down, and discussed real and imagined pain. Is imagined pain any the less painful than actual pain? Impossible to conclude, intricate to discuss, we followed each other's threads over and under until the pauses stretched and yawned back at us and it was time to go.

"A beautiful night. There's Rigel. Happy sailing, Hugh. The oars are in the Giannellis' boathouse; the dinghy's at their dock. I wish I could come with you."

"Likewise, Philip. Good night, and thank you."

We walked home, close together in the soft sea air, Consuela's warmth against my side added to my reflective savorings of recent pleasures—my swim with the children, dinner, the promises of a boat and love. The rumble of our bad-tempered scene died away, no room for that now. The garden smelled good as we passed through, headed for the cheer of the lighted kitchen.

The Giannelli girls were sitting at the kitchen table portentously sorting nuts and seeds and unrecognizable dried things. They glanced up at us and woodenly prepared to go, quite oblivious to our blatant good humor. Consuela was settling accounts with them when the telephone rang. It was Margaret, their mother, asking if they had left yet.

"No, Margaret. I'm just about to walk them home."

"Oh, thanks, Hugh. I just wanted to make sure that if they walked back alone they went along the shore. The screaming has started again and it makes me uneasy. I'm glad you'll escort them."

"Screaming . . . ?"

"You don't know? Well, don't worry about it. I'll explain when you get here."

"O.K., we'll be right over. I can hardly wait to hear." I returned the receiver to its cradle. Screaming? What could Margaret mean? And on such a peaceful night. I went to corral the girls.

"Ready, ladies?" Off we went down the path to the beach, me singing, foolish with booze, "Francesca da Rimini, nimini pimini da da da da, dada." Anything to lighten the leaden silence of these two.

"You must be in school somewhere?" I asked them.

"Not really." Thank you, Ms. Giannelli. Now what?

"Oh?" I tried again. "Why not?" I was inexplicably hellbent on making contact if only by forcing them to reply.

"We spend our winters in England at Summerhill."

"A. S. Neill's place?" Light and sure of foot, I led them over the riprap to the Livingstons' beach, pleased as punch that I had picked up the ball on Summerhill. A point for middle age. "What do you think of it?"

"We don't think of it, we are it."

Silence. Scratch the point; middle age stinks, but I will make one last effort.

"Isn't Summerhill allegedly a school?" Fine, hardly even

an edge on the voice, except for the "allegedly," which they probably missed.

"Summerhill is a *community*." That wrapped up that one. Funny, how one's expertise in dealing with fifteen-year-old car thieves turns to dust when applied to the overfed and overprivileged one per cent.

I conceded and stood aside to let Francesca and Daisy guide me up the uncleared path from the beach to their house, two amazons in the moonlight, a beaten Dionysian victim in tow. When we saw the deck house shining through the pines, I wanted to sprint past them to conversation and equality with their mother. But I stayed behind, stuck in the mud of the establishment.

"Margaret!" At last. Did anyone notice my brandied sigh of relief? Margaret, calm and intelligent, welcomed us and took me to Val's small study, away from the girls and the electronic noise of the Grateful Dead.

"Tell me all about this screaming. Are you sure you're not just getting the horrors, living in a female dormitory?"

"Would you like a drink?" she offered.

The Giannellis, as Aunt Edith is wont to remind everyone, are of Latin blood and are newcomers to Gosnold's Bay. Consuela and I like our loaves leavened, and so were delighted when they bought the old Richards place, a monumental turreted horror of pink stucco. The Giannellis tore it down and planted herbs in the sunny shelter of the old foundation. They spent their first two summers in a camper, with sundry tents strewn about on the untended lawn.

"Like gypsies! I never in a thousand years dreamed we would be living in a *trailer park*. How do they *bathe*? Disgusting and unsanitary!" Aunt Edith had it in for them from the beginning, to no one's surprise, and hasn't altered her abuse during her six years' proximity to slum alley.

"Thanks, I'd love a drink. Here, let me make it. I really shouldn't have any more but Consuela will drag me off to Race Day tomorrow morning and I may as well go with a hangover. Now, what is going on?"

"For the past three years, in fact ever since George Living-

28

ston opened his mother's house next door, we've heard a man screaming in the night. It seems to come from the bushes on the boundary, quite close to our house.

"The first time it happened I was alone with the girls. We'd gone to bed about ten. A little after midnight, I woke to horrible screams, a man's screams, somehow more terrifying than a woman's. Under the screams I heard dull thuds, like someone beating something, and there seemed to be an animal whimpering nearby. The man's voice rose above the other sounds." Margaret paused to sip her Bourbon.

"I hadn't met George or his wife yet, but I knew he had just arrived and his lights were still on. I was uneasy and wanted to alert someone, anyone, so I rang him up. He answered immediately and was very kind and apologetic. He said he knew all about it and that 'the situation was under control,' but he offered no explanation. I didn't want to press him with questions then, and something in his manner warned me not to pursue it at all.

"He did say to please call him anytime we were bothered again and he would take care of it. We hear it often, always the same noises, always from the same spot. We call him, from time to time, and the screaming always stops right away. We're so used to it now that I rarely bother him about it; it's just a part of our lives. But I don't like the girls loose when it's going on."

"Do Edith and Oliver know about this?"

"I don't know. We don't see much of them."

"I can imagine."

Margaret made a face.

"So who do you think the screamer is?" I asked.

"How should I know?" She downed the rest of her drink. "You think maybe they're hiding a toadlike uncle in the attic? Or maybe it's a weird gardener. For all I know Miss Havisham lives in the barn!" Margaret giggled nervously and got up. "Drink?"

"Thanks, just a little. What about George? Maybe it's him?"

"George?" Margaret stared in disbelief. "Oh really, Hugh,

you've met him! Do you think he looks like the type who would prowl around the bushes, screaming uncontrollably in the dead of night?"

Margaret was right; it was ridiculous. George Livingston in his alligator shirt and yellow baggy pants, sockless pink feet in polished penny loafers, crying out in agony and clipping coupons or sinking putts eight hours later?

"Besides," Margaret continued, "if George is in the bushes carrying on, how can he answer the phone?" Good point.

"I'd like to hear this screaming," I said. "We took your advice and walked over here along the shore. Never heard a thing. If I go home the inland route across the lawn maybe I'll hear him. Is it all right to trespass through the Livingstons'?"

"Oh yes, they're very friendly. But I don't think you'll hear anything now. He stopped just after I rang you up, and once he stops, he usually doesn't go at it again for a day or two. Do you want me to call you up the next time I hear him?"

"Would you? I don't know why I'm so fascinated. It's just that screaming in the night . . ." Deep breath. "It's not Gosnold's Bay. Well, I must go." I stretched and got up.

"Glad you came over," Margaret said as we walked to the door.

"Oh, I almost forgot. Consuela said something about you and Val coming to dinner tomorrow. She'll call you about it. We'd love to see you both. Good night."

I nudged my way between the rhododendrons and the cinder block underpinnings of the Giannellis' house until I spied an opening in the bushes and crossed the border to the Livingstons' property. Cosmetically perfect, the lawns swept wide to the beach, swallowing humps and bumps put there, no doubt, by landscape architects. A ponderosa pine, uncommon to Cape Cod, showed off its contortions in the moonlight, the only faintly sinister object on an otherwise tranquil set. No unnatural noises, no nervous east winds or scudding clouds, clearly poor timing for a scream-monger. Instead of making for home across the grass, I veered down to the water and the *Melande,* who halfheartedly tugged at her mooring. Her clean Herreshoff lines did not betray her conversion from a racing S Boat to an adequate boat for two to cruise aboard.

Where will we be on Monday night? Cuttyhunk Harbor? Menemsha Pond? As I remembered safe harbors, riding lights winked back at me, small and secure as they stood vigil on the visiting boats anchored in the yacht basin beyond.

I took off my sandals, eager to leave the land, the California pine, the night screams. My feet, unused to nakedness, hit the sand; its lingering warmth was a jolt to my memory. I stripped down and jumped into the water, delighted as it rolled like mercury off my private, coddled skin in great shining sheets of phosphorescence. I illuminated the depths with my friction, feeling the night weight of water settle above me while it continued to support me from below. I needed air and stood up, shaking sparks from my hair, to leave that festival of lights for Consuela.

Cold now, and less drunk, I hurried up the path to Edith's bastion of sobriety, where hall lights pointed the way to stairs and bathrooms. Justin's door was open to let the light in and keep the monsters out, and I paused to look at him, sleeping with the same purposefulness he applies to all the business of living. One sturdy brown leg hung out of a wrinkled pajama and I touched it. He flipped his head over and sighed. I kissed his damp, sweet cheek.

Consuela was asleep too, but unlike her son she was neatly settled like an undertaker's arrangement. I let my sandy clothes litter the seersucker spread on my bed; shirt sleeves and trouser legs spilled over its narrow width. I shut the door and in the dark I crossed the scatter-rug alley between our matching white iron beds to squeeze in beside her, blood quickening under my chilly skin.

She tilted toward me, and murmured sleepily of summer colds and chunks of ice, but soon she gave in to wordless love. The perils of our stingy, virginal cot added to our suspense, and the tired bedsprings grudgingly joined in and jostled to our beat. Spent at last, we slept as we were, heedless to the probability of numb arms and prodding elbows.

Not so many hours later, we lay in the morning sun,

31

weakly trying to block out the strident singsong of taunts rising from the kitchen. A persecuted screech sailed up from little Ward. He is our runt and true to type much picked on by his elders and babied by them, too.

For one suspended second we lay there listening and alert to the pandemonium below. We each waited for the other to do something about it. I lasted longer.

"Oh shit, why can't they ever leave him alone?" Consuela sighed and disentangled herself from me, leaving a gap by my side. Cross and desirable, she went to the door.

"You boys cut that out and, Ward, why don't you come up here?"

She sat down on the bed and removed my hands from her shoulders. "Well, I guess *you're* not getting up."

Ward skittered in not certain which to expect, a lecture or a hug. Consuela picked him up and dropped him on top of me with a quick kiss and left us. Ward scuffled over me like a small burrowing creature, poking and pushing me to life. My head hurt horribly and I remembered my conversation with Philip the night before. Are hangovers real? You bet, self-inflicted but as real as a splinter.

Time to get up, you win, Ward. I pulled on some shorts and carefully made my way downstairs, Ward's small hand in mine as tough and bony as a sparrow. We crunched across the corn flakes on the floor, on Mabel's floor, and for once the disorder of children made me glad. Consuela handed me a mug of coffee and sat down with the cereal boxes and me. I drank my coffee with a shiver and a thick tongue, not paying much attention to the children's incessant talk until I heard someone say Race Day.

Race Day? Aargh, not today. But yes, today. Within an hour I must turn respectable and face all those dreary people. I ran my hand over the stubble on my face.

"Polly Miller said I could go with her in the Boston Whaler. Can I, Mummy?" asked Rebecca.

"Yes, you may. What time are they leaving?" Sometimes I don't know how Consuela can operate so efficiently, especially before she's had time to wake up. She and the children made plans. I drank my coffee.

"We've decided to row to the inner harbor."

"Huh?"

"Come on, Hugh, it's already ten past nine. The first race starts at ten."

I tried to mobilize the boys while Consuela made a stab at cleaning up the mess in the kitchen.

"Aren't you going to shave?" she asked.

"No. You afraid I'll shock your tacky friends?"

"I really don't care if you do. They'll survive."

"I'm sure they will, the question is, will I? Anyway, a beard at noon is a vacation luxury and I intend to enjoy it." I went off to stuff two cans of beer in the ditty bag, under the towels, and sent the boys down to the boat to get the oars ready and to get rid of the constant chatter. Consuela and I started down the path.

"Who is this Polly Miller with the Boston Whaler anyway?" I asked Consuela. "I've never heard of her before."

"Don't you remember?" Consuela was typically incredulous that I did not carry family trees as part of my workaday machinery. "Helen Livingston has three Miller children by a former marriage, two older boys and Polly. The boys spend their summers with Papa in Colorado, and Polly used to go to camp. But this summer she's here. Rebecca has seen quite a bit of her."

"Hmm. What's she like?"

"Oh, I don't know. I guess she's all right. A bit common maybe. It could be her age. She's thirteen and much more developed than Rebecca, and more savvy, too, if you know what I mean."

"I'm not sure I want to. You don't sound very enthusiastic." And I knew I sounded overprotective. I would rather have had Rebecca come with us, but I wasn't clear as to the reasons. I couldn't be jealous of Polly what's-her-name.

"Don't be stuffy. After all, we can't insulate Rebecca forever from the vast middle class." My head throbbed a little louder, but I said nothing.

"I haven't had a chance to ask you how everything is at the farm. Are Kip and Jenny managing without me?"

"Everything is just fine," I told Consuela. "Sometimes I think we're superfluous, discounting the checkbook, of course."

"That's the way I tried to set it up," she agreed. "Is Jen doing my garden?" And then I remembered the melons, still in the car.

"She's been out picking and weeding. I brought you some melons and tomatoes and other stuff I picked on the way to work yesterday, but I forgot to bring them in. They're doubtless baked by now. Sorry."

"Don't worry about it." Consuela laughed at my negligence. "Uncle O has a good vegetable plot this year. Poor Hugh, you were nice to pick before work." This last reduced me to another Cam or Justin, and I felt stupid.

We reached the end of the dock and Consuela jumped lightly into the bow of the old wooden skiff, balancing the weight of the three boys astern. I tossed her the painter and landed noisily amidships. The oars were in the oarlocks and out we went. A typical heavy August morning, the sun burned yellow through the haze and the heavy air seemed to press and flatten the metallic water. Snarls of seaweed lay scattered on the surface, and occasional cans and bottles, motionless detritus, were disturbed by our ripples as we passed. We drew closer to the gathering crowd on the Yard Arm Pier. The high-pitched social babble swelled and I set each oar stroke with a grim resignation.

The Ascusset Yacht Club, gold-plated sponsor of this affair, is so chic it does not even have a clubhouse. Quite unlike the newer yacht clubs which dot the coast of the United States and cater to the fiberglass weekend sailor, Ascusset eschews all material manifestations. It exists in name and members only, the ultimate in conservative good taste. The annual meeting is held in the largest available house; the annual dance at the Gosnold's Bay Golf (not Country) Club; Race Day at the dock of the only hotel, the Yard Arm, a crumbling firetrap and practically a club in itself.

The boys became restive, wiggling to wave and shout to

their friends. The inner harbor was crowded with boats, and several had been lashed together to clear the water between the float and the dock. Four vacant moorings waited there as if in quarantine, until this miserable racing stopped and life resumed as usual. Cam and Justin were unable to tolerate my slow progress and dove in, racing us to the dock.

"This water is foul, how can they stand it?" I stopped to let the boys cross my bow and turned in disgust from the thick, tepid mess, a summer's waste to be finally flushed by autumn tides and storms. We bumped a passage through the tangle of dinghies tied to the float, where Justin and Cam jumped with their cronies, wet bare feet leaving patterns on the tastefully weathered wood. Ward stuck fast to Consuela as we exchanged meaningless pleasantries with the pack. I saw that Rebecca had arrived in the Livingstons' Whaler, which they parked just like any other suburban vehicle: George pocketed the keys in his knee-length madras shorts; Helen, tinted hair aglow, staggered up the ramp in her slippery-soled leather flats. I decided to greet them, to Consuela's surprise.

"After all, they *are* neighbors. Are you coming?" She turned to follow me when her old school chums, Dorcas and Piper, intercepted.

I went on alone to reacquaint myself with the Livingstons. Poor George. It was clear he could not place me, though he wore an affable look and extended his plump, hairy hand. I introduced myself. "Hugh Murray, Consuela's husband from next door. It's good to see you again." I shook his hand and turned to his wife. She fidgeted. George guided her towards me. "Glad you came over," he said. "We don't see much of you. You remember Hugh, don't you, Helen?" She probably didn't, but pretended she did.

"Why, of course. And we've enjoyed Rebecca so much. The perfect playmate for Polly." Helen stopped her nervous staccato gushing and waited uncomfortably for someone to take over. She spun a big flashy diamond around her finger and looked everywhere except directly at me. Then she fished in her straw handbag for some sunglasses to hide behind.

George, meanwhile, was spreading geniality across the

dock, backing and filling like a balloon man at the circus, while Helen and I stood frozen on the fringe of the crowd. I all at once realized that we were, Helen and I, pariahs. Helen involuntarily, shunned for her brassy taste and Texas breeding; while my ostracism was more of my own making. I decided to stick with her for a while. She, unlike the others, at least retained some individuality and might tell me something I didn't already know. In this I was disappointed, for she mainly confided in short bursts her bewilderment at the unfriendliness displayed by "the folks around here."

"Now, you take George. One of a kind in these parts. Outgoing and warm. Back home everyone's like that." Helen sighed.

I sighed and squinted at the sun to get away from her sunglass stare, not knowing what she was really looking at.

"Well, some people call it 'Yankee reserve,' but you mustn't let it get you down," I reassured her. "We're not all like that." Big phony smile. Too bad Consuela missed that one; she really would have enjoyed seeing me as social arbiter.

"You and George been doing much fishing lately?" Helen's drooping face perked up and I was grateful to have surprisingly remembered her passion for "landing the big ones."

"Why, yes. Two grand swordfish yesterday. Over two hundred pounds of steaks. Waiting in the kitchen. I'd surely like to share it. With you. Stop by later. Please." Helen, you are boring, simpleminded, generous. You have a surfeit of swordfish and are afraid to yield to your munificent instincts and give it away. Does the entrenched local hierarchy scare you? Are you afraid they'll refuse your kind offer with chilly sneers? O.K. Helen, I'm right with you, maybe not as a steady diet, not full time, but you affect me. You give me true charity; most people don't bother, don't recognize it. You make me taller. Can I give you something? Hope? The semblance of an attentive ear? A drink in my house? I'll take your fish, for openers. I'll take you.

"I would love to. We were thinking of having the Giannellis come for dinner. Why don't you and George join us and we'll all have an orgy of fish. A block party!" I felt proud of myself, foreseeing Consuela's disbelief and probably horror at such an unlikely gathering. The shreds of Helen's face hanging beneath the huge colored glasses gathered themselves together and she almost glittered with popularity. The prom queen reborn. She would, of course, have to check with George. And then I steered her to Consuela, knowing that I would very soon need rescuing.

Consuela took Helen's arm and they made their way through the crush of flesh to the end of the dock, where a yacht-club stentor, megaphone to mouth, urged all girls eleven through thirteen to assemble for the diving contest. I watched them go, staying back away from the crowd. Then I thought of Rebecca about to dive. Maybe she would be diving for me? Reluctantly I squeezed around and between, finding a vantage point near the edge of the dock. Rebecca and Polly climbed into the crowded dinghy, waving to their mothers, and were rowed out to the diving float. I had my first good look at Polly and winced. Full bosomed and flabby, she seemed to take up more than her share of the boat with her awkward body, and trailed one arm in the water until admonished by the rower to "ship it." Rebecca raised a cool hand as she passed by, and then shot a wry grin to my call at good luck. Polly looked dumbly up as I yelled, rubbery fat lips turned down, and I knew I would dislike her, given the chance. Someone took my hand and I saw Ward peering up from the fringe of my frayed shorts.

"You certainly charmed Helen Livingston. Whatever possessed you?" Consuela shook her head in wonder. "Are you looking for lame ducks in Gosnold's Bay?"

"Just tried to brighten her day. She's vapid and kind and snubbed, quite unlike your backbiting, self-assured girlfriends. Besides, she has to suffer Edith as a neighbor." I picked up Ward and put him on my shoulders, out the forest of knees and into the air. Consuela put her hand through my arm.

"I suppose you're right. But, it will be a fascinating evening. Hey, there goes Rebecca!" Consuela's attention and enthusiasm focused on the diving, on her daughter's excellence, and I tried to match it, to pull my wife and children to me as a magnet draws filings from sand. We stand apart from all these others; I am sure we do. We have to.

But the morning crawled on. The sun dimmed and the air grew moist. Styrofoam cups of ice cubes appeared, and terrycloth robes. At last we climbed into the skiff, and left the dock to the losers. A boat full of victors! The thought horrified me.

The children were quiet, thinking of lunch and of the array of blue ribbons to be pinned on their chests at the dance next Saturday.

It was after one when we got back to the house, and the fog bank moved all the way in. Warmed by two Bourbons and some chowder, I settled down with the children in front of a smoking fire, raging fairly good-naturedly at the poorly designed chimney. Consuela dug out an elderly jigsaw puzzle from under the window seat, the cardboard box yellow and brittle, and we groused and groped for that piece of windmill arm—probably lost—compelled to complete the badly reproduced Dutch landscape.

Consuela shook me out of my therapeutic absorption.

"Who's going to pick up the fish?" Consuela did not seem eager.

"I'll go, since this was all my idea anyway. Do you need anything else?" Too bad, to leave the warmth. Rebecca stirred and wanted to come, so we pulled on our slickers and set out across the grass, feeling like intruders on a silent planet. Everything baffled by fog, no lapping waves or crying gulls. The foghorn bleated, light-years away, then answered its own query. No need for us to talk. As we approached the Livingstons' terrace Rebecca's mood changed and she turned talkative.

"Too bad Polly didn't win anything today. She's nice." Rebecca waited for me to confirm her sentiments, which I couldn't honestly do, so I fudged a bit.

"I'm afraid I don't really know her. In fact, up until today, I had never laid eyes on her before." The negative impact of my reply would never have slipped by Rebecca, so I quickly tacked on a turn-about question. "And what do you like most about Polly?" Rebecca hunched over, thoughtfully, then took my arm.

"She really cares about me. She said she didn't care

whether she won anything or not as long as I got all the blue ribbons. I don't know anyone else that generous." I looked hard at her.

"Are you generous with Polly?"

"Not very. Sometimes I'm sort of mean and bossy and she doesn't even seem to notice. Once when I was particularly nasty, in a bad mood, I apologized. She said she liked me best when I was in a bad mood because probably she was the only one who would want to be with me and she didn't worry about sharing me. She's funny sometimes."

"Funny?" Jesus! Was Helen funny on the dock?

Rebecca preceded me to the Livingstons' front door, and before I had rung the bell she pushed the door open and walked in. Her familiarity with this household was a shock. I did not feel at home with these people, how could she?

"Don't just stand there, Pa. Let's go find Polly."

But I did "just stand there," like a cigar store Indian, waiting for someone to see me in. Rebecca shrugged and mooched off, "What's wrong with you, Pa?" leaving me to drip quietly into the Chinese rug. I tried to concentrate on the funereal arrangement of gladioli and lupine, tried not to peer beyond to the living room, where I could see through the doorway corners of polished tables and faded chintz. The clock in the front hall ticked. I wanted to get out.

Helen materialized like a whirlpool, blasting staccato apologies: for keeping me waiting, for her curlers, for the fog, while she led me to the kitchen and the fish. I took the tinfoil package "5 lb. swordfish steak, 8/20" and thanked her.

"I know it will be delicious. You and George are coming to help us eat it, aren't you?"

Helen gave me a nervous glance, smiled thinly and turned to wipe her hands.

"We would like to come. Really. But George. He's feeling bad. Again. He's resting. Maybe when he wakes . . ." Her voice trailed away and she seemed to follow it out of the kitchen to the front door.

"Sorry to hear George isn't feeling well. Is there anything I can do?"

Helen shook her ravaged head, eyes tired and watery without the glasses. "Just one of his spells. Dizzy spells. He may wake up chipper as a lark. May I leave it open? Call you at the last minute?" She tugged at her ring, then pushed it down again. "I'd like to come. Truly I would." Of that I had no doubt.

"Of course you can leave it open. I just hope George is feeling better and that we'll see you. Now, where's Rebecca?" Helen took me into the library, where the girls lay in an ungainly sprawl drinking in the Saturday super flick. Rebecca seemed glad to see me and said good-by to Polly, who didn't bother to look up from June Allyson's tear-stained image. I thanked Helen and we let ourselves out, happy to be back in the fresh fog again. Curious that so pleasant a house should have such a repressive and uncomfortable effect. Perhaps it was only an extension of Helen's own tension, but whatever the reason, I was relieved to walk away and leave my uneasiness behind me, pocketed in fog.

"How well do you know the Livingstons?" I asked Rebecca.

"I know Polly pretty well, you know that."

"What about Mr. Livingston?"

"Him? I don't know him much. Just what Polly says about him. Why are you asking me all these questions about the Livingstons?"

"Because I am. What does Polly say about him?"

"Oh, she thinks he's O.K. but she doesn't think he likes her much."

"Why not?"

"I dunno. She doesn't think anyone likes her much."

"Do you like her?"

"Yeah, mostly. Sometimes she bugs me."

"Rebecca, I wish you wouldn't use expressions like that. 'Bugs me.'"

"Bugs you?" She giggled.

"Touché. Are you eating with the grown-ups tonight?"

"No, I'd rather not. Can I get my ears pierced?"

Rebecca, my love, you are right in the middle of adolescence, of nowhere. Hang on. "No, you may not. At least, not now. Not until you are older."

"Why not? Mummy has them. Mummy had them when she was a baby."

"Mummy's mother was from South America and they do things differently down there."

Rebecca let out a sigh of misunderstanding and gave up, for the time being.

Consuela must have heard us as we stomped up the back steps, for she opened the door and started talking as we came in.

"Guess what? Philip is leaving for New York tonight. Caroline called and said we could have the boat tomorrow if the fog lifts. I called Jenny and she's driving down tonight to stay with the little boys while we sail. Cam is desperate to come with us, and I think it would be nice if he and Rebecca came along." Consuela hugged me and hurried out. "That means Mass today—in twenty minutes. You better get ready." Her voice fell down the stairwell as she ran up to assist the little boys in their ablutions. Water coursed through the ancient copper pipes, which made the boiler complain in the laundry room, which in turn reminded me to shower and shave with speed before the hot water ran out.

Brushed and scoured, we piled into the cluttered station wagon, me with a tatter of toilet paper stuck to my neck where I let the razor slip. We careered over unkempt back roads through the modest settlement of new cottages ("camps" Aunt Edith called them) where backyard barbecues were in full swing.

St. Irene's Roman Catholic Church stands on a treeless plot of scorched grass, the better to display its lumpish shape and gaudy windows. It remains one of the few churches where seat money is still demanded, and at every Mass I have been to there, the pitiful congregation has been badgered and scolded by the doddering priest into putting at least a dollar in the basket. The chink of pennies, nickels and dimes from our pew has never failed to trigger a bitter stare from him. When Consuela and I were married, Aunt Edith put up such a fuss ("Why, I have never set a foot in that place; the closest I've been is to take the maids; I can't possibly attend, much less give, a wedding there!") that we were married in Chestnut Hill instead, in June, where at least the church had once been Dutch Reform, and where they eschewed pastel statues of the blessed Virgin.

When the liturgy was switched into English—a left-wing deviation for St. Irene's—they solved the problem by muttering rapidly, *sotto voce,* and keeping the same pitch as the Latin drone, thus maintaining the old-Church incomprehensibility. It is hard to work up much spiritual enthusiasm. We really only perform our "weekly duty," despite repetitious reassurances that the Baudyacriste is the Body of Christ even in St. Irene's. Repeat after me: "catholic, universal; of use or interest to all men; all-embracing, of wide sympathies, broad-minded, tolerant." Believe it if you can.

Hurtling home through the fog in a rush to program the children before our guests arrived, Consuela and I tried to organize our cruise above the hungry complaints of the little boys. I was glad to see Jenny's battered pickup truck in the driveway.

"Hi, Jenny!"

Jenny scooped up Ward and everyone else crowded around her, talking, bragging, questioning. I fled the friendly commotion to set up the bar, uncertain which I would welcome more, the Livingstons' absence or presence; puzzling over George's peculiar selection of a spouse. Why after fifty-odd years of bachelorhood should he marry at all, and why a woman like Helen, unglamorous and from outside his restricted milieu? I wondered where George could have even met her, for the Livingstons were reputed to surpass all the others in insularity and caution, including Aunt Edith. Aside from that, I really knew very little about them, concluding that I hoped they would come. With the Giannellis to liven things up, it might be an interesting party. Rebecca came in, with Polly Miller slouching behind her.

"Pa, the Livingstons *are* coming. Polly wants to know if I can stay with her, spend the night. It was hard to tell from

Rebecca's voice and face whether or not she wanted to. I took a stand.

"I don't think so, not tonight. We're leaving early tomorrow on the Potters' boat. This may be your last dry bed for five days. You'd better take advantage of it." The girls exchanged a look. Polly pouted.

"But, Mr. Murray, it's our last chance to see each other." I might have predicted Polly's rasping whine.

"Sorry, Polly, not this time. I want Rebecca rested, to begin with, anyway. We'll be back on Friday. Perhaps you girls could plan something for then." I heard the door slam, Polly's exit, and Rebecca returned to set the table.

"Hope you understand, Rebecca. I didn't mean to ruin your plans."

"It's O.K. I didn't really want to go much anyway."

"Thank you. What's the matter? Did you and Polly have a falling-out?"

"No. I just want to stay here and read my book and stuff." Sometimes children are such rational, if unpredictable, creatures. I wanted to give her a hug, but her businesslike manner held me off, so I mixed a martini instead and tried to poke up the fire to accommodate the freaky chimney.

Consuela came in wearing a long skirt, her shoulders wrapped in a soft shawl. Even to the cow barn she brings beauty and charm, quite unknowingly. I poured her some Lillet, renewed my martini, and we sat erect yet close on the sofa before the fire for one expanded common moment. I guess we loved each other. It is for rare seconds like that that we plow through the dreck from day to day, a windfall to sustain us over the next hurdle.

Then the Giannellis and the Livingstons came together, neighbors after all. Val Giannelli is a smoldering crusader for civil liberties who knows he must set aside time for play and does so with diligence. It does not come to him naturally. He and Margaret are as surefooted intellectually as George Livingston is socially. Likewise, they are not at home in the other's pasture. We fall somewhere in the middle, a halfway house.

Consuela guided quivering Helen around the social quicksand which Helen expected at any party in Gosnold's Bay; eventually Helen's shoulders relaxed, while her Ping-Pong conversation stretched to almost a drawl. The evening must have been a success. I leaned back in my chair, surveying the ruins of dinner, smug in my role of host, masterful and hospitable in gin and Montrachet, washed in the blood of the Lamb.

The Livingstons left early: George tired from his afternoon malaise, Helen animated and grateful. The Giannellis lingered for one last drink and meatier conversation. Consuela and I were just loading the glasses in the dishwasher, rehashing the evening, when I recalled how subdued George had seemed. Amicable as ever, but quiet and almost sad. When I escorted them out, George had turned and put his hand on my shoulder.

"Thank you, Hugh. I wish we could do this again. Happy sailing and safe landfalls." His eyes were cloudy, his face calm and resolved. Although I knew him only slightly, he seemed totally out of character. Remembering now made me uneasy. Not "I hope we can do this again," but "I wish." Perhaps I seemed as enigmatic to him. After all, no one can truly know another, or even himself. It's called the human condition. Consuela bustled away the rest of the detritus as I stood there, rooted, heels of my hands rotating hard against my eyeballs, itch begetting itch, no comfort.

"Hey, sweetheart, you all right? You look worried." Consuela stopped wiping the counter and came to me.

"I'm just tired, and claustrophobic. Maybe I'll walk to the beach and see if this miserable fog is lifting. I'll be back in a few minutes." Consuela handed me a slicker, looking bleak.

"I'd come with you but I'm beat, also cold. Do you mind if I stay and take a hot bath?"

"Not at all. I'm not good company anyway. Shouldn't have had that last drink. Have a bath. I'll see you soon." The fog was still there as I had expected, but I went down to the beach anyway. The tide was out so I walked over the slippery stones to the Giannellis' segment of shore, and out to the end of their jetty. I couldn't even see the *Melande* through the fog, so I turned back toward home. The fog and food and drink made me feel closed in.

I was struggling for a foothold on the slimy rocks when I heard it, a muted, muffled scream, which hardly penetrated the fog at all. I waited, poised precariously on the rocks for confirmation. It came and I followed, to answer whatever strange supplication quickly. My pulse throbbed as I picked my way over the rocks, wishing I could go faster. It was rather like hurrying to an exam with a head full of Dexedrine. The cries continued, still distant. I began to run, past the ugly pine and up the hill, not seeing much of anything except the uniform gray of the fog. The screams were louder, one was followed by a yelp, and seemed to come from ahead of me. The lawn hooked and I swerved, brushing the bushes that I had come through the night before. I was close to the Giannellis' house, possibly just beyond it, and very near to the screams. Out of the fog I saw a stand of clipped arborvitae. I headed for it, then circled around, looking for a way in. My feet felt flagstone and I turned, just as a monstrous anguished cry escaped from the opening in the hedge.

A few feet away from me George Livingston lunged toward a cowering whippet pup, kicked him savagely, and raised his far arm, in which he held some sort of club. Under the shrieks of the puppy grew a low, guttural crescendo, unrecognizable, unearthly and wholly terrifying. I watched, paralyzed, as George's shoulders tensed. I was aware of an awful power. He threw his head back and opened wide his distorted mouth, loosing the vilest, most tortured bellow, as he swung at his dog. The hypnosis of the observer snapped, and I sprang at George. I came down hard on his free side and stretched for his arm which held the club. Our opposing powers seemed to lock against each other, and for a second to melt together, motionless, like the eye of a hurricane. I felt him sway, then topple like a drunken giant to the ground. I looked at him, all in a heap. I watched the quivering dog timidly nose toward him. I noticed that the fog was lifting.

Unwilling, repulsed, I dropped to the grass to help George to his feet. When I touched him a foul acrid taste flooded my mouth and then my nose. I looked hard at George. His head lay tilted against a rock, obscuring some sort of an in-

scription: ". . . ing memory . . . Mandarin . . . ful and forgiving . . . . . . 1974." Some sort of grave. Then I made myself
look at George's face, totally unprepared for the look of pure
horror on it. Horror, disbelief—an agony of revelation. The
look I had read about in books when one sees Pan. As if to answer me, his eyes shifted to mine and then slid away. I tightened my grip on his arm and tried to help him to his feet. He
protested with a gurgling noise and plucked at the front of my
slicker. I realized only then that he was in physical pain.

"Jesus, you're hurt. Don't move, George. I'll get help."

I put him back on the ground as gently as I could and took
off my slicker to cover him. He began to talk.

"No. Don't go. Stay with me."

I stopped fumbling with the coat and leaned over closer to
him, straining to understand his clumsy speech.

"Sorry, Hugh. Too late." Then something very garbled
about a curse; "allegiance curse," it sounded like, and he tried
to raise his hand and pointed to the dog. "Take him. Careful.
Always careful." Then the awful look of recognition faded and
his eyes went blank. His muscles let go and he yielded to gravity. The slack jaw completed his anonymity; he became just another corpse.

I took his wrist and patiently waited for the reassurance of
a pulse, though I knew there would be none. Kneeling on the
wet turf, I held my neighbor's limp hand and swallowed the
foul juices in my mouth, the dog trembling against my thigh. I
waited for the web of panic to break.

At last I felt some energy stir and breathed harder. I
thought of getting to my feet. I had to leave this place, get help.
Hurry, hurry. I looked for the little slit in the grim wall of ever-
greens and saw I was enclosed in a tight circle of midget tombs,
one of them George's final headstone.

The battered whippet, like a last remnant of fog, piloted
me out into the open. I ran toward the Potters' thinking that
Philip as a doctor could help. I remembered halfway that he
had already left for New York. I changed course and struck out
to the Giannellis. Their house was silent and dark. I hesitated
at the door; I could not knock. Embarrassed and guilty, I

swallowed and sneaked away like a child, until another cramp of panic seized me and I started running again. Helen. Helen must be told. I should have gone there first, must compensate by running faster, up the hill toward the sprawling battery of lighted uncurtained windows. I slowed and finally stopped, panting when I crossed into the limits of her lamplight. The callous reality of self-preservation took over. I had tried to restrain George from bludgeoning the dog: in fact, I had pushed him, had killed him.

"Hi, Helen. Guess what? I just killed George, that's what." Sure, I just walk right in and tell her that I, Hugh Cameron Murray, LL.B., General Counsel for the Juvenile Court of the Commonwealth of Massachusetts, subscriber to both the New York Social Register, and, by marriage, to the Boston one, have just killed her husband after a pleasant dinner together. The dog whimpered, snaking his long neck around parallel to his shaking hindquarters, staring back at me. The white froth from his mouth had dried, leaving an arrowhead of yellow scum across his pointed face.

"Go home, boy. Go on. Go." I walked away, back to the shore, past the circle of trees without a pause. After all, no one had seen me. George was beyond any physical assistance. He and I both knew I had not meant to kill him or even to hurt him. He had clearly lost his mind, left his senses, to attack an animal that way. Why should I become involved? Why should I have ever known about it? What good can I do, telling Helen? Resolved to put it all away, I waded knee-deep into the water, bent double to get my face in, and washed out my mouth with salt water. I spat and looked up at the *Melande,* ready to spirit us to unsoiled islands in the morning. I practiced walking naturally on the way back, but no matter how I shrugged or twitched I did not seem to fit in my skin properly. My mouth closed, set wrong; opened, was crooked. Filling it again with Bourbon didn't help. I was glad Consuela was already asleep and stiffly got into my separate clammy cot, unable to face her, or even a mirror.

Leaden and slow, I resisted Consuela's bright voice and firm hands with the oxlike resolve of a drugged sleeper. I had not slept well, hardly at all until after first light, when I finally managed to get beyond the initial moment of letting go, when sleep is suddenly smashed by involuntary snaps and jerks of unknown muscles. Sleep ultimately won out, but it was a poor victory, for my tortured conscience continued its rebukes, twisted accusations spun in the corners of my mind and nightmares flashed behind my closed eyes. Why not wake up? Consuela rubbed her cheek on mine, then went, leaving me a tall glass of orange juice and privacy. Deceit tainted the clear sky and steady breeze. I mechanically stuffed my gear on top of Consuela's in the duffel bag, anxious only to leave, the joy of being at sea unfathomable, remote, possibly just a tired memory. I tried on my face again and it still felt like someone else's, but I shaved it anyway, afraid of what might sprout there, given the chance, or maybe I was trying to scrape and shear it clean from my own disgust. I descended, a brave and cheerful fraud, a Macy's Santa emanating jollity from a bleak soul, duffel on my back.

We dressed the *Melande* in her glorious main and jenny, yards of canvas billowed on her teak deck as she waited for us, flapping her wings. We finished stowing the gear and kissed the two boys good-by. Cam stood on the bow, mooring buoy in hand, as I trimmed the sails and Consuela held the tiller, ready to head us off and out.

"O.K., Cam. Stand by to cast off." My voice sounded normal.

I pulled the clew of the jib to port, and watched the jenny fill in the light air. Slowly the bow swung against the mooring line over to the other side, and then I heard the almost silent slap, slap that meant we were making way. Conscientiously, I ran the jib clew around the mast (can't foul anything now) and leapt aft to catch the wind in the mainsail.

"Ready to cast off, Pa." Cam was solemn with the importance of his duty. I squinted at Consuela. "Ready aft," she answered. I took a breath: "Cast off!"

The buoy splashed into the water.

I cleated down the mainsheet and hauled in fast on the port jib-sheet, some old instinct making me sure to coil it as I hauled. When my city hands began to hurt with the strain, I ran it around the winch and rang it, as one would ring a churchbell. "This is living," I thought. But an echo nagged at me: George is dead. A last look ashore, where up the green lawn that used to be George Livingston's stood a tall clump of trees, now sliding backwards, still reproaching me even in retreat. I looked at Consuela and grinned to prove what a successful liar I was. And I looked back once more, defiantly, to see a bleached dog at the end of the dock and a figure running down the hill.

"Look, Pa!" Rebecca called, her face turned away toward land. "Here comes Polly to say good-by. Please, can't we come about and get close enough to yell to her?" Rebecca's question bounced off my ears on little airborne bubbles while her eyes remained riveted to the shore.

"No, we can't get closer. It will ruin our course and we'll have to spend another half-hour just fetching the channel buoys. You'll see her Friday." I dove below to end any further pleas from Rebecca, and shuffled through the charts. Rebecca poked her head through the companionway.

"You're mean. Polly was yelling something and it might have been important."

"Tough." Well, that is certainly true. Tough, like, hey, Rebecca, someone's killed my stepfather; I tripped on his dead body on my way down to the dock to say good-by to you. Is that what fat little Polly was shrieking? Oh shit, George Livingston, it's really not my fault, you know. Are you going to ride with me all the way to Cuttyhunk? Where are you anyway? Bobbing behind us in the dinghy? Leave me alone, God dammit. Go to hell. And the last thought broke my cracked head. I emerged from the cabin into the sunshine, laughter lashing crazily out of every split and rent. A volcano of merriment. A burst boil. The laughter subsided, shuddered, slithered down the other side of the peak, the sobbing side. I was all at once aware of Consuela and Rebecca, four dark eyes, nails of disbelief piercing through my hysteria like nickel-plated lances of reality and saneness.

"What's so funny? What's wrong, Hugh?" Consuela, sailing the boat, taking me away, brought me back.

"Nothing's wrong, love. Nothing at all. I don't know what it was that started me laughing, but I couldn't stop. Oh, sweet Jesus, I am so glad to get out." I tidied up the lines, trimmed the sails and took over from Consuela.

"Ready about," I said.

We anchored in Tarpaulin Cove for lunch and a swim. I felt better and dove off the stern to rinse off the last grains of guilt. Newly baptized, I arrived at my gin in the cockpit. The children ate quickly and took off for shore in the dinghy, while Consuela and I lay in the sun on the deck under the protection of the white lighthouse on the cliff. The gin loosened my joints, took the pain out of new blisters.

I figured it would take us about two and a half hours to get to Cuttyhunk given the wind and tide. Cam and I wrestled with the anchor and we swept out, down along Naushon and Pasque to the mouth of Quicks Hole.

Rebecca sighted the entrance buoy to the Hole and we trimmed the sails, keeping the *Melande* close to the wind for a straight shoot through. We'd timed it right. The flood tide was pulling us into Buzzards Bay. An old Concordia, twin to the one my father sold, heeled past us, drum major for the parade of smaller boats which had collected behind her. We were occupied with comradely waves and buoys when out of nowhere a fog bank strode in, swallowing us one by one from behind until nothing was visible beyond the twenty-eight-foot limits of the *Melande,* and even her forestay was eventually erased.

The wind dropped, half deadened by the fog, and most of our progress came from the current tugging below. Consuela blew loud blats on the tin foghorn, and hushed the children in between so we could try to hear other horns. Complaints from spluttering engines joined the brass, and we became a muffled orchestra, Consuela our soloist, as we slid, unseeing, unseen, all of us, into the eddies and maybe the rocks of Quicks Hole.

Philip was a sail snob (as am I). He refused to defile the *Melande* with an engine. We had just wind enough to fill our sails and maintain way. Thank God the tide was flooding! We saw, in a hole in the fog, the specter of the Concordia. She was

50

in irons, her engine stilled and alarmingly close to our starboard bow. But we were wrapped again so quickly that we couldn't get an accurate comparison of our positions and headings, or do much to keep a healthy distance.

In the narrowest part of the Hole, the full force of the water caught us. Our course became drunken as we met successive vortices which pulled against the rudder, sliding us sideways, closer to where I supposed the drifting yawl lurked, and closer to the black, jagged margin of rocks.

Not much I could do, except try to keep on course. I steered by the compass, trying to remember how the currents ran, and cursing my lunchtime gin. All of us strained to spot the crucial red buoy, and we hallucinated in the unrelenting monotony of gray. We were victims of vertigo and foolish faith.

The crunch of keel on hard stone stopped the honk of foghorns. I wondered who would be next. Muffled orders and confirmations from the grounded boat sounded.

"Pa, there's a buoy," Cam shouted from the bow.

"Cam, we all hallucinate in the fog. . . . Jesus! you're right! Number Four?"

As a reward for desperate prayer, perhaps, the fickle fog drew back, just for a second, long enough for us to see not only Buoy Number Four, but the whole passage, salvation pointing west. We also saw the keel of the yawl as she listed on the rocks, and we looked away.

"Listen," I said to Consuela, "you take her while I work out some sort of compass course."

The light and blessed wind persevered through the fog enough to blow us andante up the deserted shore of Nashawena. We got to the brackish safety of Cuttyhunk Pond, where our crowded anchorage was, for once, a delight. How splendid to see, if dimly, neighbors on all sides.

Archie comics and Orange Crush below with the children, while we blotted out our memory of cold sweat and imminent danger with dewy sweaters, whiskey and cigarettes and listened to the friendly purr of the outboards, tripping from ship to shore. I stretched and slumped back, limp from exertion; Consuela curled against my ribs. Happiness, I thought. But heavy

George, and the nervous wriggles of the misused whippet burbled up. Move. Move away from these thoughts, from thinking.

"Hey, Consuela, let's all go ashore and eat at Bosworth House. No cooking aboard first night out, and certainly not after what we've just come through." We had another drink for deeper anesthesia, took sandals and ditty bag, and went ashore. We lurched up the hill on staggery sea legs. Cam and Rebecca were delighted to be on land and exaggerated the lingering pitch and roll of the boat. Remorse and George waited, obligingly, outside with the fog while we enjoyed the simple, ample pleasure of chowder, steak and service.

Replete, we stepped back out into the fog. The children erupted with energy from their recent refueling, and tore past us down the hill. I sprinted after them, stumbled on the stones at the bottom of the hill where the road leveled to the scruffy dock and caught Cam's sweater. He skidded to a stop.

"Look, Cam, over there, can you see the fire engine?" I pointed to the largest of several misty rusty shapes, mechanical dinosaurs in the fog.

"Neat-o!" yelped Cam. "Can I climb on it?" And he dashed off without waiting, hollering over his shoulder to Rebecca.

"Be quiet, Cam!" I hurried over to him. "Listen, you creep, Charlie Snow lives in this house, or used to, and he's probably trying to sleep."

"At this hour?" Cam was scornful. "Who's asleep? Is he a grown-up or what?"

It was eight-thirty. Except for the full dining room at Bosworth House, we had not seen or heard anyone since we left the dinghy in the lee of the carpeted color TV equipped stinkpots berthed at the marina.

"O.K. Cam, off. Let's come back in the morning. We'll need some ice anyway." I pulled him down from the square back of the 1928 engine, heartened to find it much as it was when I had climbed on it over twenty years ago. "Charlie's parlor," we called it, my cousin Lucy and I, and we paid calls on

Charlie daily during the four summers we spent together on Cuttyhunk. Tomorrow, I resolved, I'll visit Charlie again. Last summer, Consuela and I cruised south, to Newport and Long Island Sound, to visit friends with accommodating moorings, bathtubs and booze, and we never stopped by Cuttyhunk.

Only once before, in fact, had I ever brought Consuela to Cuttyhunk, and that was just to prove to myself that I could— the way some people burn their love letters. Lucy and I licked the sores of adolescence together here, and because I knew that I could never share that bond with Consuela, I tried at least to break its continuing spell by bringing her here. I was struck to find that Consuela's presence made no difference whatever. Some spells are fed internally, and nothing physical can alter them at all.

After Consuela bedded down Cam and Rebecca we sat in the cockpit under the canvas tent, one last drink for me, and a cigarette to put off the moment when we climbed into our separate sleeping bags, stretched on skinny cushions on the cockpit deck. I felt for my lighter and remembered that I had forgotten to bring it.

"Sweetheart," began Consuela, "are you sure you're all right?"

"Sure. . . . Why?" I was grateful for the lack of light.

"Something is wrong, I know it and so do you but you're pretending you don't."

"That doesn't make sense, love." Only it did and I knew it.

"Well, for one thing, when you were laughing; that was hysteria. You did it once before, when Rebecca was born." Consuela paused. "Only then, it took me six months to find out why. How long will it take this time?"

I reached for the Bourbon, remembering Rebecca's hasty birth by cesarean section, and the doctor's admission that she might be brain-damaged from loss of oxygen. He couldn't tell for six months anyway, so I had seen no reason to worry Consuela, and place double scrutiny on the baby. Determined to keep this to myself, I damned near blew it right away in the hospital room, when Consuela, breaking through the shroud of pain-killers to receive Holy Communion, told me afterward how she had given thanks for her perfect baby. I shook and bleated with mirth, and tears. In the end, Consuela was right to have thanked our Lord. Rebecca was perfect.

"I'm not sure; not sure if I'll keep you waiting, not sure if anything is wrong. I am sure that I got us through the fog to Cuttyhunk. Let's worry about getting to the next port. No more talk about it, I can't." I stopped abruptly, closing my lips on the glass, swallowing the Bourbon down to silence any percolating confession. Please, Consuela, don't force me. Not yet.

"You're drinking a lot." Her voice was soft and low, not nagging but stating an observation.

"Trust me, please. I'm not a lush like my father. I enjoy drinking, but I keep track, so don't worry."

I crawled around the edge of the tarp and went forward for one last check on the anchor. The fog hadn't changed, and I could see only the riding lights suspended with halos in the damp, and disembodied from their spars and stays. I stood a minute, constricted and claustrophobic despite the alcohol.

When I resignedly threaded my way around the tent lines to the cockpit I found Consuela motionless in her sleeping bag cocoon. I blotted my feet on a towel, climbed into my own bag and zipped it to my chin. Either just before I slept or just as I woke, I heard a dog whining, like an internal mosquito.

It was still dark and foggy when I woke up. The boat rocked, a lone cradle like so many others hiding in the crowded pond. My mind rushed with technicolor memories of schoolboy summers, and hot embarrassed experimental love, and Cousin Lucy. And for the first time in many years I let myself remember Lucy. Odd things, like her elbows, arcs not angles, and the day when I noticed that her hips and breasts filled the same curve, to my awe and admiration. I had touched her breasts quickly and tentatively and afterward had relished both my courage and her body.

I was no longer sleepy, so I inched out of the sleeping bag, careful not to waken Consuela. The deck was wet and cold but I sat down on the stern anyway, head on arms, arms on tiller, while fragmented memories darted in my head, more vivid than reality had ever been. But they soon petered out and I sat there in the fog empty, lonely, out of time, out of place. Foolish to think you can belong to a place. Foolish and, more to the point, vain. Once I had felt whole; I had had a sense of purpose and peace. Why did I feel that this wholeness was labeled "Cuttyhunk"? It had been mine, with my name tape. Somehow, I'd mislaid it.

I was wrung out, too unsprung to sleep, with a widening rim of hollowness pressing from my inside out. A warning whimper sounded like a subconscious alarm and I thought again of Gosnold's Bay and George and of the shivering pinkish puppy. I missed them. I wanted to go home, through the looking glass as it were.

Reversing the reel, I let the frames flicker by from finished yesterday backward: Cuttyhunk, Quicks Hole, Tarpaulin Cove, the dock in Gosnold's Bay, click. I reviewed Polly pummeling downhill toward me, and my subsequent heartless vision of her finding George's body.

George, oh, George, will you haunt me? I believe in you, if that's what you want. I believe in the Holy Ghost, even if they've changed His Name to Spirit, why not you? What do you want? A confession? I am trying to work that out, but it's nasty, admitting I was scared. Your dying like that was nasty too. Will you demand an eye for an eye? No, you wouldn't. I don't know why thoughts of you and your damn dog keep intruding. Or do I invite them? You knew something, George, you saw something as you died. Do you want me to know it, to see it, too? Are you warning me perhaps? Will I know? Will I sleep? is more to the point. Time out, George. I must attend to my body. You understand surely? You would have understood.

I carefully wrapped myself in the now damp wads of my sleeping bag and slept.

I didn't wake until seven, when Rebecca began to pump the head with anvil blows as she tried to sluice out the full bowl.

I greeted my hangover like an old friend, and sat up pleased to see Rebecca's smile of triumph through the companionway, pleased to bask in Consuela's lazy feline yawn and pretty face.

At four a clean wind sliced in and dissipated the sticky fog and George. We hoisted sail and left our anchorage to monkey around in the bay, the afternoon too old to find a new port. The children took turns at the tiller and the sheets, eager pupils whose interest and questions kept me alert and occupied.

We went ashore to visit Charlie and his fire engine, leaving Consuela and Rebecca on the dock to haggle over fresh flounder with a surly local, someone I didn't recognize. Charlie and two cronies tipped on the porch as they traded toothless yarns. Their old men's talk stopped as we came near, and I dreaded their evaluation of Cam and me as they gnawed on their pipestems: tourists, that's what we were. And I knew because Lucy and I used to sit there on the engine and judge the cattle right along with Charlie. Oh, Charlie, what a reception!

Time had tried to change me to a man, but had left Charlie alone, having completed the job already. He didn't know me, and never had. Our "friendship" was something I had fabricated, like my own worth. I wanted to go past the house, past the past, but Cam had already turned in, to the engine. He waited for my introduction. It stuck in my throat. Cam stood in the sun between the rusty engine and the rusty men and returned their steady wordless stare.

"Hello, Mr. Snow. I'm Cameron Murray. May I climb on your fire engine?"

Charlie nodded. "Sure can, boy. How d'ya know my name? Do I know you?"

"Not 'til now, sir. But my father used to know you, I guess it was ages ago. He's over there." Cam pointed a brown finger and vaulted into the driver's seat.

I was proud of him for doing what I didn't dare to do. Now I could come forward, led by my son.

"Hugh Murray. How are you, Charlie?" I asked. "I used to spend summers here with my cousin, Lucy Carter." He got up to shake my extended hand and smiled briefly, a glimpse of pink gums. Then he gazed at Cam, who was confidently rushing his team of firemen off to a fantasy holocaust in his polished finely turned machine. Charlie turned back to me.

"Looks just like you, don't he? What happened to yer friend? Pretty little thing; Charlie's Parler she used to call it." Charlie shuffled into his chair. "Never came back."

"She was in a car accident twenty years ago, and she hasn't walked since. She remembers you, Charlie, and the talks we used to have."

"Too bad, she was such a pretty little thing. You see her, you tell her hello from Charlie. Tell her her parler's waiting."

"Whose parlor?" Consuela and Rebecca flanked me, curiosity on their faces. I introduced them and called to Cam. Time to go and leave Charlie to his old men and memories.

A glassy new telephone booth stuck out from the side of Charlie's house, chrome trim incongruous against the peeling wood. When I lived here the public telephone, a crank phone like all the rest, had been fixed to the bumpy back wall of a lean-to. Everyone knew what it was. The present one boasted a neatly printed identification tag—T E L E P H O N E—in blue, with a little picture next to the letters for the illiterate. I turned back to the porch.

"Hey, Charlie, what's this thing?" I shouted, outraged.

"Classy ain't it? Phone's the same, though. Only now we got two public ones, so the line's twice as busy." Charlie gave a short cackle, thinking no doubt of the impatient trippers who continue to queue up by the phones as soon as they get off their yachts.

For the people who live in Cuttyhunk, telephones are necessary solely as instruments of retaliation. We all used to do it. Late in the afternoon, when the first boats started to trickle in, that is the time for talking. Both lines would reliably be in use for the rest of the day, and again early in the morning, until Cuttyhunk Pond emptied and the island returned to normal. The tourists would take their urgent messages off with them, undelivered, to harbors which depended on the sea-dog tourist dollar.

"Hey, children, look at the phone."

"This is a telephone?" Rebecca was incredulous. "It looks more like that thing in our attic, that coffee grinder."

"Why's it got a handle?" asked Cam.

"It's a crank phone. You pick up the earpiece and wind the crank. That makes all the phones on the line ring, and tells the operator you want to make a call. She comes on and asks you for the number."

"You mean she talks to you? You don't just dial?" Cam talked to us last year through the echo of a satellite from Still River to Paris. No wonder he was astounded by this functioning antique.

"Right. She says, 'Number please.' When you're done, you ring off—two rings—to let everyone else know the line is free. Got it?"

"Can I do it? Call home?" Cam hopped and ran his fingers over the crank.

"Sure, go ahead. Make it collect."

He stood on tiptoe and lifted off the receiver. A nasal drone came whining out. We listened.

"Someone's on, Esther. Some New Yorker most like." Then louder, "Just a minute, can't you? I'll ring off when I've done." Cam stood, phone in hand, spellbound.

"Hang up, Cam." I grabbed the earpiece and replaced it, "New Yorker" not native that I was. "No point waiting, they'll gossip forever, especially now they know someone wants to make a call. Let's go up to the top of the hill."

We trudged up the hill, past the one store, where the flies buzzed in a black cloud around the hot trash barrels just outside. On the top of the hill we stood like cranes in the sun and looked down on the crowded harbor tucked between the thin claws of land. We tried to spot the *Melande*.

I suddenly felt isolated. The boats belonged at their anchors, but I was adrift again, a transient. Lucy and I had cut our lines and Cuttyhunk had never really belonged to us at all. It had been a rosy, callow conceit that wherever we were was ours. Focus. I must focus on particulars and try to regain some touch with here and now. Consuela helped me, by accident or maybe by intention.

"Oh, Hugh"—she tugged at my arm—"look over there, down the other side."

The hill sheared off to the other pond, the inland pond, and then the land rose up again to the looming bluff and the lighthouse. I made myself concentrate on the view. From our summit Cuttyhunk followed every detailed cliff and inlet of the Coast and Geodetic Survey chart. Contour lines drawn on paper marked each knoll and dip, a firm black line limited the island, and the blue sea in contrast seemed terrifyingly infinite.

"What's that?" Cam pointed to a raised concrete platform, out of place in the scrubby tangle of salt grass and broom. He took off along the narrow path and climbed up. Then he squatted to peer down the hole in the top.

"Bunkers! Just like in 'Combat'! Come on, Rebecca! I'm going down!" And he vanished into the pit. I followed him, with Rebecca trailing behind me. When I lowered myself down the cool metal ladder I remembered at once the stench of stale urine and the dirty litter of beer cans and Trojans befouling the bunker floors. The smell was the same, and as my eyes adjusted to the darkness I looked for the wastes of passion. A poor crop and I thought of the Pill and then of Rebecca, whose legs were lengthening down the ladder.

She hesitated when the trapped smell met her nostrils.

"How can you breathe down here? I'm going up." Rebecca gasped and began to retrace her steps. Over my head I watched her legs as the sunlight struck them making the fine hairs shine, hairs still soft in unshaved infancy. Always go up, Rebecca. Get used to it now, while you are young and agile.

Cam scuttled after her, leading his company of GI's over the top, the machine guns left unmanned, entrusted by him to my care even though I meanly said I couldn't see them. Cam had pointed to an empty smelly corner, confident that I would hold the fort.

The puff of sulphur as I struck a match to light my Pall Mall soon mingled with the reek of old piss, and I stood like a dazed tick in the bottom of a concrete carton. What had happened to me? I was the same old Hugh, the same young Hugh somewhere under the ugly veneer of George Livingston's unholy death, under the shroud of Lucy's accident and our separation. Lucy.

Lucy and I. We leaned over the opening in the noonday sun and saw down in the gloom two people screwing. They grunted and writhed like animals and we were revolted. And excited. We ran away fast, down the hill through the grass, and trotted to a stop halfway up to the lighthouse. The edge of our raw craving for each other was smoother from all the running, but it was still there. So was the sense of horror. We sat facing Spain.

"We do love each other." My voice had sounded gritty.

"We do."

"Would you like to do that?"

"No," Lucy had answered. "Not that. Not like them . . . I feel funny." We were sitting very close, skins tingling where they touched at shoulders and bare feet.

"I do too." I knew it was the same. What we had seen had triggered the same physical reaction in both of us, our blood racing straight to that vortex, that wild pulse between the V of our legs.

"They weren't making love, Lucy. They were fucking."

"I know. But we can't do that. Not us."

"You do want to do something, don't you? I do." I must have sounded desperate, I was desperate.

"Oh, I do! I want you to love me, and touch me. I want to touch you. But not like them. I wish we hadn't seen them."

Lucy and I lay in the grass, our clothes spread out beneath us. We touched and kissed. Kissing we knew wasn't bad, until I came in her mouth. I was embarrassed and relieved. She gulped my semen down. I had thought she might throw up.

"How could I? It's you!" said Lucy. But she rinsed her mouth out in the sea when we swam a few minutes later.

"You taste like the ocean," I told her. I loved her taste.

We called our love-making our "seasoning." Our lives revolved around it for three years. Everything we did, together or alone, was connected to the tastes and touches of our love. It was pure because *we* weren't fucking. It wasn't until just before Lucy's accident that I became aware of perversion. It was my brother Omar who told me about blow jobs and fellatio and cunnilingus, and made me feel guilty and dirty.

With our love had come promises. Promises of purity, duty and godliness. Lucy and I were obsessed with religion, worshiping God through each other. If man was created in the image and likeness of God, then it followed that we could adore him in this way. Another corollary was our mutual dependence, which was a kind of insurance against losing each other.

"Bang! That's a grenade. You're dead."

I jumped. Dead?

"Christ, Cam!" Too loud. "Sorry," my voice trying for normality. "You made me jump."

"Oh, sorry." His voice echoed in the bunker, whose fetidness shook me as it had twenty years before.

I climbed out fast and breathed the salt southwest wind off Vineyard Sound.

Consuela was drowsing on the other slope out of the wind. The distant monument to Bartholomew Gosnold stood tall, blackened by the sunset behind it. The monument seemed an urban tribute mistakenly erected in a salt marsh. I stared at it but didn't really see it because from the confused blur in my head a solitary thought took shape; I had to tell. I had to tell Consuela and I had to go back to the mainland and tell Helen, too, that I had seen, helped George die.

I'd killed him. Panic. Like George's face as he died. Why had he looked like that? Because he knew that I would run away? What else had he known?

The sinking sun glittered on the water and made the grass into gold. *I will go back, I will change everything, I will confess.*

Consuela tossed back her hair and got to her feet. "Where are the children?" she asked me.

"Playing down on the hill. See? Here they come."

Cam and Rebecca, the retreating army, fled through the grass, disappearing from time to time as they dove to duck rear fire.

Close apart, Consuela and I stood near the top of the bunker. We faced the monument which was to me then a lifeline to Gosnold's Bay and a clear conscience. Separately, privately, we shared an evening benediction in the shadow of Gosnold. I resolved then to come clean and for that night at least, to stay sober. One step at a time.

We ate our eggs and rolls early the next morning with a placid one-legged laughing gull, who then watched, unruffled from his crumb-strewn perch on the stern, as we hoisted sails and anchor. Cuttyhunk released us from her impersonal, picture-postcard perfection, glad, no doubt, to see the trippers leave, Indian file down the narrow channel. I glanced at my bare arms and saw muscle and bone working under newly weather-tarnished skin. My head was as clear as any teetotaler's, my stomach quiet under a single cup of coffee and two poached eggs.

A steady little southwest wind blew us straight to Menemsha, an uncomplicated reach so we all took turns at the helm. Perfect conditions to sort out one's head, which I did. Two confessions took shape; curiously enough, the one to Consuela was the hardest, I guess because I like to think she knows me so well.

The sea gull hitchhiked along, attended by Rebecca, who cleverly insisted we call him Jonathan.

"That's not very original," I protested.

"Then his name is George," announced Cam.

I was dumb and the moment passed when I could have changed the unfortunate name of our albatross. George he stayed. Perspective was growing, true, but I did not find the coincidence humorous. The name and the gull stuck fast until we settled late in the afternoon in Menemsha Pond, after a leisurely day on Vineyard Sound. We swam; the children struck for shore to explore the poison ivy thicket, and George after a few tentative bobs for fish, discovered some distant relations to visit.

Consuela and I lay peacefully stretched out on the warm deck, letting the sun soak to our marrow. The alcohol alarm buzzed in my master nerve and sent little impulses all around, but I lay on, consciously postponing the knock of ice cubes. I played the child's waiting game; if I wait five minutes we will have a clear night, ten and it will be sunny tomorrow. Consuela moved first, and brought me the last of the gin.

"We had better get to a 'wet' port tomorrow," she warned, sinking the empty bottle. "There's still vermouth, beer and some Bourbon, but not much, considering it's only Tuesday."

"Sorry for the heavy damage. I was in bad shape on Sunday, I guess you knew that, but things are better now. I do want to talk to you, but this boat is too damn crowded with the children." I watched them busy excavating on the beach, and wondered if maybe I could blurt it out before they returned.

"You could do it now," said Consuela, languidly mind reading.

"Yeah, but it might take a while, and I don't want to have to do it in installments." True, but I was more afraid of false starts, and I wasn't quite ready to lay it on Consuela, away from the mainland and with the children.

She shrugged. "It's up to you."

"Listen, why don't we head back tomorrow? Jenny's planning to stay until Friday night anyway, isn't she? We could leave Cam and Rebecca with her and have two nights to ourselves on the boat." I knew I sounded like an unaffectionate father and added, "This hasn't anything to do with the children, they've been great, but I need some time with only you."

"Fine, but make sure they understand it, especially Rebecca. She takes offense easily these days." Consuela gave me a tough look, making me feel that I knew my daughter only slightly, an uncomfortable truth, I supposed.

Consuela put her hand against her forehead like a visor, and smiled across the sun at me, encouraging, omniscient and vaguely irritating. I got up and switched to Bourbon, discarding unanswerable questions: How can Consuela pretend to see me so clearly when she makes so little effort? Is she pretending, or does she really know me, heart and soul and soft, white underbelly? What do I know of her?

"I'm ready to listen," she said. "But, I guess you aren't ready to talk."

Evidently, Consuela was plugged in to her psychic Telex and received, if not the questions themselves, the gist of my discomfort. She shunned my gathering uncertainties and rowed ashore to get Cam and Rebecca, while I sat on the berth, doubts banging in my mind.

Consuela's cool intuition was infuriating to me, odd. Lucy and I had built a union, a pure and exclusive trust on our effortless communication. We talk, Lucy and I, or we used to, with an ecomomy and clarity bewildering to eavesdroppers. With Consuela I often toil and pray for patience as I try to strip her thoughts from husk to kernel. Obviously, the key words here are pure and exclusive. With Lucy, I followed the straight way; we faltered and stumbled side by side, no distant opportunity for individual treachery or deceit, we were in it together, welded. And we were alone. We excluded everyone from our unique communion; it was only ours.

My love and respect for Consuela continue deep and steadfast; we have been soldered physically to be sure, and when we burst in simultaneous orgasm I know our separate souls enjoy a brief and blinding merge as well. But day to day, our paths are not the same. They are more than different, to me they seem charged with competition, and I lose by default again and again.

I had no doubt that when I finally told Consuela about killing George she would understand perfectly. She would offer excellent advice, and what's more, she might not even show much surprise. I despaired of ever discovering all she, on the other hand, pondered in her heart. The business with Aunt Edith was the nearest I had been allowed to venture to Consuela's quick. I had dealt with that so poorly, how could I hope for other disclosures?

Glum in my own pale self-importance, I was glad to hear the gentle bump of the dinghy against the side of the *Melande*, it roused me from dejection and drink to dinner. After we had eaten, Consuela pulled her mandolin out of the sail-locker, and we sat in the dewy cockpit, letting "Sloop John 'B'" and "Lemon Tree" settle on the dark, still water of Menemsha Pond. We ended with the Navy Hymn:

> Eternal Father, strong to save,
> Whose arm hath bound the restless wave,
> Who bidd'st the mighty ocean deep
> Its own appointed limits keep:
> O hear us when we cry to thee
> For those in peril on the sea.

Consuela's voice hitched in a speck of a sob on "those." Her broken alto weakened me like an electric shock. She sat with the mandolin on her lap, looking into the night with a straight back and wet cheeks.

I left to shepherd the children below, closing off the companionway when I returned to sit alone with Consuela, privy, I hoped, to her sadness.

"Something's very wrong, Hugh. I don't know yet what it is. Please pray that it will come right. I love you so much but it's hard and lonely now. Together, we seem to be all screwed up."

I wanted to reply and accept the blame, but my tongue and palate stuck together. The best I could manage was to take her tight in my arms. We sat, constricted by each other's tension, both of us needing comfort, both of us trying to offer it. We slept that way as well, in miserable, sexless affection.

Compassionate strangers in the haze of early morning, Consuela and I set the sails and fled Menemsha Pond on a racing ebb tide. We spoke softly and kindly and only when we had to. Cam and Rebecca were subdued and vibrated like tuning forks to the static which crackled over the great distance between Consuela and me.

We were all relieved to be going home, to a known destination which might bring a change to our faltering egos and bolster us up so we could resume our lives. Confronted head on with George's death, as I knew we would all be, I also knew that that alone would catapult me from my limbo. Whether or not I could pull Consuela out of hers was another question.

I tended the helm automatically, while in my mind I rehearsed my speech to Consuela and planned the details of delivering the children. Young Polly might well rush to the dock, eager to spill the beans, and if possible, I wanted to tell Consuela myself. With each passing headland I plotted the mechanics of going ashore in Gosnold's Bay. Recognizable harbor mouths gaped at us as we sailed past, but my eyes were fixed only on the enlarging tumor of land which was Gosnold's Neck.

Fetching the channel buoys demanded more attention, and we all came to life. Once around the Neck I saw the five little beaches, and in the middle the green scar of George Livingston's lawn.

"I have an idea." They all looked at me, waiting. "Instead of pulling up to the Giannellis' dock, let's sail down right to Aunt Edith's beach. If Justin and Ward are down there they'd love to see us come in. Consuela, you take the tiller. Sail her in as close as you can, and Rebecca, Cam and I will dive in and swim ashore. You just sail around while I find Jenny and tell her our plans." That way, I hoped to isolate Consuela from some of the gossip, for a while.

The beach was empty, happy my luck. Poised to dive in, I glanced across the water to the Livingstons' dock and was suddenly sickened by the ugly sight of the whippet swimming toward me, his head a faded pimple barely above the water. He stuggled to keep his nose dry and looked as if he might drown. But he wasn't drowning; he was heading directly for me. My toes curled tightly over the edge of the deck. I did not want to dive in.

"What are you waiting for, Pa?" asked Cam.

I turned just in time to see his grin as he pushed me into the water. Both the children jumped after me and we paddled in together, met halfway by the dog. He poked his pointed snout into my face with a pathetic, if disgusting, servility and yet in some unfathomable way I was flattered by his interest in me.

66

Jenny and the little boys were out when we reached the house, so I left Cam and Rebecca with a covering note and hurried back to the boat, the wet dog trotting a few steps ahead of me. I rejoiced in the good fortune of being undetected and thus spared from feigning surprise at the news of George's death, but too soon, for I bumped headlong into Polly at the foot of the path.

"My stepfather's—" she blurted.

"I know, Polly." I broke in, chopping off her banner head-lines, and then added in utter honesty, "And I'm terribly sorry. Is there anything I can do to help?"

"Who told you?" Polly challenged in an accusing voice.

"Everyone knows, Polly." Everyone that is, except Consuela. Polly gave me a sour look, but she at least accepted my inadequate answer to her question.

"Where's Rebecca?"

"She's at the house, with Cam. Why don't you go over? Oh, please tell your mother that I'll come to see her soon."

Polly lumbered up the path. The dog stood next to me, watching her go.

"Hey, Polly, call your dog. He keeps following me."

"He isn't mine," replied Polly with scorn. "He was my stepfather's. He's yours, now. That's what my mother said. Name is Waffles." With that, she disappeared.

Waffles and I regarded one another. Then with a confirming wag of his stalk of a tail, he continued to the water and swam off toward the waiting *Melande*. We arrived simultaneously, and he looked reproachful as I hoisted myself on board and left him to struggle in the deep water. I trimmed the sheet and the sails filled; the gap between the dog and me widened. I felt cruel, abandoning him, and wondered what Polly had meant when she had said the dog was mine now. Why would anyone imagine that I would want him?

We sailed down to the inner harbor for ice and other essential stores. On the way I told Consuela that George was dead.

"Dead? Oh no, I can't believe it. How did he die? Who told you? Oh, poor Helen. When did it happen?"

I waited before I attempted to answer her artillery of questions, clinging to a wire of faith in her ESP—hoping she might just guess that it had something to do with me.

Disappointed, I finally replied.

"All Polly said was that he was dead. Please don't rush around town asking everyone about it. They'll all be dying to tell you about it anyway, I suppose. Oh shit, I don't care what you do, but I have got to talk with you."

"Not about George?" Consuela was puzzled. "I thought you wanted to talk about you, and me?" And then I think she began to put the shapeless puzzle pieces at least in a row.

"About all of us; you, me, George, Lucy—"

"Lucy? Your cousin? I don't see what she can possibly have to do with it!" Neither did I, but I knew that she figured somewhere in my guilt.

"Listen, just wait, all right?" I testily implored Consuela. "Let's stock the boat and go back to Tarpaulin Cove. There won't be many boats in there now, and we can be back here in two hours if we want to be."

"Anything. Fine. . . . I don't like this."

"Do you think I do? Oh, God, I wish it were over, or not done." I shut up and applied myself to docking the boat.

An hour later we sailed past Aunt Edith's beach again, sticking close to the lee shore as far away as we could from the beach and the children and the dog. Once out of Gosnold's Bay I relaxed a little, had a beer and a roast beef sandwich, and tightened up the boat to boil along, close on the afternoon southwest wind.

Consuela doesn't like to shilly-shally. She waited as long as she could, but when lunch and the boat were under control, she put it to me directly.

"Are you going to start now, or will you wait some more?"

"I'm going to sail this boat and wait until we are at anchor before I start. Telling you will take all my attention and nerve, can't you understand?" She returned my stare but didn't speak again until we entered the cove and prepared to drop anchor.

Before I began, I mixed a weak whiskey and water and silently invoked the third person of my Triune God to touch my tongue with His own fiery one and shade me with His snowy wing, a trite and basic supplication. I told Consuela, beginning with Margaret's rumor of the screams, and related with honest shame every cowardly step of my ordeal. They were sins of omission, I told her (after all, I had not meant to push George so hard, had not meant to run away), but sins just the same. Mea culpas for the thing I should have done were registered in Consuela's computer. I finished.

"What about Lucy? Where does she come in?"

"She comes in later, last, after you have had your turn. It is your turn, you know."

Consuela didn't say anything.

"Jesus Christ, I have killed a man, your neighbor, in fact. Will you just sit there, speechless? Come on, Consuela, if we are ever going to patch up our lives we had damn well better start now. Please, say something."

To admit wrong is one thing but if, after you make yourself tell, there is no priest behind the confessional curtain, no forgiveness after all the humility and courage, what is the point? I really did expect shrift from Consuela, and now she withheld it.

"I'll try. There is so much to say and starting's hard." Held in another hiatus she scanned the horizon with her eyes while her mind plunged. "First, about George," she began. "It, his death, it isn't your fault at all."

"Isn't it? Why not?" Having made a clean breast of my guilt I could now afford to be hard on myself.

"No, it's not your fault. But you shouldn't have run away. That immediately breeds suspicion, doesn't it?"

"Yeah, I'd say that's a big part of my problem." Hurry up, Consuela, let's get to the meat.

"But it isn't your fault that George died as he did. Don't you know about his family?"

"Stop asking dumb questions. Of course I don't know about his family. For Christ's sake, I didn't even know him until the day he died."

"Well, you don't have to be so rude."

"I'm sorry. I'm just impatient. I want to hear about George."

"Evidently. I'll tell you the whole story, but it's long and complicated, and maybe we should talk about 'us' first."

"No, I want to hear about the Livingstons." Which I did, but I also wanted to put off the part about "us" until after dinner, when maybe our tongues would be more used to talking and the dusk kinder to our drawn faces. "Please tell me."

"Here goes, then. The first George Livingston (there are three generations of them in this history), the first George Livingston was a railway mogul from Pittsburgh. He was very proud of his fortune and was determined to become a social success as well, so in the 1880's he moved to New York and built the house in Gosnold's Bay. He was an expert polo player and earned quite a reputation for his skill and cold-bloodedness. He didn't quite make the "Four Hundred" in New York, but he achieved a certain popularity for his horsey house parties in Gosnold's Bay (often inviting two full polo teams and their assorted ladies), and for his availability as an extra man at dinner parties. Gossip has it that he was basically stingy, and when he married his first cousin everyone said he only did it to keep the money in the family. He was fifty when he married her, while she was right off the floor of the Pittsburgh Cotillion. A year after the wedding George II was born, and the trouble began."

"What do you mean, 'trouble'?"

"Look, I said it was a long story. Wait a minute and you'll find out. Now, George's wife did not like the house parties or the polo set. But George didn't care and kept right on enjoying both. That is, until someone was killed on the polo field in Gosnold's Bay. George was suspected of foul play, but no one could prove anything. His wife asked him to stop playing polo. He was furious, and left Gosnold's Bay. She and George II spent most of their summers there without him.

"Uncle O and George II were about the same age, in fact there is a picture of them together in an album in Chestnut Hill —two little boys in sailor suits. Uncle O is recognizable, and the child next to him is George II, looking like a mongoloid with a huge puffy face and skinny body. When I asked Aunt Edith who he was she said, 'Very unfortunate, dear. We don't talk about it,' so I asked Uncle O. He told me almost everything I know. Mrs. Livingston was a tyrant, and wouldn't let George out of her sight. On special occasions, like birthdays, Uncle O might be allowed in or possibly young George allowed out, but rarely. They never liked each other much anyway. Uncle O said George was a 'queer lot.' "

"Queer? How?"

"I don't know. Bad blood, I guess." Consuela resumed. "I think George I did still come to Gosnold's Bay in the spring and fall with his polo friends, but he only came when his wife was in New York. They say he grew odder and odder."

"In what way?" I wished Consuela could be more specific.

"He had a nasty temper for one thing, and for another, he and his wife were never seen together, in New York or Cape Cod."

"What's so odd about that?"

"I wish you would stop interrupting me. How can I know exactly how George I was odd? I wasn't there, you know. This is all based on what Uncle O and the Potters have told me. And they say George got peculiar.

"Then, after showing no interest in his son, he suddenly began to take him everywhere. Young George was in his early teens, and his father in his sixties. They played polo, went to Europe and spent a lot of time together in New York. Mrs. Livingston was fit to be tied. She was domineering and possessive and terrified of losing her son. She felt old George was corrupting her boy, and in fact it may well have been she who tipped off the police."

"Police! Jesus, Consuela, you take the cryptic prize today. What do you mean?"

"Let me finish. When young George was eighteen, he was followed by the police to a house on West Fifty-first Street in New York which was supposed to be a dormitory for actresses. It was actually George I's private brothel. Instead of polo ponies, he kept a stable of very young girls and I think a couple of boys as well. The police questioned both Georges and the residents and someone, no one will say who, finally admitted that George and his son found their pleasure there, not just in the usual way, but with whips and other perversions. The scandal was hushed up, of course, and even now no one will talk about it at Gosnold's Bay. Old George was proved insane, and sent off to that place your father went to in the Berkshires."

"Ewell-Lowe? When was this?"

"About 1919, I think. Something like that."

"I wonder if my grandmother knew him. She was there then."

"Where? In Ewell-Lowe?"

"Yes. It seems that most of my family has been locked up there at one time or another. Go on, sorry to interrupt."

"O.K. Meanwhile, young George got married to an actress. They eloped in Maryland, I think he was still eighteen, and they came back to live with Mama. Some people think she was one of the girls in the brothel, and maybe that is why old George got so wild when he found out. He didn't get the news for almost a year, not until George III was born. Old George escaped from Ewell-Lowe right away and took a train to Gosnold's Bay. He used his railroad pass, which made it very easy for the Ewell-Lowe authorities to trace him, but when they got to Gosnold's Bay it was too late.

"When George got off the train, he walked right to the stables, got his favorite pony and a polo stick and headed for the house. George II and his wife were playing croquet on the lawn when the old boy came galloping straight at them. Young George grabbed his wife, and as they stood huddled together, old George trampled them both, swinging his stick. His horse kept on racing toward the beach, but George lost his balance and slipped out of the saddle. His foot stuck in the stirrup. It was still in the stirrup when the police came a few minutes later, and the rocks along the shore were red with his blood. Young George and his bride died some hours later."

"Jesus, you don't expect me to believe that, do you? Three at a blow?"

"You think maybe I made it up? Besides," she went on, "I'm not finished yet."

"Go on."

"After the triple funeral, Mrs. Livingston ordered a ditch dug in the lawn, where the bushes are now. That night, she had the horse brought up from the stable and she shot it, bang, into the ditch. Then she closed up the house and left with her grandson, George III."

"My George."

"Your George." Consuela drew a breath. "The bushes were planted later, by him. The house was uninhabited until the war, when George began coming down. Actually, I don't think he ever stayed in the house when he visited, I think he always stayed at the Yard Arm. He checked over the house and visited the Gomeses, who lived in the gatehouse and took care of the place for him. But I guess he didn't live in the house until he married Helen three years ago."

"What about his grandmother? Did she come back with him?"

"Oh no! She never returned until they brought her here in a casket and planted her next to her husband behind the church. That was only four years ago. Before that, she had lived with George in Arizona until he went to Dartmouth, when she moved to Hanover for four years. The year he entered Columbia Business School she bought a co-op in New York and they lived there together until she died."

"Poor George. How well did you know him?"

"Me? Hardly at all. I can remember him coming back to Gosnold's Bay when I was quite small. When I was eleven or so, Dorcas and Piper and I made the great discovery that he came back to Gosnold's Bay to bury his dogs."

I felt suddenly uneasy. "What do you mean, bury his dogs?"

"Just that. After each visit we would snoop around and find a rectangle of freshly spaded dirt in the circle of arborvitae, and a new headstone. Once we asked Mr. Gomes about it, but he was angry and sent us home. I didn't dare ask Aunt Edith or Uncle O. We were sure he was a murderer and to prove it, one night we dug up the most recent grave. We found a slightly bashed-up dog wrapped in a linen sheet. What a disappointment. He must have had a lot of dogs; he buried two or three a year."

"Was it a whippet like Waffles?"

"No, a Doberman pinscher."

I shuddered and saw a specter of George beating dog after dog, all lean, short-haired and sharp-nosed, like Waffles and the Doberman. Consuela kept on talking but I didn't really hear her. Something about consanguinity and inherited insanity brought me back in time to hear her wind up.

"So you're not to blame. You must see that now. You should be glad in a way that you helped him out of his despair and ended the chain of madness."

I really heard the last part, it shook me completely. I had no sense of finality as Consuela did, although I knew that George was dead, really dead. I knew that his spirit had not haunted me in Cuttyhunk; instead, it had been my little fantasy, a facet of general hysteria, and guilt. What terrified me was a growing feeling that George Livingston's death was a beginning, of what I didn't know. Nor did I have any idea where it would lead me. I did know that I was excited by Consuela's story, and that I was still waiting for a real conclusion to it, even though she had finished. I had no idea how long I would have to wait for the end.

part 2

MIDDLE

Gosnold's Bay

Purged by the bloodletting of two confessions—one to Consuela, and a greatly abbreviated one to Helen—tired from two nights of scanty sleep, I dozed fitfully on Friday afternoon. I wandered through various degrees of consciousness in unnatural daylight sleep. The thin white spread under me was puckered in damp wrinkles from my weight and sweat, and the dried salt on my back prickled against my shirt. I lay there, passing three hot hours deliberately supine, content in the success of the past two days and fortifying myself for Aunt Edith's return before dinner.

Consuela and I had covered years of omissions in our late night talk in Tarpaulin Cove. I tried to explain my peculiar relationship with Lucy, something I had assiduously avoided even thinking about after the scene in the Pittsfield General Hospital. I had asked Lucy to marry me, mainly out of love but also in answer to my own guilt and responsibility for having drunkenly driven the car off the road.

She had lain like sculpture on a sarcophagus lid between the starched sheets, blue eyes running over and all the more startling as isolated affirmations of life and hope. When she could speak a few days later, we became betrothed. Betrothed for a day.

My mother appeared deaf to the good news. Aunt Deborah, Lucy's mother, said, "You can't marry Lucy. She'll never walk again!" I knew that, and told her so.

She tried another argument. "Besides, you are cousins!"

"We are second cousins, not first. And we probably wouldn't have children anyway."

Cousin Deborah sighed. "You force me to tell you the plain truth, Hugh. Lucy doesn't love you."

And the next day Lucy turned away as best she could from me and sent me out, dismissed me. Said she only pitied me

77

and that pity would turn to hate, in time. "Please don't come back, Hugh. I loved you as a playmate. Now I've outgrown you. Don't wreck the past."

I left her, closed the green hospital door on her dead legs and went home, knowing that I was the cripple. Lucy's revenge.

Stumbling for a year, I gradually learned to walk. I did not exactly recover from Lucy's rejection, but kept it framed, a shrine made beautiful and untenable by hallowed memories, gilded day by day for six years. College and the Navy filled the spaces left, no room for faithless sweethearts. Better the emptiness of shameful stains on the sheets than to be untrue to Lucy, or to let another be untrue to me.

Consuela burned my defenses in an instant, and marched in like Caesar. Freed suddenly from my rituals of memory, and swept into the present, I also imagined that Consuela had thoroughly exorcised me. When lingerings of Lucy would trickle in, I would ignore them, put the stopper on the bottle.

In Cuttyhunk, I had given up, to wallow once again in Lucyland. Torn off from Consuela by the secret of George's death, I removed myself even more by letting Lucy in. This is what I said to Consuela when we talked about "us," and she understood it all, volunteering no heartaches or confessions of her own. When I pressed her for an unburdening, she only said she had been lonely, cut off by my drinking and my private horrors.

Stomach side down, I shut my eyes against the afternoon light and tried again to sleep. Hurry, hurry, before Edith comes back, before the children yodel in to fracture the thick quiet. Sleep switched on and off, with echoes of my sad talk with Helen Livingston, who had been kind to me.

She had a vague knowledge of George's troubles, and a premonition that one day soon, he would die by his own exertions. Illogically, she blamed Gosnold's Bay, said it killed him. In New York, he had been better able to control his spells, and every spring she would beg him not to come back. But he claimed he had to return; his grandmother's house "nourished" him. That last June while they were packing their bags, George had admitted outright that he was dependent on Gosnold's Bay.

Helen forced the dog on me, and I couldn't refuse her kind gesture, though I really didn't want the thing. She also entreated me repeatedly not to think ill of George.

"He was not himself when you saw him with the dog. You must believe me."

"I do believe you." I had answered Helen automatically, just the way I gave the responses at Easter Vigil.

"George loved that dog."

We beseech you to hear us, O Lord.

"The dog loved George."

We beseech you to hear us, O Lord.

"George was a good man."

I do believe. George was a good man. We beseech you to hear us, O Lord. And so the endless litany went with Helen. Went too with me now, around and around nipping through my sluggish drowsing. Suddenly a loud cry of pain broke through and split my sleep. I leapt to battle station alert, and ran down the hall to Rebecca's room. I could hear her sobbing on the way.

The door was locked.

"Rebecca, what's wrong? Open the door, sweetheart." I pounded hard, as if to bash it down, and heard whispers and stifled crying.

"Open the door now! Who's in there?"

The lock clicked in and I pushed the door open into Polly Miller's ugly face. The veneer of mock innocence staring at me round-eyed only underlined her guilt. I felt something close to hate for puddingfaced Polly.

Rebecca lay on the bed, face to the wall. Her narrow shoulders were shaking, and her hands were over her ears.

"What happened? Rebecca, are you all right?" I crossed to the bed and tried to roll her toward me, so I could see her face, but she buried her face in the pillow and resisted my hands.

Polly was hovering near the open door, and I wheeled on her.

"It's your fault, you. What have you done to Rebecca?"

"Nothing." Polly sidled closer to the hall.

"Pa, it's O.K. now, it's nothing." Rebecca raised her head

from the pillow and pleaded through her sniffles. She still refused to turn her face to me. "Please, Pa, don't blame Polly. I
wanted her to."

"Wanted her to what, for Christ's sake? Why can't you tell
me what happened?"

Rebecca sat up and faced me. As she started to speak,
Polly broke in.

"No. No, don't, Rebecca. You promised. He'll kill me, I
know he will. You promised."

"I did promise, Pa. I know I shouldn't have." Rebecca
lowered her head so she wouldn't see me, hurting to tell me
and split by conflicting loyalties.

I tried to pull the right words from my mouth but couldn't
do it, so I stood silent, my eyes fastened on Rebecca's bowed
head. That was when I saw the thin stream of blood trace the
ridge of her jaw beside her brown pigtail.

"You're bleeding!" I pulled her hand away from her head
and saw the red oozing hole in her earlobe. "Oh no!" Polly
tried to insinuate herself into the dark hall, but I grabbed her
and shook her hard.

"You little bitch, you butcher! How dare you defile Rebecca
like that, cheapen her like you. Get out. Get out and don't
come back." I gave her a shove and closed the door, returning
to Rebecca, who by this time was pale and scared by my outburst.

"Let me see it. Here, spit on this." I held out my shirttail.
"Now, once the blood's wiped off, it won't look so bad. There.
Not a very good job. What the hell did she use, a six penny
nail?" The hole was big, but clean enough. I thought it would
heal quickly.

"Pa," said Rebecca quietly, "you shouldn't have yelled at
Polly. It's my fault. I asked her to." She still didn't look at me.

"Don't you really mean that Polly offered to do it and you
said yes?" I tilted her chin up so that she had to look at me.
When her eyes met mine she nodded. "Well, why didn't you
say so?" I let her chin go, poor baby, she was like a frightened
rabbit.

"I couldn't Pa, because you were so mad at her."

"You bet I'm mad at her. Go wash your face and put some peroxide on your ear. I shouldn't have lost my temper like that, I know." I followed Rebecca down the hall to the bathroom. "I'll apologize to Polly, O.K.?"

"O.K. Right now?" asked Rebecca.

"This minute. And when I come back, I'm going for a quick swim. Will you meet me at the beach?" Somehow, I just couldn't leave her like that.

"Maybe. Thanks, Pa," and she shut the bathroom door.

I picked up my bathing suit and set off for the Livingstons'. The bad taste in my mouth had returned, I supposed from my nap, and I stopped to rinse out my mouth with Listerine, anything to get rid of that unbearable taste.

At the front door I whistled for Waffles. I felt I needed some company when I tendered my apology to Polly, and I was disappointed when he didn't come bounding up the steps. I went off alone.

I turned off the path and headed once again for the Livingstons' house, not much wanting to face either Polly or her mother. But I had to tell Polly I was sorry. And it would be easier to do without Helen around. I scanned the lawn, hoping to nab Polly before she reached home, when I saw Waffles come tearing out of the trees around the animal cemetery. His thin white coat allowed the blush of skin to tint it and he seemed even pinker against the green grass. I paused to admire him in action; his skinny angles and gawky proportions took on an unexpected grace and usefulness as he sped toward me.

"Come on, Waffles, come on." I clapped my hands and he pounded faster, until he reached my knees and pranced to a stop. He wriggled like a nervous snake as I reached to pat his bony head, and then he began to yap and dance around my toes.

"What's your fuss, friend? Simmer down, good dog." My words had no effect and he kept on darting ahead of me and then swerving back to nose my ankles. All the while he barked in his high, adolescent voice in the most irritating way.

The taste in my mouth had risen above the antiseptic and my stomach muscles tensed. Waffles seemed to have communicated his skittishness to me. Bubbly juices drooled from the velvet corners of his lips, and he revolted me. I started running, in a hurry to find Polly, to finish my business in this place, to exhaust my neurotic dog, to brush my teeth and gargle.

We dashed across the lawn toward the circle of trees, Waffles slightly in the lead turning his head back often to make sure I followed. My pulse drummed in my ears as I chased him. Then, through the thumping in my head I heard someone calling faintly. Polly? I slowed to a jog around the trees, and saw her as she straggled through the opening, her clothes torn and bloodstained, face covered with her red hands. Waffles stood near Polly, watching and wagging his tail.

"Oh, dear God! Polly, Polly, let me help you!" Gently, I pried her hands from her face. Claw marks screeched their three-tined course at me, from brow to jaw. Her eye was spilling watery blood, the eyeball itself had capsized and was so red and tipped that it was difficult to assess the damage. Teeth marks and scratches on her arms and legs were nothing compared to that eye.

When I stooped to lift her up, I saw her halter had been ripped, and hung in tatters between her two flabby breasts. Deep teeth marks pocked the flesh around one swollen nipple. Polly was bleeding, but she wasn't crying. "Waffles did this," she whispered. I picked her up, an inanimate sanguinous hulk, and carried her home, trying to find out what had happened to her.

"Were you teasing him? Has he had his shots?" She didn't seem to hear my questions. As we stepped onto the terrace, Polly came to life.

"You made him do it, didn't you? Because of Rebecca! I hate you! I hate your dog! Oh, Mom, help me." Helen opened the door and I put Polly down on the chintz couch, her wounds glaring more loudly against the faded printed roses.

"You start sponging her off, Helen, while I try to get hold of Philip Potter. With any luck, he will have just got in from New York. Has the dog had his shots?" Helen nodded but was not mobilized by my orders, in fact she looked utterly helpless, so I left her standing there and went to the kitchen for a basin and some towels. I set the basin on the floor beside the couch and sloshed one towel in the warm water, wrung it out and handed it to Helen. She made no move to take it, only stood in shock.

"Wipe her off, Helen. Wipe Polly off. Here, take the cloth. I've got to get a doctor." I made her hands hold the towel and hoped she would do something with it while I rang Philip. He had just come in from the station and said he would be right over.

Helen was still standing with the towel when I got back. I took it from her and pushed her into a chair, and then began gingerly to clean up Polly, avoiding her listing eye.

"Please tell me what happened, Polly." Dab, dab at her wounds.

"You made Waffles do it. Just like my stepfather." Polly's voice was thin and bitter.

"What do you mean? You think I made Waffles assault you? How can you think that? I don't understand!"

"All my stepfather's dogs did horrible things to people he didn't like; that's why he killed them." Polly was matter-of-fact.

"Killed who?" I asked.

"His dogs, of course. You don't think he killed people, too?"

At that point, I would have believed almost anything.

"Listen, Polly, I was on my way over to apologize to you for having lost my temper, when I found you all beaten up. Even if I could have told the dog to punish you, you don't really think I would have done it, do you? I just lost my temper, that's all, and I am very, very sorry."

Polly didn't say anything, and I wished the hell Philip would hurry up.

"Besides," I went on, "how could I have possibly 'made him do it'? He wasn't even in the house. Are you sure you didn't tease him or make him angry in some way?" Polly squeezed out a mirthless laugh.

"All I did was get out like you told me. I went to the Magic Circle."

"To the what?"

"The Magic Circle, the cemetery. I call it the Magic Circle. Your dog was there, asleep. When I picked up the phone to call Rebecca, I noticed something in the grass and went to pick it up. That's when your dog got mad."

None of this made any sense to me; the Magic Circle, the phone and the funny triumphant ring to Polly's voice.

"Let me get all this straight. You were making a telephone call from the animal cemetery when the dog attacked you, is that right?" Jesus, we're all cracking up.

"Not exactly. I *was* making a telephone call, but I stopped to pick something up. Then your dog attacked me." Polly put an evil emphasis on "your" each time she said it, which seemed like every other word, and it was getting to me.

"I suppose I should ask you what that 'something' was?" I didn't really care but it was the next logical step in this spaced-out catechism.

"I'll bet you'd like to know, wouldn't you? But I'm not telling."

"O.K., Polly, I guess you're entitled to your little secrets. But just to prove to you that I didn't make Waffles attack you, I will have him put to sleep for good."

I tried to look her in the eye while I spoke, but I couldn't do it, flinched and looked toward the door, wishing for all the world that Philip would walk through it.

"Killing Waffles won't solve anything," muttered Polly. "It isn't him, it's you. Besides, you'll just get another dog, the way he always did, my stepfather."

Philip did walk through the door and Polly stopped talking. I have never been gladder to see anyone than I was to see Philip.

He deftly wiped the eye and examined it, while I gave him a synopsis of Polly's story. Helen continued to sit like an unstrung marionette. Philip cleansed and bandaged everything except Polly's eye, then called the hospital to tell them Polly was coming. I felt superfluous and offered to drive Polly over.

"I'll take her, Hugh. You stay with Helen. Here, let's try to bring her around with this"—he handed me a vial of spirits of ammonia—"and then I'll leave you a sedative to calm her down when the full impact hits her. She's in mild shock, probably just as well, considering."

We carried Polly to the car. I leaned in the open door as Philip turned on the engine, not anxious to return to Helen.

"What shall I do when she comes to and has her pill? Should I take her to the hospital to be with Polly? Will she know what has happened?" Stay, Philip, don't leave me here alone.

"Just play it by ear. She may remember, she may not. If she wants to come to the hospital she can. Polly's going to be all right, aren't you, Polly? Keep a low profile, Hugh, and you'll do fine," and with that, he rolled out of the driveway.

Spirits of ammonia were well and good for Helen, but what about me? I needed something too, other spirits, and located the liquor closet before returning to the living room. I poured a shot of Bourbon and swilled it down, poured one more and a little glass of brandy for Helen and brought them in.

Helen recovered her wits after a few sniffs of the ammonia and swallowed the brandy gratefully. Then she asked where Polly was. All Helen could remember visually was seeing Polly all bloody, but while Helen had sat on the chair, stony-faced, pieces of Polly's and my conversation had fluttered in her mind and she recalled them now.

"Polly. She talked about George. And his dogs. Didn't she?"

"Yes, a little," I replied quite calmly. Poor Helen, a bit mixed up in an improbable nightmare. I did try to keep a "low profile" but she pursued the subject.

"Polly never liked the dogs. Or George. She didn't seem fond of him either. Don't know why. What did she say? About the dogs? And about George? You mustn't believe her. No." Helen's color returned with her speech and I dared to hope she might soon want to leave to see Polly.

"What else, Hugh? What else did Polly say?" Oh yes, I had forgotten.

"Nothing much."

"She said he killed the dogs. Didn't she?"

"Well, something like that. She was talking wildly, poor kid. I didn't pay too close attention to her, Helen."

"No. That's right. Don't pay attention. She's very odd, Polly."

"Helen, I think perhaps I'd better have the dog put to sleep."

"Waffles?"

"Yes."

"Put to sleep? You mean killed?" Helen looked as though she might cry.

"I can't keep a dog who attacks people like that. And if the police find out I'm sure they'll impound him."

"But that dog was George's," pleaded Helen. "George wanted you to keep him. Polly did it, Hugh. We've had trouble with her before. Don't kill the dog. Promise me you won't. It's a part of George, still alive."

I couldn't refuse her. Not killing Waffles seemed to be the least I could do for poor, rattled Helen.

"Well, I'd better go to Polly now."

"I'll drive you over."

Polly was in surgery when we got there. Philip left the observation window and came to us.

"Are you taking care of that dog, Hugh?" he asked me.

"No, please," broke in Helen, "Hugh and I have settled everything. It was Polly, not the dog. She bullies, teases. You won't report it, Philip?"

Philip looked at me enquiringly and I shook my head.

"No," he said and offered Helen his arm. She took it. There was nothing more I could do for them, so I called Consuela for a ride back home.

Aunt Edith answered the call and my voice stuck.

"Where have you been, Hugh? You have worried us, why didn't you call earlier?" Edith's careful enunciation (*been* as *bean*) and condescension infuriated me.

"I'm at the hospital. Pol—"

"THE HOSPITAL! Whatever for?" If she had just shut up, I could have told her, the old bird.

"Polly Miller was attacked by her late stepfather's dog, now mine, and I found her." I was interrupted by a snort.

"I DON'T understand a thing you are saying. Here's Consuela." She let the telephone clunk on the table and stomped off to get Consuela, tugging at her girdle on the way, I bet.

"Hugh? Are you all right? Aunt Edith says you're in the hospital." Consuela's voice was like a sea anchor and I stopped drifting.

"Hi, sweetheart. I'm fine, just *at* the hospital. It's Polly who's hurt. That wretched dog attacked her and tore her to pieces. Philip came over and mopped up the superficial bites and scratches and now they're operating on her eye. It's a mess. I just brought Helen over in her car, but there's nothing for me to do now. Can you pick me up?"

I waited outside on the hospital steps, out of earshot of the PA paging doctors and away from the smell of carbolic acid. I studied the thick wood-chip mulch around the uninspired plantings to spare myself the trouble of explaining why I was there if a familiar face should happen to come up the walk. Depressing though Aunt Edith's return was, at least I hadn't been on hand for her arrival, and the announcement of George's demise. Little Polly had spared me that. Only Helen and Consuela knew that I had been there when he died, and we planned to keep it that way.

As for the damn dog, I wondered just what to do about him. It wouldn't be a great loss to have him gassed by the SPCA, if only Helen hadn't minded. No one seemed to like Waffles, and besides, our real dog is Alice: spawning Alice in Still River, part Lab, part Newfoundland, she is thick and lazy, the antithesis of Waffles.

Everyone was well into his second drink when we got back to the house. I greeted Uncle O, smirked at Aunt Edith and vanished quickly upstairs with a stiff one, to wash my hands and my stale mouth. The rancid juices had stopped but the taste lingered in my spit, and my teeth and tongue seemed coated with a putrid film. Bad breath, a dentist had told me, usually comes from the stomach. If taste were any indication, my breath could be rising from my lower bowel. I was probably getting an ulcer. Who wouldn't, after a vacation like this?

I came downstairs and freshened my drink, then settled on the horsehair sofa. The small talk which Edith finds so enjoyable bores me, and I looked for a diversion. Waffles, on cue, slunk out from under the couch, where he had hidden himself after tearing up Polly. He tentatively wagged his tail and tried to look endearing.

"Lie down, Waffles, you miserable cur. Lie down." I was stern.

He shied away from my raised arm, and obsequiously stretched his long, slithery body across my feet like a python. He lay there, playing dead, while we continued with the forms of the cocktail hour. When we rose for dinner, Waffles got up too, very sneakily, behind my back. But I saw him.

He crossed behind us and prowled around beside Aunt Edith like a sleuth. Waffles' surprise tactics worked and Aunt Edith let out a piercing shriek when his wet icy nose nuzzled her thigh. He must have grinned, under her Ban-lon slip, when he bumped into her stout rubber garter, and I imagined his leer, exposing his new white fangs.

"Hugh, get that dog! You stop it, dog, you hear? Stop it!"

Aunt Edith's voice soared as she tipped and teetered and trotted with little mincing steps, arms working like oars against her skirts to ward off the Peeping Tom.

I didn't laugh, exercising enormous self-control. Nor did I look at Consuela, but went right to Waffles, very businesslike, and firmly held him back. After the dining room doors were shut against us, I scratched behind his ears a little and ruffled the hair on his neck, something that transports shaggy Alice to Nirvana, but which held little pleasure for Waffles. I almost was afraid that I might break the thin, twitching satin of his nearly bald coat.

Conversation at the table seemed to center on the Livingstons. I introduced Polly's queer statement that she had gone to the animal graveyard to make a phone call. That stopped all talk. Until Edith launched forth.

"What nonsense you speak, Hugh. Who would put a telephone in a cemetery?"

"Mary Baker Eddy?" ventured Consuela.

"Pa's right, Aunt Edith," announced Rebecca. "There is a telephone there. Mr. Livingston had it put in, or out, because he used to sit there a lot."

"They always were so nonconformist, those Livingstons!" rankled Edith. "I knew George would come to a bad end like the others, I knew it."

"I still don't understand the telephone." Poor Uncle O could always be counted on to try to keep Aunt Edith on the subject.

"Is it an extension of the phone in the house, Rebecca?" I asked.

"You can 'listen in,' if that's what you mean."

"That is exactly what I mean." And at last I had it figured out.

"Mr. Livingston called it his alarm clock. Mrs. Livingston used to call him on it through the operator when he stayed out too long." Rebecca confirmed my theory. The telephone bell would jangle George out of his madness. And that's why he always answered Margaret Giannelli's calls about the screaming.

Aunt Edith snorted and resumed masticating the face of the rump. She loves nearly raw, red meat; sinks her teeth into the juicy flesh with a communicant's fervor and devotion to the Body of our Lord. Completing portion one of her sacrificial rite by washing down the remains of the victim with St. Émilion, she cleared her throat importantly and waited until she captured every eye. We all felt the lecture coming on.

"The Livingstons, despite the early promise they showed when they built that charming house here three generations ago," she began, "are not our sort of people. Their family genes are bad, as history will attest. They have always been inclined toward vulgarities of one kind or another. An animal cemetery is one of them, and a telephone in a cemetery, especially in a cemetery of that sort, is certainly another. That is, if we can assume that what Rebecca says is true."

"It is true!" broke in Rebecca.

"Please don't interrupt. Now, I'm not speaking ill of the dead—my Maker knows that I have never had an unkind thought toward George Livingston, but since he has 'passed on' as you Catholics believe, personally I think 'away' is more accurate, since he has passed, and without issue, I think we can all hope that Helen will move away and sell the estate as quickly as possible. We will not have to acknowledge that they ever crossed our lives.

"Let us all try, then, beginning now, to speak of the Livingstons as little as possible. I do not want people plying me with questions about their pasts"—here she paused to look pointedly at me—"nor do I want you, Rebecca"—she shifted her glare—"to let Polly linger as your friend. She is thoroughly unsuitable for a girl of your upbringing, something I hope you will appreciate later, though how, living as you do in a cow barn, I don't know. I have finished now. You may talk."

What an old fart she is, I thought to myself, and then aloud, "I'm perfectly willing to stop rehashing this thing, and in fact would welcome more interesting topics of conversation. But my dog has just hurt Polly, she may have lost her eye for all I know, and Rebecca seems to be her only friend here. So I am afraid, Aunt Edith, that you will have to suffer the Livingstons for a few days longer."

"No, Hugh, you are wrong. *You* may have to suffer them, I will not. This is *my* house, and I do not want to hear about them. If you have things to say, plans to make concerning Polly or Helen, please do so in private. Of course, I shall pay a sympathy call on Helen in the morning, something I could have avoided if only someone had thought to let me know before the funeral. Flowers are so much easier than house calls." She explored her empty plate with her fork for unseen meat, like a dowser with his willow, sighed and laid her tools to rest at four-twenty on the plate, and stifled a burp.

"More beef, Aunt Edith?" asked Consuela.

"No, I don't think so, dear." We waited. "It was good, nice and rare. I've never understood how anyone can enjoy overdone meat, one reason why I don't eat with Jewish people."

Edith toyed with a small piece of gristle, all that was left on her plate, and returned the fork to its hour-hand position.

"Are you sure you won't have just a little more, Aunt Edith?" coaxed Consuela.

"No, dear, thank you. You young people help yourselves." Sweet Edith, always thinking of others. No one felt much like eating any more.

"It's a shame to put all this meat away, with Mabel coming home tomorrow. You know how she hates dealing with other people's leftovers. How about this nice little sliver, Aunt Edith? Just perfect for you." Consuela wheedled charmingly, knowing full well the regimen of forcing food which Edith expects.

"Well, if you really insist." Consuela tucked two other bleeding "slivers" underneath the offered one and put them on Edith's plate.

"Blood?" asked Consuela.

"Thank you, yes. Where are the little silver blood cups? Rebecca, that's a good girl, just run to the breakfront and see if they're there. Now, who else would like some? One for me and one for Oliver. Oliver always drinks it, don't you, dear?" Oliver nodded glumly.

"None for me, thank you," I announced.

"Nor me," chimed Consuela.

"No juice?" Aunt Edith's eyebrows disappeared under her short, frizzled bangs. "But it's so GOOD for you. You really ought to drink some, you know. Rebecca?"

"What?"

"Not what! Yes, Aunt Edith. Would you like some blood?"

Rebecca's fingers flew to her earlobe, and she looked pale.

"No, thank you, Aunt Edith." She gave the two silver cups to Consuela and waited while they were filled with cooled-off drippings eyeing the white flotsam of coagulated fat bobbing on top. Rebecca delivered the final sacrament and asked to be excused.

"But we're not finished. We do have dessert, don't we?" More eyebrows.

"Yes, Aunt Edith, we do have dessert. Don't you think

Rebecca might stretch her legs a bit before she clears off and brings in the pie? She's not used to such late dinners," said Consuela.

"At her age? Well, she should be!" Edith humphed and chewed some more.

"At her age I was still eating in the nursery with M'amzelle." Consuela lighted her cigarette aggressively, and stared defiantly down the table at Aunt Edith, who was watching Rebecca leave.

Aunt Edith's face had a greedy look, I had to admit. In fact, it was quite the same expression she had worn when she had waited for her little silver cup to be filled. I turned to Uncle O, who filled my wineglass again.

He bent to my ear and whispered. "They say George was found with a polo stick by his side, you know. His father's. What do you think he was doing with it?" Caught off guard, I was about to tell Oliver when Edith mercifully interrupted.

"What was that, Oliver?" Her eyes may have been on Rebecca's bottom, but Edith's ears were sharp and her tone querulous.

"Just a little man talk, my dear." Oliver chortled, proud of his deliberate disobedience. He's really getting ballsy, I thought.

"About those dreadful Giannelli girls I am sure. They are loose, no morals whatever. I hope Rebecca hasn't made friends with them, as well?"

Consuela told her no and then went on to describe Race Day, to which account Edith gave rapt attention, though why, as it changes hardly at all from year to year, I didn't know. Oliver and I made murmurings about Wall Street, mainly so we wouldn't have to hear the chatter.

The instant we opened the dining room doors, Waffles played peekaboo under Edith's skirt again, and I had to put him outside. When I closed the screen door behind him he turned around, and that time I was sure he laughed. His canines did show, like small white icicles hanging from underneath his drawn-back lip. Sometimes, he was almost adorable.

Just before we went to bed the phone rang. I took it in the hall closet. It was Philip to say Polly was doing pretty well.

They had left her eye in, but were not sure either if she would ever have the use of it, or if they could keep it from getting infected. Philip said the danger of infection was great with eye injuries. I asked him if I could do anything.

"You might visit Polly tomorrow. She asked for you several times. Bring Rebecca with you; that will cheer Polly up. She's an odd one. Said the strangest things when she was coming to. Helen was most upset. Well, good night, Hugh."

"Good night, Philip."

Slowly, I returned the receiver and pulled the chain hanging from the forty watt overhead bulb. A bright stripe of kitchen light shone from under the shut door and limited my privacy on the south. The northern wall was woolly with coats. I could feel them hanging behind me, just as I felt the clammy rubber of yellow slickers which lined the east side. I sat down on the frayed rush seat of the telephone chair, and leaned against the worn slate board, expunging vital messages with my head and shoulder as I rubbed against it. I've known so many blackboards, covered them with my mark, only to have someone else wipe them clean. I wished the wipers would come now and wipe me clean of children, dogs and aunts, and clean of weariness. I lighted a match for a cigarette and noticed how my hand shook. I must watch my drinking. One more match to see the closet contents in the flickering light.

Except for me, it was a tidy cupboard: directories, binoculars, chalk and pencils in a jelly jar, a little box of paper used on one side and carefully cut to fit, placed blank side up for portable messages, two tennis rackets in a rack with a furled umbrella, a bag of golf clubs standing under a small shelf for tennis balls and two flashlights which worked. A complete inventory.

So Polly had chattered, looped on sodium pentothal. I wondered what she had said to Philip. Had she expounded her convictions that I had in some way perpetrated Waffles' bloodthirsty assault? I must talk to Philip, perhaps he could shed some light on why she insists that I was involved. If I started in with Philip, I would probably end up telling him everything, including my part in George's death, and maybe that was not such a bad idea.

Good doctors are well used to secrets, and besides, Philip is smart and cool. He would be an objective confidant, different from either Helen or Consuela, whose emotional attachments to the incident bent their view. Not that they hadn't accepted my confessions with surprising equanimity, they had been admirable. But Philip was a man.

I decided to "proceed as the way opens," a tactic I had picked up from my Quaker mother. Meanwhile, no point in lingering any longer in the airless cubby. It was time for bed, and for a thin Bourbon and water. The door opened quietly, letting in the light and humming kitchen motors, and me.

There was Aunt Edith, knife in hand, hunched over the scrubbed counter, hacking off great pieces of red meat, which she hurried to her twitching, pale wet lips. She was so engrossed in her gluttony she didn't see me. I wanted to remove myself from this revolting spectacle, but I couldn't, unless I slipped back in the closet again, and I didn't much want to do that, either. The longer I watched her, the more hypnotized I became, as I spied on the secret eater. Ten-year-old conscience twangs were reborn as I stood there, until I almost shook with the fear of being discovered. I backed into the closet and pulled the door. Slamming the phone down, I kicked the door and burst out, to see Edith on the run, stretching for a sponge, her back to me.

"I'm just cleaning up. We can't leave a mess for Mabel, you know. Some people do not understand how to leave a kitchen properly." She wiped the counter furiously. Was she hoping to expiate her greed by acts of cleanliness? I thought it likely.

"Mind if I have a nightcap?" I asked, while thinking, You'd better not or I'll get my dog.

"If you think you should." She was sanctimonious as she rinsed out her sponge and put it carefully by the sink. "Please don't leave a mess, after I've just tidied up. Good help is most difficult to find. Good night, Hugh. Please don't stay up all night. Consuela has already gone to bed, you know." What a cheap parting shot.

She left as she spoke, and was gone before I could reply. Trust Edith always to have the last word. I took my drink out to the back steps, where Waffles sat, repentant and faithful. I stroked his white coat, feeling the crusty scabs still there from George's blows. Poor Waffles, poor me. How unfair for both of us to have gotten mixed up with the Livingstons. Maybe we should stick together.

We came back inside. Waffles streaked into the living room while I put my glass, ice cubes still in it, in the sink, thinking I would leave it there as Mabel's morning perquisite. The good guest in me ultimately won out, and I washed, dried and put it away, while the ice cubes dripped down the drain. Edith had thoughtfully turned out every light downstairs, so I was left to fumble my way to the stairs, bumping into heavy carved corners of chairs and tables. Waffles had selected Edith's chair as his bed; he waved his rat tail at me as I went by, and let it fall among his legs. He was a white doughnut settled snugly in the dent Aunt Edith's fanny had left on the cushion.

I went right to my own bed, glad to resume that happy position I had been forced to abandon earlier. Was it only seven hours earlier? The hair mattress crunched under me as I resettled, flinging out one bent arm and retracting the other from a stiff stretch.

Three more nights until I could sleep with Consuela. We would be back in Still River then, in our own giant bed, which firmly supports us with silent sponge rubber, not this frugal rusty-springed cot with its pallet of uneven hair. I groaned, lowed actually, like one of our cows as I tried to resign myself to three more nights of monkish chastity. I was too tired to block out the refrain of our aborted love-making two nights before in Tarpaulin Cove.

Reunited after hours of talk and breast-beating, we had celebrated in the empty cabin with intimate pleasures. Intimate and indulged in less and less often as thirteen years of marriage carried us along. Before we were married, the spring of Consuela's senior year at Radcliffe, when she had lifted me out of the keep of Lucy's rejection, Consuela and I had given ourselves entirely to the winds of passion, like milkweed thistles.

My withheld love and semen flowed with the spring-swollen rivers. I knew their force and supply were infinite. Consuela tramped across my self-consciousness and inexperience until she wiped them out. I was a superb lover, superbly loved as well, Consuela made me sure of that. We tried to be guilty; I would take Consuela down to the musty basement of St. Paul's Church in Cambridge and wait with kerchiefed crones mumbling over their beads, while Consuela confessed our fornication.

We would try to stay out of bed. Neither of us could understand why we had been taught that our God was against this highest expression of love. Spring confirmed daily His renewal of life, how could we subscribe to the no-sex-before-marriage theory, even though our elders had tried to ingrain it in us since early puberty. In my case, it was "one doesn't fool around with 'nice' girls," a mean and unchristian maxim for a father to give to his son.

Spring vacation and Easter bore down on us, a separation too cruel to bear. It was clearly time for Consuela to Meet My Folks. Mother sent Edith a ladylike note inviting Consuela to Tyringham for Easter weekend. Our timing was perfect: Mother had just returned from a good rest with her sister in Philadelphia and my brother, Omar, was still studying turtles on the Galápagos. At that time he was a glorified schoolteacher aboard a school ship for boys whose parents could afford it.

On Holy Saturday, we decided to get married right after commencement. Consuela wooed my mother almost as enchantingly as she had wooed me. She also manipulated Aunt Edith with swift skill and convinced her that I was everything she had ever hoped for in a son-in-law, right down to a listing in the New York "stud book," a courtesy my mother continues because she thinks telephone books are so unmanageable, and she doesn't want to inconvenience her friends.

Our future was tossed in Edith's lap. After all, it was really her wedding, as Consuela pointed out, just let her do it, what did we care? Each ring of the telephone, Edith in some sort of twit over invitations, or canapés, confirmed our guiltlessness as we kicked my law cases under the chair and turned my graduate student's bed-sitter into a Persian garden of erotica. We pretended to worry about babies; that is, Consuela kept track on the calendar and we usually screwed anyway, knowing that first babies are always early for those who bother to count. We indulged ourselves then as we would never again be able to. What we lacked in practicality we more than made up for in our inventiveness and stamina.

In Tarpaulin Cove I felt I had been swept so clean that it was only natural to return, for one private night, to the joyous abandon we had had before. Our life together has brought many things into our nuptial bed: croupy babies, hungry babies, unborn babies; sore joints from bending over calving cows for hours, alcoholic stupors, February depressions, sobbing victims of nightmares, early risers pattering in for food at six just when I began to wake to Consuela's inquiring hand lightly tickling the inside of my thigh. But on the *Melande,* alone in an empty cove, maybe we could regain the selfishness of bachelorhood.

Consuela responded, blazing with desire. Hosannas rang in my ears as we remembered old pleasures. The tidal wave of orgasm rose offshore, and started moving in, building faster and faster. Kissing as I went, I turned around, half on the bunk, half on the deck, Consuela stroking me in front and kneading me behind, as I struggled for position. I irrupted big and stiff in her softness; we worked in unison for an ecstatic second, trying to prolong the tension. Consuela mumbled something but I was too engrossed to pay attention. Then Consuela stopped. "No, Hugh, no." I felt her legs kicking me and her nails biting into my groin as she tried to heave me out.

"What are you doing?" I managed to ask, still working.

"No, not inside. You can't come inside, not now. No more babies, Hugh. I can't."

So I had pulled out, feeling the gasp of her suction as I left, to go limp on her belly. No release, no relief, no anything. Until she invited me back, I would stay, waiting in suspended animation.

Consuela is physically so deceptive. She has stone mason's sinews tucked in her willow-wand limbs, vitamin D seeps from her pores. Her teeth are white and unfilled, even at thirty-three. Consuela radiates health and strength from her polished olive wood skin to her smooth hardy toenails, and yet she is female frail.

Technically, medically, Consuela is a juvenile virgin, her cervix no bigger than Rebecca's. That's why the doctor carves our babies out of her guts with his knife. Her papist blood is further tainted by the Rh negative factor. Again and again during pregnancy they puncture her belly until the test tube shows the fetal blood cells warring and we spar for time. Ward was seized from her womb almost two months early, and his blood was flushed five times until it flowed right. Consuela's battle scar is sliced afresh for each new life, to glow a livid purple for another year. Now six years healed, it is a taut white swath lumping crookedly down the fine hair line of her abdomen.

It is not in deference to the Pope that we abstain from pills and devices, but because Consuela's doctor will not let her use the surest ones, afraid of hormones or infections. I tried a pack of prophylactics once; Consuela was first incredulous and then wildly amused. Even I began to think my bathing cap absurd, and no erection can survive being laughed at. I suppose from that angle, the prophylactics were a success the same way liquor is—if you can't get it up, there's really no problem with birth control. In the long run, however, neither is satisfactory. So I wait, impatiently, for the few days grudged me, intervals of love between the ripening egg and its sloughing off.

I dreamed that night in technicolor, the detailed dreams of my youth. When I was little, I was such a skillful dreamer that I could make myself re-dream my favorites at will. Sometimes, I could even resume a broken dream, picking up again at that particular juicy moment which had waked me up seconds before. My dreams, like our love-making, have been altered by mundane responsibilities. In fact, I hadn't dreamed at all for several years.

But that night, perhaps to catch up, I had a double feature;

the Consuela-between-my-legs dream, a golden oldie, and a new one, Aunt Edith's metamorphosis. Here it is.

I walk into Aunt Edith's bedroom (something I have never done), and see her, lying on her bed, the peach-colored satin puff discarded in a rumple on the floor. She has on a dark dress, the covered buttons buttoned wrong down her front, the hem riding above her wrinkly knees. I think of the dress as being made of black bombazine, out of period but then, dreams are like that.

As I walk through the open door, she smiles, a fleshy cavern of a mouth, teeth in a glass on the bedside table. This is dream license too, as Edith still has most of her teeth and complains of "bridge work" from time to time. I notice as I approach the bed, smears of dirt, garden dirt, not grease, on the white bedspread. It looks as if an animal has tracked across it. Edith's smile grows wider, longer, a hole in her face. Meanwhile, her dress is slowly creeping up. I watch, spellbound, as more holes appear like the one that was her mouth only these are on her arms and legs. The holes spread, they follow her shrinking clothes until she is riddled with gaping cavities. What's left of her becomes fibrous and dry. Finally, the metamorphosis is complete, and on the bed is a cellular, dried-up sponge thing in the shape of Aunt Edith. I touch it long enough to feel its hardness, like coral, and then wake up.

I woke up quite fascinated with my own subconscious, and resolved to dream it again. Even now, I dream it quite often, it has become a mainstay in my repertory. Sometimes it changes a little. That first night I had two other versions. Once Rebecca's face and then Consuela's peeped out of the holes. The other run-through had blood seeping up to fill the gaps until each one looked just like the little silver cups passed round at dinner.

I was more interested than horrified by the dream, and didn't mind in the least watching it several times. The only obstacles to rest that night were physical frustration stemming from Consuela's cycle, and the return of the bad taste in my mouth. I decided to see a doctor about my stomach as soon as I got home.

In the morning, I called the hospital about Polly, asking if she would like to see Rebecca and me. The nurse said she would like to see me as soon as possible, but not Rebecca, which I thought was very strange. It was about ten o'clock before I was ready to leave. The children had gone to the beach with Rebecca in charge, and Consuela was playing tennis with her giddy girl friends. We had hoped to play singles together, Consuela and I, but Polly had ruined that plan. I felt martyred dressed in my hospital visiting clothes and went to the garden to pick some flowers for Polly. Monster dahlias so perfect they could have been molded in plastic severed easily between my nails. I was wrapping the stems in soggy newspaper in the pantry sink when I heard the screen door clap. I went into the kitchen and found Cam, sandy feet on tiptoe, reaching for the breadbox.

"Hey, what are you doing? You better not let Mabel see you. Now that she's back things will be different."

"Sure, Pa, but guess what? George is here. He's hungry."

I blanched. George. George is here? I shouldn't have been such an intellectual snob in rejecting Rebecca's choice for a name. Clearly, Jonathan Livingston Seagull would have caused fewer turns of my stomach.

"That's nice, Cam. Are you sure it's the same bird? We left him in Menemsha. That's a long way from Gosnold's Bay."

"I know it's George. After all, we brought him across the Sound from Cuttyhunk. Maybe he got another ride from Menemsha."

"Maybe. But I doubt it. Surely there is more than one begging single-legged gull?"

"I bet he really missed us!" And Cam ran off, leaving me to marvel at how little effect my deflating adult logic had on him.

In the hospital elevator I felt ridiculous with my bunch of flowers, and affected a bored stare. I checked in at the desk, which was manned by pretty, bosomy little Miss Moniz, probably from Portuguese Teaticket but working her way up, gold crucifix earrings twinkling on her ocher skin. Within a year or two she would certainly be married to a handsome young doctor, prosperity is just around the corner.

"You must be Polly's father, go right in, Room 309. She has another visitor now, but I'm sure it's all right."

"I'm not her father, just a friend." A middle-aged suitor, cradle snatching—is that what you thought, Miss Moniz? "I'll just wait outside until her guest leaves." She shrugged, disinterested, and returned to her charts.

Polly's door opened as I walked down the hall, and I was startled to see a uniformed policeman emerge, hat in hand. He closed the door and stood in front of it, looking me over as I stopped to double-check the number, Room 309.

"Good morning, I've come to see Miss Miller, I think she's expecting me. I'm Hugh Murray." I offered him my free hand, noticing the incongruity of his shrewd scrutinizing eyes and his scoured choir-boy's face. I also saw his sergeant's stripes and *Gosnold's Bay Police Department* sewn on his short-sleeved drip-dry shirt. Had Polly tattled about my vicious dog?

"Oh yes, Mr. Murray, she's expecting you. I hope we meet again." He dropped my hand abruptly and turned on his heel, never mentioning Waffles. I heard his brisk steps down the hall as I went into Polly's room.

"Hello, Polly. I hope you're feeling better? I brought you some flowers." I scanned the room for something to put them in so I could have my other hand back, and with it my dignity.

"Thank you, Mr. Murray." Polly's voice sounded more monotonic than ever coming from her bandaged swollen face to the recycled air of the sterile room. "I'll ring for a vase," she said grandly.

"Who's your friend in the blue uniform? He looked pleasant enough but a little old for you, isn't he?" Polly didn't find that funny.

"He came because I asked him to." Polly fixed me with her one eye and halted. "And it had nothing to do with the dog."

"Oh," I said. What now? I waited, then asked, "Do you mind if I smoke?"

"I don't care." Polly's stare continued steady and so did the silence until she announced, "I asked the policeman here because I had something to give him."

Was I supposed to question her about the cop? I didn't feel like it, so I prepared my smoke very slowly instead. Dragging out each slight action in a pretense of occupation. I patted all my pockets for matches, knowing exactly in which one they were, trying to hold off the final lighting, which would have to be an end to my busyness. If, however, the matches should be damp, I might squeeze out another whole minute or two before I would have to say something. The matches were dry. I inhaled with exaggerated bliss and rooted for words. Polly evidently decided that she had put me off long enough and spoke again.

"Aren't you going to ask me what I gave him?"

"Do you want me to?" Clever.

"Oh, never mind." She wiggled grumpily in the bed, mouth curving down unpleasantly. "What happened to your lighter with the boat on it, the U.S.S. *Boxer?*" Polly's eye shone hard as a jet bead.

"I don't know. I've lost it." What is she driving at? I wondered, and how the hell does she know about my lighter?

"I know where your lighter is. Do you want it?" The little pig eye, nearly lashless, stared on.

"Yes, of course I'd like it back. Do you have it?" Why don't you just give it to me, why all this beating around the bush? Polly was enjoying her production, and I was most definitely not.

"No. No, Mr. Murray, I don't have it, but I know who does!"

Smug and tantalizing, Polly folded her jellyfish hands on her belly, right under what I knew was a chewed, flaccid breast.

I blatantly pulled out my watch, sighed and put it back in my pocket.

"O.K., Polly, tell me who has it. I would love to get it back. I've had it for nearly twenty years, when I was on that ship in the Navy. Now, where is my lighter?"

"At the police station! I found it in the Magic Circle yesterday; when I picked it up your dog began biting me. I just gave it to Sergeant Lyons as evidence!" Her voice rose in victory to a squeal. I would have liked to gag her.

"Evidence of what?"

"That you were there when my stepfather died. You were with him in the Magic Circle. You maybe even killed him!" And from Polly's vituperative bawl, I think she looked forward to watching me hang from the gallows, out of pure hate.

"Polly, Polly, slow down. You found my lighter close to where your stepfather died. You also found it five days later. What does that prove? That I murdered him? Do you really think Sergeant Whatnot is going to believe that?"

"Lyons. Sergeant Lyons is his name. Listen, Mr. Murray, he is very interested in what I told him about you. He wants to talk to you, so you better go down and see him. You better face the music, Mr. Murray."

"I intend to do just that, Polly. But before I go, I want to tell you a few things." You yattering little finger-shaker. Too bad it wasn't Polly who had died in the Magic Circle. Poison Circle.

"First, I did happen to be in the animal cemetery when your father died, you guessed that one right. Second, and I doubt you guessed this, I have told your mother all about it. Third, she did not want to drag in the police; there really isn't any reason to because your stepfather died by his own hand, not mine, as the coroner has already verified.

"Something else you don't know about is scandal. The police in a summer place like Gosnold's Bay love a scandal involving the rich summer people. And that's what we are, Polly. Once you give the cops a sniff of a scandal, they waste no time digging for more and smearing it all over the papers. The *Cape Clarion* salivates for any tidbit, no matter how spurious, and turns it into pulp for the front page. Do you think that will please your mother?"

Polly smoothed her sheet and looked as if she didn't give a shit what her mother thought.

"You have done a foolish thing, Polly," I continued. "You are immature and selfish, and the consequences will be tiresome for everyone." Damn. What a dreary speech. I got up and went to the door, leaving the dahlias drooping on the foot of the bed, where I had put them for the nurse who never came. Polly had probably not even rung for her, just to be nasty. "Good-by, Polly. Rebecca thought she might visit you later. Do you want to see her?" Anger seeped into my voice against my efforts to hold an even temper.

"I don't care."

"Fine. I hope you feel better, Polly. I'm sorry Waffles was so awful to you." Lies, lies.

When the door shut her away, I leaned against the cool tile wall of the hospital corridor. If the police were in on the mess, I knew I had better move quickly before they cooked up stratagems to catch me up and twist the truth, which God knows was ugly enough untampered with. If possible, I must keep it from becoming a publicized horror. When in trouble, call a lawyer. What irony, but I did call Jim Earl in Boston, one of the best criminal lawyers in town and a good friend. He said he'd try to help. Then I went to the police station. Sergeant Lyons was sitting in a chair, reading the paper.

"Come in, Mr. Murray. I was expecting you." He led me to a back room where we could talk privately, a host ushering a favored guest to his inner sanctum. His deferential manner did not fool me; I have known many sergeants and listened to their caustic cant at roll call. Lyons would test true to form and be out to get me twice; once for being a big shot lawyer and once for being rich.

I cut short the preliminary fencing and used courtroom rhetoric, talking throne to throne.

"I am sure you see exactly why Mrs. Livingston did not want to come to you with the whole story. You must know about the family, and I'm sure you can appreciate her desire to keep the notoriety and scandal out of the papers. I was a witness to Mr. Livingston's death, and if you find it necessary to question me, just get the summons and I'll be glad to help you out. In the meantime, I hope you'll try to spare Mrs. Livingston both unnecessary questioning and publicity. The past week has been rough for her."

"Well," he drawled, pulling out the word to its utmost extent, "well, we'll have to do some looking into this. The *Cape Clarion* already seems to have gotten wind of something, you know how they are. 'Course, we'll try to keep the gossip down like we always do, but there's no telling what might get in the paper." He offered me a cigarette to show he was a gentleman, and I accepted to show he was my equal. He then tipped back in his chair and put his feet on the table so I would make no mistake about whose territory we were on, or how relaxed he was.

"You know that I'm a lawyer." The ball was in my court. "I called a colleague before I left the hospital. Here is his number. From now on, you will be in touch with me through him. My wife and I were planning to leave on Monday morning—we're only visiting here—so if you need me after that the logistics may be complicated. I'd like as much notice as possible. Let me give you my number here."

I was reaching for a pen in my jacket when I heard him snicker.

"My goodness, Mr. Murray, I've known your wife all my life. Why, my old mother, God rest her, used to work for Edith Shaw summers 'til the year she died. Washing, ironing, sometimes a little cleaning, 'do for' she called it."

"Oh? What was her name? I might not remember too well. We don't get down often." Social injustice has always made me come out in spots, and I found it impossible to keep my professional cool while I stepped all over the mystic lines of social strata. Sergeant Lyons licked his chops as I faltered, and took full advantage of his strengthened position.

"Mum's name was Nora, a little woman with a lot of brogue." He beamed, rocking in the chair, proud of his good, dear Mum. She must have died a devoted slave to Aunt Edith.

"Oh yes, I remember Nora. She always had a cheerful word." How easily the lies were coming now. I couldn't remember one single face of the indistinct corps of chirruping minions Edith used to have, only that they had constantly scurried to cupboards and pantries with their arms full. But Lyons seemed satisfied. His beam broadened and he straightened in his chair as it dropped back on its two front legs. He leaned across the table at me.

"Mum's words weren't cheerful when she found me in the

closet with Miss Consuela, I'll tell you. Why, she was fit to be tied when she found us . . ." He winked at me and began to laugh.

Jesus! But I kept an impassive face.

"Miss Consuela thought it was funny"—he stressed the "Miss" and seemed to mock me—"being caught necking like that, we were only twelve or so. But *she* didn't have to listen to Mum go on and on about fooling with a girl whose skin was as dark as a Port'gee's, with holes in her ears no better than a Gomes, Moniz or Viera. Oh, it was something, let me tell you. But I always liked your wife, Mr. Murray. All of us local boys did. She was always up for anything, not like some of the snobbish prigs who come here in the summer." He laughed again, a barroom guffaw, and I rose to excuse myself from his bawdy humor, to return to my beautiful dark wife, the wanton chippy of Gosnold's Bay.

When I got home, Mabel was keeping order in the dining room with tight lips and hands on her hips, while the children sullenly spooned in their creamed chicken, not saying a word. From their dripping hair I surmised that Aunt Edith had sent them from the beach for lunch, so that she could sit in solitary grandeur under the shade of her striped umbrella on the lookout for skinny-dipping lovers. The children were stuffed into real clothes and sandals. Their resentment matched the general oppressiveness of the room. Consuela had lost the sandwich battle once again.

I got a small glass of straight Bourbon, closed myself in the closet and pulled on the light. The telephone closet was getting to be my favorite place, very cozy. When I got through to Jim Earl again I filled him in on my visit to Sergeant Lyons.

"There really isn't any case against me as yet, but I'm sure that mick cop will do his damnedest to work one up if he can." I slumped against the blackboard. "What now?"

Jim was sympathetic and said he'd drive down first thing in the morning. In the meantime, I was to do nothing, not even talk to Helen. That was a relief—I could not face crossing her lawn again with bad news. I couldn't face her.

"Relax, Hugh. After all, it's the weekend. I doubt they'll

serve a summons before Monday. If I can spend tomorrow night with you, I'll stick around on Monday and talk to Lyons if I need to."

I hung up and finished my cigarette in the closet. Talking to Jim had calmed me down, but the added complication of a possible criminal suit being brought against me was very nearly the last straw. Well, I must tell Consuela this new bit of nastiness, so I got up and went into the kitchen and to the dining room, where the children still sat behind half-full plates under Mabel's watchful eyes. I gave them the peace sign, and once behind Mabel's back, turned it into the finger, which cheered them momentarily.

I walked through the vegetable garden and across the old polo grounds, now used only once in a while for baseball or soccer, and I thought fleetingly of the original George, who had after all landed me in this mess, albeit indirectly. I also wondered whether or not I could chide Consuela about doing whatever it was she did in the closet with Sergeant Lyons. Probably not. My touch would be too heavy, and I did not want to risk putting Consuela on the defensive for so thin a tease. And so I arrived, depressed, at the two tennis courts which were maintained quite perfectly by the Gosnold's Neck Association for the use of its few privileged members.

Consuela and Dorcas were playing vicious tennis with Piper and another horsey girl I didn't know, Mopsy, Flopsy or Cotton tail. Why didn't these ladies have normal names like Betsy or Sue? If I hadn't been in such a rush to talk to Consuela, I would have liked to watch them play. Even in my impatience, I was smitten with Consuela's grace and deft co-ordination. She never seemed to exert herself but consistently made her points with a casual wave of her racket. Fresh and neat, she glided with the control and reserve of a superior animal, in pretty contrast to the other three, who moved about like machines. Their tennis dresses and skimpy socks, pompons bouncing on their heels, looked absurdly clean and new, compared to their sweaty blotchy faces. How could Consuela enjoy the company of these women? They were like triplets, identical in forced jollity, superficiality and a compulsion to vanquish middle age. At parties they were too friendly and darted from conversation to conversation like mass-produced wind-up toys, with carefully turned-under straight hair and size-nine diet-guarded shapes. The hell with Sergeant Lyons' dirty stories, I had chosen well.

They were just finishing the set when I arrived and we all left together, like noisy geese, until Consuela and I turned to follow our narrow path and left them to theirs. I told Consuela what had happened to me since breakfast, so long ago.

"We've got to keep this out of the papers, Hugh. We've got to. Not only will it demolish Aunt Edith, and I don't want to be around when that happens, but what about you? You won't look so hot as General Counsel, will you? God damn Polly! What got into her?"

Polly, at least, was no longer my problem. No one could pin that on me, and Consuela agreed.

Edith was still monarch of the beach when we got down; she utilized all her regal privileges and kept the children out of the water "for a good hour after lunch." They were stoic and bunched on a rock with George, feeding him a midday banquet glommed from Mabel's larder.

Swimming cleared my head and rearranged the priorities crowded in it so that by the time I climbed the path to dress for lunch I felt I had regained a little perspective. Then Consuela reminded me that the Ascusset Yacht Club Dance was to-night, beginning with the usual drinks and cook-it-yourself steak dinner on the veranda of the Golf Club at six-thirty. A real family party for all the Race Day competitors, including the Midgets (who swam with life jackets) and their dues-paying parents and grandparents. Even the baby-sitters were invited to the dance with their muscular boyfriends (usually the sailing, tennis and swimming instructors, or "tutors," a fancy name for male baby-sitters necessary for school-aged boys). A truly egali-tarian evening.

In past years I had fought with Consuela about attending; we alternated between my going acrimoniously and then getting stinking drunk, and my staying home and getting just as drunk only without the acrimony or the exercise. At least at the Golf Club I could work some of it off doing a fatuous mop-dance with Dorcas or any one of Consuela's good-time girls, or I could even teach Rebecca the Ascusset samba, a hopping, kicking cousin to the smooth Latin American dance. At home, there was only Uncle O's Bourbon and faint entreaties from the commercials on Mabel's television, back in the maid's sitting room.

This year, however, my hackles didn't even stir when Consuela asked me if I would come. Yes, I would come and quite gladly. It would be a different kind of torture from the type I had been under for the past surrealistic week. I didn't care one shit about the dance, and from that angle alone it would be an oasis.

After Mabel's little lunch of chicken mousse, Aunt Edith said she was going to "ascend for her beauty rest" (she is so original), which roughly translated means stay the hell out of the house. Do Not Disturb to Aunt Edith means no toilets flushing, doors closing, telephones or voices.

As I pulled her chair from the table I saw Waffles lying right where Edith must have had her neatly crossed ankles throughout lunch. No one had complained about him, and I had assumed he was at the beach with the children. He got to his feet along with Edith, and began to follow her upstairs, sniffing eagerly the backs of her knees just under the edge of her skirt.

"Waffles! Leave Aunt Edith alone! Come here!" He turned his head at my voice and so did Edith. She had a dreamy, slightly sensual smile on her lips and in her eyes which made my neck prickle. I had seen her look that way before, but was unable to pinpoint when, and was only aware of the total incongruity of such an expression superimposed on her usual mask of righteous disapproval.

"Don't worry about the dog, Hugh. We've become very friendly. I can't think when I've liked a dog so well." She turned to the stairs again, her face still altered.

"All the same, you don't want him around during nap time, I'm sure. Come on, Waffles. Come." He didn't respond to my summons, so I went to the landing and firmly seized his collar.

Toenails scratched in protest as I pulled him down the

stairs, his rodent's tail between his legs. Those murky blue eyes were reproachful, but I shoved him out the door with my foot anyway. My stomach was tight and I felt apprehensive. I also felt something else very like jealousy. The wretched acid trickled into my mouth again. I couldn't believe that an animal could bring out such strong emotions in me. When he was with me, he affected me more than Consuela or the children, or even Edith.

Gargling got rid of that taste, and I went into the bedroom to change into my trunks. Consuela was tying back her hair and watched me in her dressing table mirror, a puzzled look in her eyes.

"Why are you staring at me like that?" I asked, watching her in return, through the mirror.

"You look awful. Are you sick or something?" Consuela's voice didn't have its usual rich timbre, but sounded thin and tense. It was the first thought I had of the pressures I had unwittingly put on her lately.

" 'I'm not sick, I'm just in love.' " I did a stupid little soft-shoe routine, and suddenly felt like crying. "Oh shit, what a hell of a week. I'm almost looking forward to that silly dance tonight, just as a change from dogs, and death and cops. Will you tango with me, love?" I put my hands on her shoulders and she put her hands on top of mine. The baroque emerald that had been my grandmother's was duller than it had been thirteen years ago, bread dough and cow dung were stuck under the gold prongs, and the wide gold wedding ring was etched with Ajax and pot scrubbers. But in a way, Consuela wore the rings better now, not just as ornaments but as military decorations. If I could love her so entirely, then she *must* know me to the core. I took a chance.

"Does that dog give you the creeps, or is it me? My general lousy state of mind that makes me so sensitive (I hate that word), so receptive to him? Or to the way I react to him?" I wanted her to sigh with relief and say, "Oh, I'm so glad you feel it too," I was desperate for some affirmation of my mixed-up and uneasy reactions.

"He certainly doesn't turn me on, not that I hate him or

anything. I do find him disgusting in an amusing way when he hovers around Aunt Edith's legs. But no, he doesn't have any effect on me. At least, not that I've noticed. I'm not really sure what you mean."

"Neither am I, I guess. It's just that I keep thinking about him. Sometimes I am quite overcome with liking him, and I have no idea why, and sometimes I practically hate him. I felt something close to jealousy when Edith bragged about how friendly she and Waffles had become. Now, that's crazy!"

"It certainly is." Consuela patted me and I tried to be content with the fact that at least I had her sympathy, if not her understanding.

"How can you try to analyze your relationship with a dog, for Pete's sake," went on Consuela, "with all the other crap that's screwing you up? Don't worry, Hugh, not about the damn dog anyway. And by the way, what's wrong with your mouth? You're always either gargling, or breathing fumes of Listerine."

"My stomach's a wreck. Come on, let's get out of here and go to the beach so Edith can take her precious nap." We started down the stairs.

"What do you mean, your stomach's a wreck? Listerine's no good for stomachs, you know that."

"I'm just nervous. Christ, do you blame me? And when I get worked up, particularly when it has anything to do with that bloody dog and everything always seems to, I get this awful bilious taste in my mouth and I have to wash it out. If it doesn't stop when we get home I'll see a doctor. I'm sure it's tension."

Consuela and I crossed the shady porch and tiptoed quickly down the stairs, where the gray paint was hot from the afternoon sun and burned the soles of our feet. The bushes next to the path were noisy with insects who stretched each warm day with their single purpose: Prepare for Winter. The goldenrod was just beginning to blossom and I thought of shiny lunch boxes and shoes, the old excitement and dread of the first day of school.

Barks and shouts from the beach broke in on my thoughts only a split second before Consuela clenched her hand on mine and began to run, pulling me down the path. We met Rebecca rushing toward us, misery on her face.

"It's George! Waffles has got him and he's tearing him apart! Quick, you've got to save him!" We raced to the beach and I knew with each footfall that it was useless. The damp-feathered dead bird was as real in my mind as it actually was when I saw Waffles carry it in his mouth from the dock to the beach. Each prance of Waffles' foot jerked the yellow beak that hung from his jaws until he carefully set the bird down in front of Edith's chaise, in the shade of her gay umbrella.

Uncle O left his fishing rod untended to help Consuela console the children, while I stood, studying first the mangled bird and then the drops of blood and entrails shaken on the sand by Waffles' triumphant trot. A haruspex bending in the blazing sun of Edith's arena, I tried to divine some meaning in yet another bloodbath, the third I had participated in in a week. Was I indeed going mad, like the three human Georges, or were my wits already pickled to irrational perfection by drink, like my father's? I would be twenty years ahead of him. Only one answer cleared in the confusion, and that one consumed me: Waffles was dominated by an animus and so was I. Something was controlling us both, or were we merely battling to control each other? The debris inside my mind settled and I saw what must surely be the only conclusion: to kill the dog and quickly. Bury his remains and whatever powers directed him in the Magic Circle, where he might have been buried five days ago but for my intervention.

Consuela was sponging off the children's teary faces with her towel, and Uncle O reeling in his fishing line as I approached them on the dock. I beckoned to Consuela, who handed the towel to Rebecca and came to me.

"I can't stand it any more. I am going to kill that fucking dog today and bury him with all the rest in the animal grave-yard. Take the children for a walk around the neck to the light-house rocks. There are tide pools there for them to explore, and breakers pound to deaden any wails from here. Ask Uncle O to go with you."

I waited while they gathered up their things to go, and felt

my heart tap fast right through my skin; the hair on my chest
rose and fell like Waffles' silky side as he panted at my feet.
Uncle O handed me his rod and turned his back on us to follow
Consuela's band of mourners down the shore.

I looked at Waffles and felt the slow hot coal of hate burn
from my bowels through each fragile layer of mortal covering,
until it wrapped me like musk wraps a ferret. The leather grip
on the slender fishing rod was imbedded in my palm and my
knuckles were white with strain, as if I tried to squeeze the grip
flat. I raised my arm high and whipped the rod like lightning
through the air. It whirred over my head and down to slash
Waffles' smooth neck and rip a straight long slash through his
baby-pink skin. The blood seeped up like thick red paint and
coated the tiny white shorn silk hairs of his coat. He stood up,
cowering, yet holding his territorial stone of the dock. He
waited for the next blow.

I came down hard, and hard again and again until I saw
not Waffles on the daylight dock, but Waffles in the night fog,
beaten by his other master. I threw down the rod and felt my
face like a blind man, feeling with my fingers for the rigid horror and demonic possession that had been so plainly etched on
George Livingston's face a week ago. I touched my own neutral
skin, and with the pressure of my flesh against my flesh, some
order and reason returned, enough at least so that I could see
the utter folly in trying to kill poor Waffles. George had tried
that, and he lay dead. No, I would not, could not kill the dog.

Instead, I carried him in my arms to the sea. I held him in
the cool water; it lapped around us both and I watched the
blood flow out of his flesh, watched it meet the water, mingle
and disperse. I cradled him; his head rested trustingly in the
crook of my arm as we rocked back and forth gently, swaying
in the sea to my croons. We stayed that way a long time, until
we both began to shiver.

Then I wrapped him in a big thick towel and bore him to
the house, soothing him with calm injunctions not to wake up
Edith. He lay in the folds of terry cloth on the counter and
waited while I fingered the bottles and tubes in the medicine
cabinet for analgesic potions. I finally chose peroxide to disin-

fect and Obtundia to comfort. Pouring on the peroxide was fairly impersonal. Rubbing in the Obtundia ointment was almost a sexual act. I squeezed a worm of balm on my finger and then stroked it lovingly in the open stripes, over and over again, thrilling and tingling as he thanked me with laps of his tongue on my wrist.

The Seth Thomas clock observed us, and measured out our affection in unemotional, precise clicks. This was our first confirmation of dependency and trust, so new to me that I didn't recognize it for what it was. I brought Waffles to the window seat in our bedroom and got him settled down. I was giving his head a last pat when Edith came down the hall, finished with her nap. She passed the open door and went by, just catching us with her eye as she disappeared from view. But she turned back and stood on the threshold.

"What are you doing to that dog, Hugh? Is he hurt?" She might just as well have said, "Did you hurt him?" so unmistakable was the blame in her voice.

"I gave him a mighty beating for killing the children's sea gull. He deserved every whack, but I didn't mean to break the skin." And I truly hadn't.

I struggled to keep emotion out of my voice and off my face, but it was difficult to hide the crossness I felt for Edith's interruption, or my own shame. I dwelt on the former and remembered how Edith never allowed anyone a private moment if she could arrange to interfere. Which made me wonder fleetingly about her own secrecy, but there was no time for tangent thoughts.

"Let me look at him." She barged in, pushed me aside and blocked my view.

"You brute! How could you be so cruel to this sweet helpless puppy. Why, you should have given him a steak bone for getting rid of that dirty gull. I didn't like it hanging around my beach and splattering everything with its droppings anyway. And the children would leave all sorts of filthy garbage on the dock for it to eat. That dog knows a thing or two that you do not know, Hugh. You mark my words."

114

Funnily enough, I did mark her words, and for once Aunt Edith was right; Waffles did know a thing or two.

I put away the veterinarian clutter in the kitchen and swiped at the counter in a slapdash way, thinking how outraged Mabel and Aunt Edith would be if they knew Waffles had flicked their counter with his penis, and let his anus rest against the cold water tap.

Then I went back to the beach to bury the slain bird. Consuela and Uncle O came down the Giannellis' beach arm in arm, the children scattered behind them, heads lowered, obviously looking for something in the sand. I met them halfway, and linked Consuela's free arm in mine. I told them of the beating and of my repentance, but did not divulge the powerful emotions that had seized me. Uncle O picked up his fishing rod and started up the path for a nap.

"You look really wasted, I guess you had a bad time with the dog. I hope it wasn't like the George scene you watched before?" Relief weakened me and all my pretenses of control and confidence ebbed. I could have stood there and sobbed nakedly if I had had the strength. But I didn't, so I just said yes, it was like the other beating, horrible, and why didn't we bury the bird?

"The children are collecting beach glass for his grave. The prospect of a funeral cheered them up completely, so we don't have to worry about them. You dig the grave while I pick some clover and goldenrod. It's got to be a speedy funeral so we can all have a rest before the shindig tonight."

I dug a hole on the edge of the beach grass and wrapped the corpse in an old red flag I found in a wet corner of the boathouse. The children assembled, solemn on the edge of the dock, their fists full of bits of sand-smoothed glass. Gaudy green from ginger ale bottles, Phillips' Milk of Magnesia blue, Coke sage, Schlitz brown, all frosted yet still colorful, jewels for a king, and one small piece of red, the rarest of all; nobody knew what kind of bottle made this ruby.

Consuela was pallbearer and sang the *Dies Irae* in her full alto voice. Behind her the children shuffled slowly across the beach. When the cortege reached the grave, I looked back and saw that the drops of blood and matted feathers were lost forever under a dusting of fresh sand from our feet. The incoming tide would complete the job in another hour.

Upstairs, we all lay down and slept, lulled by fiddling crickets in the grass and the creak of Aunt Edith's glider where she sat enjoying the wind off the water in the lengthening shadows.

The dance was, as I had hoped it would be, normality itself. I got very drunk as I always have, only this time on half as much booze and twice as fast. That meant practically no hangover the next day, something most untraditional.

I do remember the children and Consuela, arresting in their beauty especially beside the regular features of their dull contemporaries, all alike in conventional good looks. Rebecca and Consuela brushed their thick long hair so it shone with the dark luster of old black cherry, hand rubbed with an oiled glove. No chemically dyed acrylic frocks for them from Saks Fifth Avenue, but brilliant Mexican cotton aired in the sunshine to sweetness and pressed evenly by Mabel's firm iron. In February, Consuela had embroidered columbine and trillium, lady's slippers and stars-of-Bethlehem on the bodices to flower in three-dimensional splendor on my ladies' bosoms. The other women were splashy in sloppily designed bouquets of blue roses and green poppies stamped on the cloth by machines and then stitched up by the ILGWU.

The boys bowed and whirled, danced jigs with style in starched sailor suits handed down and down. They stood apart from the other sons, who were all dressed up to look like Dad in madras jackets and pastel linen-like acrylic shorts from Brooks Brothers, cut for seven-year-olds with middle-aged paunches. They danced, these other boys, in pure white sneakers whose nonskid soles sucked the floor with every glide, not in the slick sandals, glowing with spit and Kiwi, which shod the dancing Murrays.

I remember Aunt Edith, guardian of the grill, seated at the table closest to the fire, where she could watch the meat continuously from firm raw red to seared black, when it was taken from the fire to a plate, to ooze its juices out in a vampire's puddle on the way to the table. She nodded and wiggled her eyebrows at her friends, but she flirted with the meat.

I remember sitting at our table with three Dorcases and three Dorcasmen, waiting for the gin to snap the wire in my frontal lobe, while I automatically assumed all the right attitudes and expletives, adeptly skimming any given topic of small talk, just like everyone else. Once in a while I would explore Consuela's thigh, to keep in touch with reality.

I clapped hard for the winners and admired their ribbons. I danced with Aunt Edith and Rebecca and with each indistinct lady at my table. I did a hug-and-rub méringue with Consuela and had to sidle around, face to the wall, for a moment afterward to hide the disgraceful bulge in my pants.

I also remember that Waffles was happy to see me when I finally rolled in.

Jim Earl appeared in the driveway about ten-thirty the next morning and I left the dining room to greet him, hands gummy from cutting Ward's pancakes with his syrupy fork. We took our coffee into the living room and shut the door.

"Can I take your jacket?" Jim had come dressed like a lawyer in spite of the enervating heat and humidity of an August dog day.

"Thanks, Hugh. I'm surprised it's just as muggy here as it is in town. This room is cool, though." We sat facing each other on two severe China trade chairs, carved octagon table set between us for pencils and yellow pads, which stuck to its damp top. It was cool enough in here, but the dampness and heaviness of the air made the slightest motion an exertion.

I cut emotional corners and spoke with professional brevity and lucidity, or tried to, when I went over the whole horrific week with Jim. I got through it fast and left out nothing pertinent. Less than an hour later, I drove him to Helen Livingston's, introduced them and left so Jim could talk to her about the police and how he proposed to deal with the mess. Back at the house, I gathered bodies in need of spiritual nourishment and we trundled off to noon Mass.

There was a traffic jam in front of St. Andrew's-by-the-Sea, the coastal counterpart of the Church in the Wildwood. Morning Prayer and Sermon were just over, and the rector was standing on the front steps pressing white-gloved hands as we waited for the people who had skipped out early to get their cars out of the parking lot. The boys hung out of the car windows hollering to Aunt Edith's corseted bulk. She nodded curtly to us, wishing, I am sure, that we would move on and stop calling attention to our heretical worship in St. Irene's.

The pasty-faced priest there was no more pleased to see us arrive late in his church than Aunt Edith had been to see us pass by hers. He stopped in the middle of the Epistle as we filed in and glared. Past the holy water font, past the boxes for seat money, past the stations of the cross we marched to genuflect one by one by the empty pew too near the front. Twelve sandals thwacked the kneeling bench as we squeezed in, to kneel in tardy piety.

None of us paid much attention that Sunday. I tried to apply myself to the obvious needs of my soiled and twisted spirit, but my concentration lingered instead on the sheer nonsense of the sappy hymns, on the meanness prompting each stammered word of the dreary sermon, and on the silly games the children were playing with their fingers on the varnished oak seat. It was hot. I knew I needed something, some help to see through the smoke screen confusion of my life, but I did not know specifically what it was I wanted. I thought or prayed vaguely, asking in a kind of blanket supplication for strength, grace and forgiveness, figuring that covered just about everything. But there was one flash of a second when I saw myself in sharp clarity and clenched my fists as I thought, *Save me—save my soul, I can't do it alone*. I didn't make a sound and yet I felt the same quick energy and immediate exhaustion that one feels while screaming for help and in the silent second afterward. Then my thoughts wandered to a pre-lunch drink.

Aunt Edith had held Jim Earl in importunate cross-examination for a good half-hour when we returned. Circumspect fellow that he is, he was polite and uninformative and had nearly driven Aunt Edith beyond civility in her famine for gossip. All she knew was that Jim was here to "do some business" with me. But she must have suspected something else.

We had martinis on the porch in the damp heat and made pleasant noncontroversial conversation. This somewhat restricted our selection of topics, but Uncle O was splendid and not only reconstructed Bartholomew Gosnold's itinerary, but also a great hunk of his locally interesting life. We sat listening, too warm even to anticipate Mabel's Sunday dinner.

The children, still stuffed with late breakfast piggishness, were mannerly about concealing their uneaten salmon under dollops of mayonnaise, or swiftly swigging down unchewed mouthfuls with watered wine. Aunt Edith started in on politics, but Uncle O was aware that the uninformed tenets which she parroted from John Birch propaganda would make most of us uncomfortable and all of us bored and he doggedly persisted over her parlor prattle to find out more about his guest. Jim capitalized on his sandy hair and freckles, and did not mention his son's Bar Mitzvah, or which country club he belonged to. He was awarded full marks for handling his finger bowl doily with nonchalance. Edith's hawk eyes missed nothing.

Uncle O kindly offered us asylum in his study; he went off to fish with Cam and Justin. Here at least the chairs were squashy leather that hissed pneumatically as you sank on the cool seats, and the frayed buckram books which lined the walls lessened the pervading austerity of the house. We pulled off our coats and ties again and opened our shirts, ready to draw up battle plans.

Helen was abashed that Polly called in the police about my lighter. She was willing to do anything she could to help hush the matter up, and that included buying off the cops. Jim had assured her that payola would be disastrous and exactly what the locals would be waiting to jump us for. Polly would have to stay in the hospital for at least a week, which meant that Helen's plans to leave for Texas would have to be postponed. She wanted to get out of Gosnold's Bay as soon as she could and was very upset at the probability of reporters snooping around the house asking questions. I had foreseen this and suggested to Jim during our morning talk that he urge Helen to close the house, send her cook back to New York, and take a room at the Yard Arm.

She had asked Jim if he could represent us both, as our positions and intentions were common, and he had agreed. We all thought it would be helpful if I remained in Gosnold's Bay until Wednesday, when the weekly *Cape Clarion* came out. Jim suggested that I call the Chief Counsel for the Commonwealth, my boss, on Monday morning and inform him of my predicament and also offer my resignation.

Obviously, Aunt Edith and Uncle O would have to be told fairly soon, before they read about it in the papers, and Jim volunteered to tell them after supper. Consuela and I didn't want the children, Rebecca in particular, to know any more about the Livingstons than they already did, and we figured the best way of protecting their ignorance was to take them back to Still River. Consuela was beginning to miss the cows anyway, and said she'd go home with the children Tuesday morning. I had no desire whatsoever to leave. Even at the time I thought it was strange that I should almost want to stay with Aunt Edith and Uncle O in Gosnold's Bay. The idea of packing up my suitcase and moving out was awesome; just thinking about it made me tired.

Aunt Edith was aghast when Jim laid bare the sticky truth that I had seen George die and then had run away. I had left out the part about my pushing George when I briefed Jim; the push was coincidental, not essential, and I didn't see how it would help Jim in his defense to know about it. Besides, I really didn't want to mention that particular detail again—it had been hard enough to tell Helen and Consuela.

What riled Aunt Edith was not that I had been a witness or even that I had run away, but that I had not told *her*. She was at first affronted and then vituperative. She hurled diatribe upon diatribe across the demitasse tray with vitriolic allusions to Chappaquiddick, Roman Catholicism, the Democratic Party and Welfare. No one tried to pour oil on her sceptic waters; we just waited until she ran down, quite a while. Finding no supporters in the silent living room, Aunt Edith finally picked up the chattering coffee tray and was propelled out of the room by the force of her own supreme opprobrium.

I could almost hear the telephone wires hum as she spread her disgrace and the injustice I had done her, indignation hissing into the mouthpiece of her princess phone until like a stale actor, she no longer thought about her lines. Uncle O wished us a good night and went heavily up the stairs to calm her down. We had one tall drink and listened to Edith bawling and banging around over our heads. I considered racing Helen to the reservation desk at the Yard Arm. What was I going to do without Jim or Consuela as baffles against Aunt Edith's spleen? Oh well, there's always Uncle O's fishing rod. And with this consoling thought, I put the house to bed.

The telephone closet was as cheerful and comforting by dawn's early light as it had been at noon and after dark. My own Skinner Box. I meditated behind its barrier door for a minute, pulled in my dangling nerve ends and began another wearing day with a call to the Chief Counsel. It was too early, so I went into the kitchen for more coffee. My hand was unsteady and the coffee slopped into the saucer under Mabel's scornful face. I was tempted to give her a saucy grin and a pat on her flat rump.

Standoffish but courteous, the Chief Counsel didn't think much of my involvement in George Livingston's death. He accepted my resignation punctiliously, adding that I would be reinstated as soon as the dirty linen was back in the basket. He was relieved that I had hired Jim Earl, and wished me well. Punkt. That's all it took to release me from the bondage of employment, one telephone call and I was a truant on the loose. Hello, endless holiday.

I was still light-headed when I took Jim down to the police station to meet Sergeant Lyons an hour later, possibly more carefree than before. No longer responsible as a public defender, my own defense was out of my hands as well. Sergeant Lyons scratched his rusty curls and told us to sit down in his back room. Jim's visitation was a disquieting surprise. Jim admired the sergeant's view of the fish pier and said he wished he'd brought his paints. Sergeant Lyons said he wondered why we'd come and handed me a summons. I gave it to Jim without looking. Jim accepted it as if it were a parking ticket and pleasantly began to drop red flags of criminal prestige. He mentioned, by-the-by two publicized tough cases he had won recently. He wasn't bragging, he just adroitly maneuvered Lyons into asking all the right questions. Jim answered them with proficient mastery of the understatement, a technique which made Lyons pull out his defenses.

They were playing their own game and I was O-U-T out and left them together in the back room while I loitered down Main Street. I picked up some horsemeat for Waffles (a reward? for what?), and for Rebecca and Consuela earrings from a local goldsmith. Rebecca's I would wrap in a promissory note "Due on your thirteenth birthday, 10 December, two professionally pierced ears." Finding myself on an inadvertent buying binge, I couldn't leave out the boys and sucker that I am bought three overpriced and undersized fishing rods. That left Aunt Edith and Uncle O. What about that nice barrel of fish heads and other inedible parts in front of the fish market? The idea amused me, the occasional obscenity which makes you giggle, and I turned to look at the entrails again. But I saw one fish head peering up from the side with the eye half eaten and it reminded me of Polly, so I quickly crossed the street to the liquor store. The selection of wines was meager but I found two bottles of Lacrima Christi and bought them both, prey to title and taste.

Over an hour later, Jim came out of the police station.

"How did it go?" I asked him.

"Aside from the fact that Lyons has it in for you, not too badly. The arraignment is set for tomorrow morning in Barnstable."

"Fast work. Who's the judge?"

"With any luck, the Honorable Faith Willet." Jim slammed the car door and we started off. "I think I can convince her that there is not sufficient evidence to make a case against you."

"Hmm." I drove on toward the Yard Arm not really interested in what Jim was saying. It didn't seem to have anything to do with me. What was he saying now?

". . . suppressing information. In that case, I'll plead inebriation if that's all right. You didn't report it because you were drunk. A minor incident. Are you listening?"

"Oh yes." Oh no. "You said a minor incident. That's fine." We followed the curve of the harbor basin and I marveled in silence that killing George had suddenly dwindled to an incident. Very soothing. My life was chock-full of incidents lately; you might, in fact, consider it an incidental life. I laughed and pulled up to the hotel.

"Glad to see you're so cheerful, Hugh. You look strained though." Jim leaned in the window and studied me.

"Strained? Wouldn't you be?" I tried to laugh again but this time it came out all wrong.

"Take it easy. You aren't getting hysterical on me, are you? Go home and have a drink."

"I will. Thanks." I started to drive off.

"Wait, Hugh! What about tomorrow? Shall I pick you up?"

"Oh yes, I'd forgotten. Pick me up at eight-thirty."

Helen Livingston's car drove into the Yard Arm as I drove out. So, she was checking in too. Nice. I liked the idea of the Livingstons' house being empty. Maybe I would take a walk around the Magic Circle some time soon, I might even take Waffles with me. Just us and the Livingston ghosts, it would be a bloodless stroll.

Dinner was almost festive with my wine and presents, even if Edith did pick at the capon and complain of a headache. Consuela and I went to bed right after the children for our long-awaited screw. But it was a disappointment to us both. Disappointment is the wrong word. And it was all my fault, basically one of timing.

I guess Consuela reached her climax early on. For some reason, horny though I was, I did not have one. Instead my attention spun off with a host of unrelated fantasies, all of them absorbing, all of them vile. Edith in drag necking with Consuela, Uncle O on the slippery raft connected to both Giannelli girls simultaneously, Polly titillating Rebecca while Rebecca let her, unprotesting, and all the while I worked on top of Con-

123

suela. I chafed her dry with impersonal brutality and watched the orgies in my head. A voyeur. Not until Consuela moaned was I actually aware of what I was doing to her. To her and for me. I was fucking alone, masturbating in Consuela. Had I really become so warped that I could rape the one person I loved above all others? I heaved myself off her and buried my head in the pillow. What I had just done was worse by far than the human animals Lucy and I had watched in the Cuttyhunk bunker.

Consuela lay very close against me in the narrow bed. She tentatively rubbed my back with a light hand and said she was sorry.

"I couldn't help coming, Hugh, and then I sort of dried up. What can I do to give you some pleasure?"

"It's not your fault, love. I drank too much. And you did give me pleasure. That's why I was so greedy. I was having too good a time."

And with the little white lie "I was having too good a time," I unwittingly began to drive the wedge of separation between us.

She left early the next morning with the children.

"Good luck in court. Please call me tonight and let me know how it went. I'll miss you." She kissed me and they rattled down the driveway, bye-bye, bye-bye.

A few minutes later Jim's car drove in and I tucked a Cloret under my tongue and picked up my seersucker jacket. Uncle O was on his way upstairs with Aunt Edith's tray, Waffles weaving around his legs in an effort to get past him.

"You off, Hugh? Good luck and let the dog out, will you?"

I did and climbed into Jim's car. Helen was in the front seat looking more nervous than usual and I wondered if we would have to listen to her short blasts of talk all the way to Barnstable. But she was quiet. I felt awful. The business with Consuela scared me. I had betrayed her in a very real way without knowing it until the deed was done. I had lost control over my mind. And my mouth tasted terrible.

The courthouse was like any other and Judge Willet presided. I did not, could not pay attention, in fact halfway through the proceedings I realized that I had no interest in my own case at all, not personally, not professionally. I continued to think about the sexual perversions I had seen in my mind. What was particularly repugnant was how much I had enjoyed what I saw. The other thing I did in the courthouse which shocked me was to reach down under my seat twice to scratch Waffles. It was almost like clearing your throat, a reflex action. At one point I did pay attention. The judge was questioning Helen, and she nearly blew it about my pushing George.

". . . reached out to stop, I mean help him." She looked at me, terrified and apologetic. But when I was questioned and explicitly asked if I had touched George before he fell, I lied under oath, just so as not to complicate the case, and said no. At the time I thought, What the hell, the whole thing is hoked up anyway, has nothing to do with me, or with dead George Livingston either, for that matter. What difference does it make? I was astounded at how easy it was.

The case was dismissed for lack of evidence as Jim had hoped and the court was adjourned just before noon. Helen came over and hugged me, I wondered why, and realized it was because we had "won," something else that didn't seem to affect me much. Right outside the courtroom doors the press was waiting for us, their cameras blinked as we pushed our way through. Jim brushed the questions away and Helen and I had the good sense to shut up. But we knew it was only the beginning.

Halfway home we stopped at Howard Johnson's for lunch. Jim and Helen were worried that the reporters might have been allowed into Polly's room at the hospital. They decided to drop me off and go straight to her.

"Do you want me to help you?" I asked.

"It isn't necessary," said Jim. "You don't look so great, you know, Hugh. You ought to get some rest."

I agreed and wondered if rest, like honesty, would be increasingly difficult for me to manage. But it was nap time when I got back to Aunt Edith's, so I thought I'd lie down and try to sleep. It was so damn hot I couldn't do much else anyway, except go to the beach and that was too much trouble. The house was very still. When I opened the refrigerator to get some ice, the noise accused me. I placed the ice in a glass, rather than dropping it, and sloshed gin and tonic on top. I didn't see Waffles, probably he was outside somewhere, so I tiptoed up to my room alone, trying fruitlessly to keep my glass from tinkling. When I reached the top of the stairs, I heard a soft scratch and looked down the hall. Aunt Edith's door was opening slowly, and then I saw Waffles slink out. I didn't like it at all and looked at him sternly. He licked my hand. Why didn't old Edith just leave him alone, for Christ's sake? He's my dog after all.

"Come on, Waffles. Let's take a nap." I downed my drink, gargling with the last mouthful, and lay down on the bed. Waffles stretched out on Consuela's, and we slept. I was in the middle of the Metamorphosed Aunt Edith dream when Uncle O woke me up, pounding on the door.

"Hugh, you awake? It's quarter of six, you know, time for a drink. Helen Livingston wants you to call her at the hotel."

I took a shower and felt much better than I had that morning. Even my mouth didn't taste too terrible, and I had been able to sleep.

I mixed a martini and took it into the telephone closet to return Helen's call. She sounded far away and vague and I suspect that Jim had given her a few drinks to calm her down. The press had not gotten to Polly and though there was sure to be some mention of the episode in tomorrow's paper, it at least wouldn't make the headlines.

"The reason I called you, Hugh, was to see if you and Consuela would be interested in buying the house. I thought I'd list it tomorrow. With the real estate agents. If you want it, call me before noon."

I thanked her and hung up. Buy the Livingston house, what a curious idea. Imagine living here, spending every summer in Gosnold's Bay right next door to Aunt Edith. I could even keep the telephone hooked up in the Magic Circle. I waited in the closet with my martini to soothe me until the impact of that wild arrangement lessened. How could I live in George Livingston's house? The astounding part was that I could imagine it so very well, in fact it was completely natural to me that I should. I inherited his dog, why not his house too? What else had he left me?

I went back into the living room and mixed myself another drink. Waffles was curled up next to Aunt Edith's feet. He raised his head when I came in and then got up and stretched. I sat down on the sofa and he sat in front of me, curled his lip slightly and energetically began to clean his personal parts, damn him, while Aunt Edith pretended not to notice.

"Well, what did Helen want?" asked Aunt Edith after dinner.

"She wondered if Consuela and I would like to buy the house. It was nice of her to think of us."

"It wasn't nice at all," snapped Edith. "It would have been quite rude if she hadn't asked you. And she should ask me if I know of anyone, as well. In a community like this that is always the way it is done. Well, would you?"

"What? Oh, like to buy the house? I don't know. Maybe."

"Humpf. You had better call Consuela. Yes, you better ask her what *she* would like to do. It *is* her money."

Normally, a remark like that from anyone, especially from Aunt Edith, would have put me right over the edge. This time it had very little instant effect. I remember thinking, *Someday, Sweet Edith, you're going to get YOURS,* and then I got up obediently and went to the closet again, calling behind me, "You're absolutely right, Aunt Edith, you're absolutely right."

But once inside the telephone closet I did not call Consuela. I snapped on the light and looked at the phone. I sat there for a long time, stubbornly *not* calling Consuela, even though I had promised her this morning that I would. To me it seemed funny, a contrary little joke on Aunt Edith. And I didn't feel like talking to Consuela, not yet.

That night I dreamt the Aunt Edith dream completely through and it had a new twist. After she had changed into the sponge, Waffles entered, jumped up on her bed and took the Edith sponge in his teeth. He shook it furiously but it was too rigid and big to be any fun, so he finally just hauled it off the bed and dragged it around the room, biting off little pieces and leaving them on the rug.

Uncle O had taken Mabel off to do the marketing by the time I got up the next morning. A cold front had moved in during the night and the sultry atmosphere was gone. Edith gave me some coffee in the chilly kitchen and went off to "write letters" in the dark hole she calls her morning room. I called Consuela. She sounded hurt that I hadn't called her yesterday with the good news of the trial, and I couldn't think of an excuse, so I changed the subject and told her about the Livingstons' house. She burst out laughing.

"I bet you're really eager to buy it, aren't you? Can you imagine anything worse? Oh, it's ridiculous!"

"Ridiculous?" I asked. "Is it? Why?"

"Oh, come on, Hugh, I know you despise Gosnold's Bay. The only thing worse than living *with* Aunt Edith would be living *next* to her."

"Maybe not."

"Are you serious? I mean, you're not really considering buying that house, are you?"

"I guess not." Consuela was right, it was silly of me, but I decided to have my walk over there just the same. I called Waffles and off we went. The reporters and cameramen were not in evidence, everything was deserted and peaceful in the clear air. Waffles gamboled beside me on the Livingstons' lawn. I threw some sticks, which he retrieved, and patted him for "fetching." His wounds, the ones I had inflicted, were healing but they still stood out like the marks of a branding iron, which, in a way, is exactly what they were.

A beautiful day; I am unencumbered, no job, no wife, no children and to boot, I am going back, like the proverbial criminal, to the scene of the crime. I was pleased with myself. I may have been returning to the scene of the crime, but when we got to the trees that form the Magic Circle, it was clear that Waffles was not. He barked and skittered nervously, did not come when I called him. I watched him racing across the grass to Aunt Edith's house, and I entered the Magic Circle alone.

It seemed quite ordinary. I looked at the stones with cool appraisal. They were strangely placed not in a circle as I had thought, because that was what the design of the trees had suggested, but in a complete pentagon, with a few stones left over. I looked at the stone in the center.

It was dated 1921 and there was no name. It must mark the place where Mrs. Livingston had shot the horse. The other stones were newer and had elaborate inscriptions. The sides of the pentagon were capped with triangles of thyme so the whole thing formed a five-pointed star. At the tip of each point was another tombstone, each of these very recent. I found the one on which George had struck his head. "IN LOVING MEMORY OF MANDARIN, FAITHFUL AND FORGIVING, APRIL 30, 1974." I checked the other dates and Mandarin had been the last to die, the one before George.

The telephone was under a small stone bench, where I imagined George might have sat to meditate on all his slaughters. It was still connected. I started back towards Aunt Edith's feeling neutral and not really wanting to live in George's house. I would call Helen and tell her.

I squinted against the glare from the painted porch steps, remarked to myself that I felt nearly normal, and climbed up to the dark veranda. Just as I opened my eyes wide in the shadows, I suddenly felt a tremendous pressure building inside me. My spit turned sour and my pulse raced. I made myself stand still and swallow several times, took deep breaths and felt kinks of excitement twitch in my chest. What now? I won't be fooled again. These are signals of some sort. A paranoid's premonitions and this time I will pay attention, yield to them.

Indian style, I walked down the porch on flat silent feet. When I was abreast of the first window, which was open to Aunt Edith's morning room, I stopped and edged against the shutter. It was hard to see inside, but as my eyes became more used to the gloom I could see Waffles. My nervousness accelerated and my mouth tasted worse. The dog crouched in front of the love seat. There was a fearful intensity about him which scared me.

Then I made out Aunt Edith in her green shirtwaist dress. She was sitting on the love seat and I could see a blur of a face and her dingy teeth. She was smiling. My own face was almost against the screen now, and I thought I saw too clearly.

Waffles' snout appeared to be moving rhythmically between Aunt Edith's spread-eagled legs. I could hear her breathing stertorously, and I heard Waffles' toenails scratch against the bare floor. Damn you, damn you, you uncanny dog. At which point Waffles must have beamed in on my thought, for he stopped whatever he was doing to Aunt Edith and craned his head around toward the window, an edge of green chambray skirt resting over one ear. For a second our eyes met. He flicked his tongue across his loose lips, wagged his tail and returned to Aunt Edith. She is so trusting of those sharp little teeth, I thought, or is she drugged by his soft, active tongue? What am I watching? Why am I watching it? Why do I enjoy watching it? Oh, sweet Jesus.

When Waffles pushed her skirt higher, above the cushion on the love seat, I wanted to scream, "Stop it, both of you!" But I didn't, I was stealthy, quiet, watching through the window, hating myself. Hating Waffles and Aunt Edith. Hating the orgiastic tremors riffling through me. I will go. One last look and I will go. Waffles heard that, too, and turned again to look at me. Then Aunt Edith called him.

"Come here, Waffles. Good doggy, come." And her voice sounded perfectly normal in my ears as I crept away from the window, down the steps and into the sun.

Bone tired, I lay on the grass and tried to put it all together: murder, cowardice, cruelty to children and now voyeurism and bestiality. Not once had I tried to stop watching; I liked watching. True, I didn't like Aunt Edith. I remembered Consuela's talk with me and could see them tongue to tongue the night before we were married. I also remembered the way Aunt Edith had looked at Rebecca, and her outrage at the Giannelli girls. Maybe I should give Waffles my blessing. Maybe Aunt Edith got what she deserved.

I went up the front steps and through the door with heavy feet so that Aunt Edith would hear me. I heard her Old Maine Trotters clip-clop down the hall as I tightly closed the door of the telephone closet and pulled the light chain. I sat in my sanctuary for quite a while, playing with the dial and trying to compose myself. It was odd that her voice had sounded so ordinary. She wasn't even out of breath. As I sat thinking with the coats behind me, I began to have doubts that I had seen what I had seen. The room had been dark, and I had been wildly excited. If I can dream in sleep with clarity and recall, then perhaps I can also have daylight delusions. Or was it that I hallucinated something that I really wished would happen? I heard Aunt Edith clomp deliberately up the stairs, and I opened the closet door.

I opened the door right in Waffles' eager pointed face.

"Oh, you. What have you done?"

He licked my hand and wagged his tail, perfectly normal, for him, including his conspiratorial look. Or did I imagine that, too?

"Mmmm. Well, whatever you did, I suppose it's not your fault exactly, is it? You better go out all the same. Enough is enough."

"Hugh? Is that you? Who are you talking to?" Aunt Edith called down the stairs.

"Yes, Aunt Edith, it's me. I'm just talking to Waffles, that's all."

"Well, you had better get ready for lunch." I heard her walk down the hall.

Waffles had ignored this exchange. Then he pattered to the door ahead of me and waited. I let him out and watched him sniff the bushes around the driveway, positive that in some strange way we had become conspirators, in what I didn't know. He may have.

The next few days were murky ones for me. I felt unconnected to everything and everyone except my dog and myself. Those few minutes on the porch outside the morning room window had left me exhausted and confused. I couldn't suppress or divert the almost continual recollections of what I thought I had seen, but even the thoughts were limp. They just passed through and around my wan mind, always present, as I shuffled from bed to table to porch. Waffles dropped into the shadows, too, and was barely visible as he dragged along

131

behind me, never more than a few inches away. We were without energy.

Aunt Edith and Uncle O went about their usual business, I guess, although I was so on the periphery of the slight routine activities of that household that I really don't know just what they did. They, however, were aware of my listlessness and preoccupation. Oliver was downright worried and must have asked Philip Potter to "drop in and have a look" at me. Which Philip did.

I was stretched out on two wicker chairs on the porch, the Boston *Globe* still folded on my lap, Waffles asleep under the bridge of my stiff legs in my shadow. Philip pulled another chair over next to mine and sat down.

"H'lo, Philip. What brings you here?" I raised my head up from the back of the chair and opened my eyes.

"Don't move, Hugh. You look so comfortable." He leaned back and we sat with our eyes closed against the light while the wicker chairs twigged and creaked. After a few seconds, Philip continued.

"I rather thought you'd call me after the trial. I understand you're off the hook?"

"Seems so."

"You don't sound jubilant, I must say!"

"Should I? I suppose I should, but it all seems insignificant. Did at the time, too. I meant to talk with you a while back, but things happened so fast. . . ." Had they really happened "so fast"? I wondered. ". . . and I . . . I, what was I saying?" I gave a feeble try at remembering, then yawned. "Sorry, Philip. Oh well, what does it matter anyway?"

Philip yawned and resettled himself in the chair. "In a minute," he said, "we'll both be asleep."

"I doubt it. At least I won't be. Sleep comes hard these days." My eyes were still shut, but I could feel Philip's examining me. So? I thought, the cat may look at the king, and I didn't move.

"You look a bit seedy. In fact, Oliver is worried about you."

"Is that why you came? Did he ask you to?"

132

"He did, yes. That was one of my reasons for coming. The other is to ask you if you'd like to sail around this weekend. I said I'd look in on Mrs. Jensen before I leave—her husband works the farm on Nashawena—and then I thought I'd spend Saturday night in Cuttyhunk. The tides are right Sunday morning to shoot Canapitsit Channel, something I like to do each summer. How about it?"

"What about Caroline?"

"She can't come, the church fair is Saturday, and Caro is running the flower table. She always does that, it's her only concession to organized religion. No, I'll be by myself unless you keep me company."

"That's just it, I'm rotten company. I really think you'd have a better time without me, much as I'd like to come."

"You flatter yourself. That boat has too much canvas for me to handle easily by myself. My arms aren't what they used to be. You didn't guess it's your muscle I want, not your companionship? Such vanity!"

Skillful weasel, Philip. I took my feet off the other chair, carelessly knocking Waffles as I put them on the porch floor and sat up.

"Unanswerable as ever," I stated, knowing that the tedious lethargy was beginning to break. "Just for that, I'll come. When do we shove off?"

"Eight-thirty Saturday morning too early?"

"The earlier the better."

Waffles had gotten to his feet, and began to push his nose against my leg insistently, just like the children when they tug at my sleeve to distract me from conversations which bore them. I patted his head mechanically and asked Philip for a couple of tranquilizers.

"If you think you need them, sure. I'll drop off a couple of Valium when I go to the post office. Right now, you look pretty relaxed."

"Beat is more like it. Waffles, cut it out!" I pushed the dog away and stood up. "I haven't slept well to speak of since this business with the Livingstons started."

Philip gave me a shrewd look, which made me think that

perhaps he knew more than I thought he did about my role in the disasters next door, and here.

"That's their dog, isn't it?" he asked.

"It was. Helen asked me to keep him. Which reminds me, do you know of a kennel where I can leave him this weekend?"

"Try the Potts Puppy Palace in West Falmouth. I think Mrs. Potts still runs it. She's quite a character. Well, I'll be back with the pills." And he went down the steps.

I turned to go in for lunch. Waffles stood in my path in front of the door, browbeaten and reproachful, his tail between his legs.

"Move, stupid. It's not that bad, going to a kennel." I squatted in front of him and added softly, "Besides, you don't think I'd leave you here with *her?*" But Waffles was not consoled.

He stuck to me all day. When I walked, he edged just enough ahead of me to slow me down or make me trip over him, an effective way of saying, "Notice me, God dammit, here I am. Me!" I couldn't move one step without him. Finally, my irritation mounting, I threw him outside, swallowed a Valium and lay down on my bed.

The shriek of brakes outside my window woke me instantly and I knew something terrible had happened. Uncle O's Chrysler stood dead in the middle of the driveway, a thick cloud of dust slowly settling around it. Uncle O was stooped by the left headlight, looking under the front of the car. Waffles!

"Did you hit him?" I shouted from the window.

"I'm not sure. He isn't moving."

"Be right there." And I ran down the stairs, terrified, and out into the late afternoon sun.

I crawled under the front of the car, where Waffles lay motionless until I was close enough to touch him. When my hand met his head, I saw him blink, the only movement I saw him make. I tentatively reconnoitered his head, neck and trunk. He continued to lie very still.

"Did I hit him?" asked Uncle O.

"Can't tell. He looks O.K. Why don't you back up so I can get to him?"

Uncle O rolled the car back a few yards. Waffles looked perfectly normal but frozen, except for his blinking eyes. I stood up. "I wonder. . . . Maybe he's faking." I walked away to the house, turned back to the driveway and gave a cheery whistle. "Here, Waffles, come here!" No response.

"What's wrong with you?" I pushed him gently over on his side, then on his back. He seemed to roll partly by himself. On an impulse, watching him lie there, paws up, I said, "Dead Dog," and scratched his stomach. His tail moved back and forth on the driveway.

"Good dog! Up! Sit up, Waffles!"

He sat up, tail wagging, clearly unhurt.

"What a fake!"

"Isn't he the limit!" said Uncle O, incredulous, then added with obvious relief, "Nothing wrong at all."

"I'll get him out of the driveway so you can get in." But Waffles wouldn't budge. I finally dragged him off by his collar and held him until the car got past. When I let go, he went right back to the same spot, just beyond the curve in the shadows, where he was nearly invisible.

"Looks like he wants to get himself killed, doesn't it?" remarked Oliver.

"That, or he wants us to think he does. Well, I'm not taking any chances." I took Waffles' collar and pulled him to the porch, up the steps, inside. He glued his right rear haunch to my left leg, thus keeping his front quarters a little ahead of my feet. By this time, I was so mad at him that I didn't dare kick him away for fear I would lose all control and kick the hell out of him. I put him in my room alone and closed the door, hoping he wouldn't complain. After a few wails and scratches at the door, he was so quiet that I nearly forgot him altogether. In fact, it was Edith who reminded me to feed him when I went upstairs to change for dinner.

I opened the door of my room to an awful stink. Waffles looked up from his nest on Consuela's bed, but he didn't jump down to greet me. My bedspread was rumpled. I began to straighten it out and found that it was stained with runny diarrhea. Oh, damn you, not on my bed!

135

"Are you sick or merely punishing me for going sailing?" I bundled up the smelly spread and waited for Waffles to resume his annoying position in front of my foot. "Suppertime, Waffles. Let's go."

He had turned into such a nuisance that I really didn't give a damn when he turned down his horsemeat.

"Oh, go ahead, starve if you want to!" I left him in the kitchen, went into the living room and sat down with Aunt Edith and Uncle O and my Bourbon and water, very little water. Surprisingly, Waffles stayed in the kitchen, alone by his own choice for the first time that day. It was Thursday, Mabel's day off.

Aunt Edith seemed pleased when I told her I was going sailing with Philip. Perhaps she was glad to get rid of me?

"You are leaving the dog here, Hugh, aren't you?" she asked. Aren't you being a trifle overeager, Edith? I thought so, especially when she added, "I don't think he'd be much trouble. We get along so nicely."

"Thanks, Aunt Edith, but I thought I'd leave him at that Puppy Palace place in West Falmouth. He's been out of sorts today anyway. And he messed on my bedspread, I'm ashamed to say. It's in the set tub, soaking."

"Not sick I hope?" Aunt Edith sounded concerned.

"No, just a little put out. I think he knows I'm going away." I ground out my cigarette more vigorously than was necessary, still annoyed with the dog, and now with Aunt Edith as well.

She went to the kitchen to do something about dinner. Oliver and I sat silently, he worked on the *Times* crossword puzzle and I worked on my scowl. When we heard Aunt Edith scream, both of us jumped up and ran to the kitchen.

"Hugh? Huu-uugh! Oh, you dreadful, dreadful dog!"

By this time we were at the door. She was swatting away at Waffles with a folded-up newspaper. The kitchen floor was covered with trash. Shredded butter paper stuck to the floor, a milk carton had been torn to pieces, and everywhere were cigarette butts, ashes and tea leaves which had been put mistakenly in the open wastebasket, not in the step-on garbage can.

136

Waffles was cowering under Aunt Edith's quite justifiable rage, and a thin dribble leaked from under his droopy tail. I put him out and cleaned up the mess.

"Surely you don't regret his leaving now, do you?"

Aunt Edith didn't reply except to humpff as she passed into the dining room with the cold cuts.

After dinner, I called Mrs. Potts at the Puppy Palace, who said she'd "be delighted to have the little fellow visit for a few days. I just love making new friends, don't you?" she continued. "You mustn't worry about him, why he'll have a holiday too. I do everything possible to make our guests happy. In addition to three leash walks and continuous access to his very own spacious run, puppy will have a special treat with me alone, no leash, on the beach both mornings. My little way of saying welcome to all the first-timers. Getting to know each guest personally is so very important to me."

"Just wait until you get to know Waffles!" I said. "He's ah, he's most . . . unusual."

"But of course!" Mrs. Potts ran on, not understanding me. "Every visitor here is an individual, Mr. Murray!"

Ha, you've never had one like this, I bet!

"Don't forget now, to bring puppy's medical history. And of course, his favorite toy or blanket."

Favorite toy? Would that be me or Aunt Edith? Who are you kidding, Mrs. Potts? I had a suspicion that Mrs. Potts wouldn't think much of Waffles' scabs and scars.

Once more I called Helen Livingston, politely asking how Polly was (better, with partial vision restored to her eye), and to ask about Waffles' shots. Helen thought that he had had them all.

"George was conscientious. Very conscientious about those things." Helen sounded teary and I wished she'd hang up. "He'd be glad, Hugh. Glad you are being so good to him. To the dog. Waffles."

Helen's voice stabbing through the receiver made my ear feel like a pin cushion. I hurriedly got through the farewells, relieved that she and Polly were leaving Gosnold's Bay for good on Sunday.

"Good-by, Helen, and good luck." Good-by forever.

I practically had to carry Waffles off to bed. He had little more energy than a taxidermist's specimen, and lay pathetically limp in my arms as I lifted him onto Consuela's bed. Even though I was still annoyed with him, I couldn't ignore him, or the twangs of pity and self-reproach I felt as he stared sadly at me.

He didn't move all night that I was aware of, until I woke up in the morning and discovered a drying puddle of shit on my sandals. The buckles were coated and the closet stank, but for some reason, I wasn't really angry with him any more, just bothered.

All day he seemed too tired even to follow me. He stayed curled up on Consuela's bed, with his eyes open. Physically free of him, I thought about him more, almost constantly. Supposing he really *was* sick? That he died at Mrs. Potts's while I was sailing? And if he *did* die? So what? After all, he's only a dog. I knew that, of course, I really knew that Waffles was only a stupid, ugly dog. I reminded myself all day long, over and over. But the notion of Waffles' dying grew increasingly upsetting to me, and I couldn't put it from my mind. It was absurd, I thought, and then, *It is crazy. I am crazy.*

I watched the clock counting down to 5 P.M., when I could bundle him into the car and drive him to West Falmouth. We actually left at quarter of. I was desperate to get it over with.

Waffles shivered and cried all the way to the Puppy Palace, and by the time we got there, I was nearly in the same condition. The Puppy Palace itself was so outrageous and pretentious an establishment that just seeing it brought me back somewhat.

No doubt about it, this is the canine Ritz. Perched on several acres of marsh, the pink cottage with attached pink kennels seemed to command an awesome authority simply by its raging, plastic garishness. Too many petunias, pink and white, grew next to the chain link fence, but the final touch of Forest Lawn was the massive bed of white petunias shaped like a clipped poodle on the sloping lawn which faced the road. Below the poodle, another petunia bed, pink this time and edged in a double *P*, like the Plaza Hotel.

Mrs. Potts came flying out the door before we reached the end of the driveway, all six feet of her. Her pink angora sweater and white pants were as I had imagined, as were her short blondine curls. But her big bony frame, her wide mouth and horse teeth, that prominent nose, those were a real shock. She boomed a hearty welcome, quite different from her cooing telephone voice, and practically ripped off the car door in her excitement to meet the new boarder. She was a leviathan, masquerading as a powder puff. Remarkable! Waffles quaked against me and bleated, forgotten again. He looked miserable.

Mrs. Potts seemed to think so too, and her face fell with a visible if not audible crash when she looked down at him.

"Oh-me-oh-my," said Mrs. Potts, stepping back a few steps. "Oh dear, I think we have a sick visitor. Nonononono, *think* of infection. You'll have to take the little lamb home, Mr. Murray. Oh-oh, we can't have sick guests, we can't." She slammed the door hard as if she meant to lock in Waffles' germs, then turned and waved emphatically in an excess of goodwill to compensate, and charged into her blushing house.

I lighted a cigarette and considered my dog. He gazed up at me lovingly and gave his tail a little wag, then nestled himself down beside me and slept all the way home.

Philip didn't sound overjoyed when I asked him if I could bring Waffles along.

"He's practically glabrous—no hair in the scuppers, Philip." And then I added, "Love me, love my dog!" with a strained laugh.

"Bring him along, I guess there's no alternative."

Philip was polite but I knew he didn't like it, especially when he tacked on, "If he is sick, Hugh, maybe you should take him to a vet."

"Sick?" This time I did laugh. "Smart! Two days of playacting and his nose is as cold and wet as it ever was." The indulgent master, proud of his impish pet. Even to myself, I sounded a bit like Mrs. Potts.

Waffles and I ate well that night, and slept peacefully. I

didn't need a Valium either, and the room was clean and sweet in the morning, Waffles having "done his business" in Aunt Edith's words, in the bushes outside.

September air had moved in during the night, and we had a perfect sail to Nashawena. The water sparkled as it only does in the spring and fall. The wind was fresh, and Waffles had the tact to make himself invisible below, giving me every opportunity to talk to Philip. But I didn't, in fact; neither of us spoke much. I wanted to talk to him but I couldn't seem to begin. Relaxed as I was, more relaxed than I had been in several weeks without the help of alcohol, I nevertheless shied away from introducing all the recent unpleasantness in my life.

Ashore on Nashawena, Waffles and I left Philip with Mrs. Jensen and roamed the stony fields together. For the most part, Waffles trotted along beside me, with an occasional foray into the scotch broom. He ignored the grazing sheep and the flock of chickens and was a model dog, Fido himself.

We sailed into Cuttyhunk Pond about a half-hour before sunset, when the island is at its most charming. Whitewashed houses stood out, simple and clean as they leaned into the rise of the hill. The pond was full of boats, Labor Day weekend tourists, but Philip had had the foresight to call the Veeder boys and reserve a mooring. He had also reserved two rooms at Bosworth House for the night.

"We'll have a drink here as soon as we finish battening down for the night," said Philip as we laced up the sail cover. "Then a bath ashore and dinner."

"Sounds good. I could do with all those luxuries." I was indeed getting thirsty. "You wouldn't mind if I wasted that room at Bosworth House and slept aboard with Waffles, would you? I doubt they'll let him in, and besides, I can't bear to sleep on land when I could be afloat."

Philip shrugged. "Suit yourself." He finished coiling the jib-sheets and stowed them in the rope locker, then looked fore and aft, nodded and sat down in the stern with his pipe. "Get the ice, Hugh, and whatever poison you like. Bourbon whiskey for me."

When I came up with the drinks Philip was contentedly

140

sucking on his pipe, surveying the peaceful harbor. I stopped halfway up the companionway, stunned to see Philip as an old man for the first time. He seemed to read my mind.

"I know what you mean about sleeping aboard. Five years ago I'd never have been caught in a bed, but now, well, it seems that the duck on the berths gets stiffer every year, while the foam rubber underneath grows calcium deposits in one spot, and disappears altogether in others. Ironed sheets and real mattresses for me now, terrible isn't it?"

I agreed, it *was* terrible. We filled up a ditty bag with clean underwear, toothbrush for Philip and Bourbon for me, and went ashore.

Someone had painted a huge compass rose on the cracked macadam road at the foot of the hill. Philip and I stopped to look closely at it on our way to Bosworth House, when suddenly the church doors opened wide, letting out what must have been almost every year-'round inhabitant of Cuttyhunk. They were a somber lot, in both mien and dress, and they filed down the hill, dignified and silent. Obviously, an island cortege. A few women and children carried little bunches of flowers, goldenrod and wild asters, hard to come by on that poor soil. Two men at the end brought floral tributes from the mainland, which stuck out in gaudiness against the monochrome simplicity of the rest of the procession.

We stood aside to let the mourners pass, watching as they crossed the compass rose and stopped by the telephone booths. Six men climbed the rickety steps to Charlie Snow's porch, picked up a large pine box and carried it to the town pier. An old wooden dory was tied to the piling. They placed the coffin in the boat, cast off and rowed down the channel. Some of the others followed in a launch, engine barely above idle, while the cluster of people on the dock stood quietly in the raw sunset. The women pulled their dark jackets about them more closely, and children crowded against their mothers. The older boys and few remaining men stood apart. They all watched the two boats go slowly between the breakwaters and turn toward the open water out of sight. Charlie Snow was dead.

The dining room at Bosworth House was full of eaters,

whose chins and fingers were shiny with melted butter. I
watched them crack lobsters and noisily suck on the claws. It
revolted me, perhaps because this greedy scene was so far away
from the one I had just observed on the dock. I felt that I was a
part of the mourners, and while feeling that emotional kinship
with them, I knew, rationally, that I really belonged up here on
the hill, with the fat cats.

"Hugh?" Philip took my elbow and broke my thread of
morose concentration. "Let's see about our rooms."

And another drink, I thought, as I followed him to the
front desk. I looked out the window to the porch to make sure
Waffles was still there. He was.

The girl who showed us to our rooms was an islander, not
one of the usual summer help flown over from Fairhaven, so I
asked her about Charlie.

"Died in his sleep two nights ago. Eighty-four he was.
Nobody left now, no Snows except for Esther Veeder, his
sister. Know her? Runs the post office."

"Oh yes. I didn't know she was Charlie's sister. So she's
the last one?"

"That's right. Charlie's son Caleb was killed in the war,
World War II, and his wife died soon after, I guess."

"I wonder who will live in the house?" I said this more to
myself than to the girl, but she answered anyway.

"Charlie's house? Who knows? It's not much of a house,
more like a shack. There've been rumors that old Hilton wants
to sell the other shack next to Charlie's and he's been talking to
some young kids from the mainland. They want to put up some
kind of hamburger place. Maybe they'll buy Charlie's, too. Sure
will change this place if they do."

And she left. The hot water ran out halfway through my
shower, but in a spartan sort of masochism, I enjoyed the icy
water which pelted down on me and forced me to jump and
fling my arms around under the freezing needles. My mind felt
as brisk as my body and the squashy pity I had initially felt for
Charlie I had to recognize for what it really was—a narrow,
sentimental self-pity, and not very pious or noble.

After dinner, Philip and I had our talk. The beginning was

somewhat forced until I gave up trying to speak well and just told Philip straight out what a mess I was in. I talked too much.

For instance, I told Philip of the rigid terror on George's face as he died, which two weeks later was more boldly drawn in my mind than it may have been in life. I told him over and over again about that. I had to make him understand my overwhelming panic at seeing George's face then, because it was something very like that panic and tension which continued now between Waffles and me. I was certain that this exchange of energy began with George, and now Waffles and I were stuck with his peculiar legacy.

Philip listened, considered a moment and then spoke.

"Energy. You keep using that word, energy. As an M.D., I've never felt comfortable with parapsychology, in fact, I thought it was a lot of bunk. Until recently."

"Parapsychology?" Philip? I couldn't believe it.

"Not that I'm a true believer," he went on. "But as I acquire more general knowledge the ratio of that knowledge to what I cannot know or scientifically explain remains constant. That which I cannot explain but nonetheless believe exists, such as the dynamism between you and the dog, I hold as preternatural. I accept the preternatural, do you understand? I cannot explain it, but I am aware of it, aware, too, that as I know more, I know how much more I cannot know. This begins to sound like a schoolroom conundrum."

"It is one, in a way," I said. "You are the only person so far to beam in on this queer bond between the dog and me. You really do believe it exists, don't you?"

"You say it does. The problem now is to put it in some sort of perspective so that you can deal with it, live with or around it, make your life productive because of or in spite of it."

"How?"

"Think back. Do you remember our old dialogue, real versus imagined pain?"

I nodded, wondering what Philip was leading up to.

"If believing in a fever can actually drive the mercury up,

it stands to reason that faith in a current, a 'tension,' as you said, or a dependence, which I think may be what you mean—"

"It is," I broke in. "It's a mutual dependence, as if we were in some way linked together, Waffles and me."

"Don't get so excited. Let me finish this. So you believe that you and the dog are in some way linked? Why then, isn't that belief *alone* enough to generate the link or tension or dependence?"

"In other words, I'm creating it by believing that it's there?" I asked him.

"Exactly. Now we come to the next point. *Why* do you believe this?"

"Because it is there! Philip, this is getting into a chicken-and-egg situation."

"No, I don't think so. Now listen for a minute. If you do not believe in this relationship then it will not exist. You just said that it exists, so I must take it for granted that you believe in it. Again I ask, *why* do you believe in it? Or put another way, *why* is there this dependence, etc.? Could it be connected to your own physical and psychological condition? Think on it a minute, Hugh. You've already admitted your own feelings of guilt over George's death. Surely that has something to do with it. What about exhaustion? Nerves? And I suspect drink enters in here too, don't you?"

"In other words, you propose that this highly unlikely condition between my dog and myself is the result of actual, accountable facts of my life?"

"That's right. The reasons why you believe what you believe are perfectly credible in themselves."

I was stunned at how easily Philip had reduced my unnatural relationship with Waffles to the lowest common denominator—drink.

"Alcoholism can be inherited, can't it?" I asked him.

"Possibly. You could find hundreds of reputable doctors who would say so."

"Are you among them?"

Philip shook his head. "No, I'm not. I do think that proximity to alcoholism produces more alcoholism, but that's geography, not genes. Welfare parents tend to produce welfare children, but no one would attribute it to Mendel's law."

"You know my father was an alcoholic?"

"So you said."

"What I'm wondering is whether the weakness in him which made him drink has been passed down to me. And whether he inherited his frailty from his mother, who eventually went slightly crazy. Even my uncle was locked up from time to time when he went into one of his 'deep depressions.' And then of course, there's Lucy."

"A sister?"

Another strange relationship to explain away to poor Philip. He listened to me carefully once again, and I thought I left out nothing. When I finished he spoke.

"When did you see her last? What happened to her after she rejected you? You switched your focus suddenly, Hugh, I don't know if you realize it, but it becomes *your* story as you tell it, from the hospital on."

"My story? Oh, I see, yes, I guess you're right. That's because I haven't really seen Lucy since she was in the hospital, except for my father's funeral, and then not to speak to. She was skeletonic then, it was when she was having her 'breakdown.'"

"What exactly do you mean, 'breakdown'?"

"I don't know, that's just what everyone at home called it. She stopped eating for three or four years, I mean, she just refused to eat. Finally she, too, ended up in Ewell-Lowe, like everyone else in our family. We don't talk about it much. The few times I've gone home to Tyringham my mother and I have avoided talking about Lucy, aside from the standard 'How's Lucy?' 'better/worse/about the same' exchange. She's not in Ewell-Lowe now, of course. She's all over that problem as far as I know. It still puzzles me, her trying to starve that way. I've heard of other girls doing it since then, too."

"Anorexia nervosa," said Philip.

"Excuse me?"

"That's what it's called, the skinny disease of Lucy's."

"You know about it?"

"Some. Voluntary starvation is usually what it is, and it nearly always leaves the victims permanently damaged. I doubt Lucy's 'over it.' Food becomes a means to an end to these girls, and remains an obsession, even when they learn to control it. Not eating can be a very powerful weapon, especially when a child uses it against her mother, which is what generally happens. Of course, like any death wish, starvation is also used against the victim herself. But I don't know why I'm going into all this."

"I want you to. We're finishing Lucy's story, remember?" There was an insistent note in my voice, and I wondered if Philip noticed it.

"I doubt very much if we are finishing anyone's story, but as long as you are so interested in this sickness, I'll tell you what I know. Where were we?"

"Starving is a weapon."

"Oh yes. These girls use it against people they feel most strongly about. In this case, I would guess that Lucy was using it against you. Like just about every psychological illness, this one involves sex. Starving diminishes sexuality."

"I didn't know that."

"Yes. If Lucy kept at it long enough, and I would judge from you that she did, I am sure her breasts shrunk along with everything else, her periods probably stopped and, in short, Lucy approximated a return to prepubescence and a simpler life."

"I wonder what has happened to her since, what is she like now?"

"Why don't you find out?"

"Maybe I will, maybe I'll go to Tyringham and see her, and my mother." Suddenly, I longed to see Lucy again, to close the gap between us. I wanted to talk and talk away to her. I wanted her to talk back. I held on to the notion that two lives as close as Lucy's and mine had once been would have continued on somewhat parallel courses. The rational self, Hugh-the-lawyer, knew this was absurd, while the secret self, Hugh-the-Cuttyhunk-adolescent, cried out to see Lucy and pick up the stitches we had both dropped over the years.

"It's a mystery to me why you and Lucy haven't kept up with each other at all." I heard Philip say this, but didn't bother to answer him, as I supposed any reply would have to involve Consuela, and I couldn't make the leap from Lucy to Consuela, not then anyway. Philip pulled out his pipe, considered it, knocked it, stuffed it and lighted it. He watched it burn and made the leap for me.

"I gather this has something to do with Consuela. Nothing wrong between you two, I hope?"

His question slammed against me and I was totally unprepared to answer it. "No, not wrong, exactly." I fumbled for the answer, the real answer to a question I had begged for some time. "Not wrong, but maybe not right, either. I don't know what *is* between us. Is that what I mean to say?"

My feeble little question dangled in the air for a minute.

"Can you explain? Do you want to?" His voice was kind, so kind I wanted to cry. "I don't mean to pry. You do know that?"

"You're not prying, Philip. God, I wish you would." My defenses and control began to slip-slide off as I said the words. Maybe to hide that, I got up quickly and filled a glass with ice and water, poured a splash of Bourbon on the top and sat down again, stirring with my finger.

"Consuela. I adore her, that hasn't changed," I began. "From the beginning I adored her, but more than that, I trusted her, felt safe with her. She has always been steady and assured. Invulnerable is what I mean."

"Invulnerable? Is she?" asked Philip.

"So far, yes."

"And?"

"And I'm not. There is an awful imbalance between us. All the security comes from her, all the strength and confidence. There's nothing I can give her, maybe that's why I feel so isolated." I paused for a second, realizing that I had gone too far to stop, that I was hardly aware of Philip's presence, that I was in fact talking to myself. "I don't know Consuela, except superficially. I've never tried to know her, I guess. But the shocking part is that I wasn't even aware of how slightly I knew her or how little effort I had made in that direction until a few weeks ago, when she let me glimpse another, private Consuela. I was a little afraid of this stranger, and at the same time, fascinated. I wanted to know her better but before I could pursue her, I stumbled on George and the dog, and now *they* have pursued me instead. They have consumed me, taken me over more and more, crowding Consuela out completely. I was relieved when she went back to Still River with the children." I stopped to get my breath.

"So you don't think everything began to fall apart from the time of George's death? Not with you and Consuela?"

"I do. Before he died we got along all right, with enough understanding and care to keep going. No, it was the distraction of George and the dog that ultimately threw everything out of kilter. I'm sure of it." Philip frowned slightly at me. "Don't you agree?"

"No, Hugh. The night you came to dinner, Caroline and I noticed how nerved up you were. I thought you might split in two while you waited for the booze to work."

"Believe me, I was fine then, just tired. But now, now it's almost as if I were, well, possessed." I tried to laugh at the preposterousness of this idea, but the laugh was forced and Philip didn't join me.

"Possessed? Well I don't know about that, but it's pretty obvious that you are close to some sort of a breakdown. Obvious to me, and I think you know it too."

And so Philip removed any remaining barriers, there was nothing at all to hold me back, and it all came out, the dreams; the business with Aunt Edith and the blood, Edith and Waffles, which by this time I was doubtful had ever really happened; my guilt over Polly's accident—how I felt that my anger toward her for piercing Rebecca's ear was somehow transferred to Waffles, so when he attacked Polly it was in a sense I who attacked her and tore her eye. Everything spilled out while Philip smoked his pipe and, empty at last, I wept.

"What can I do, Philip? What?"

"First, have a shot of this." He gave me a slug of whiskey.

I drank it down, like medicine, and went to the bathroom. When I came out, Philip was there, with Waffles.

"It's raining out, so I let the dog in. No one seemed to care. Now, sit down." I sat.

"Here is my advice, for what it's worth," began Philip. "I think you should go home, first of all. Get away from here. See your doctor. I doubt that he'll find anything wrong but you probably need a checkup anyway. Ask him to recommend a shrink, and go to him. Most important, cut down on the booze. It's certainly adding to your problems, if not the chief cause of them. About Consuela, I think you should talk to her more. I have a hunch that you feel in some way humiliated talking to her about yourself, but I really think you must. And keep in touch with me. If I can help you, let me know."

"Thanks, Philip. You already have. Helped me, that is, and I will keep in touch. What about working? I don't look forward to going back, at least not like this."

"But I think you ought to, if you can. What else would you do? Hang around mulling over all your worries? Try to return to normal. And try to forget the dog."

"How can I?" My voice was high and petulant. It disgusted me.

"You can *try*. Why shouldn't you work, like everyone else? Be careful not to think of yourself as such a special case, and I think you'll find life easier. More fun even."

"You're right, I'm acting spoiled."

"It's getting late and we've got to get a good start tomorrow to shoot the channel. You need anything to help you sleep?"

"Not tonight, thanks. I might as well sleep here if it's raining."

"I figured you would," said Philip. "I asked them to pound on our doors at quarter of eight so we can have breakfast. The dining room closes at eight-thirty."

We said good night and Waffles and I went to our room. He settled down on the braided rug and I in my bed and we fell asleep at once, without "tension" or "current" or anything between us.

Waffles woke me up before seven, in a hurry to go out. The rain had stopped and the day was fair and sharp. The guests in Bosworth House were still in their rooms but the kitchen was awake and pots clanged over the voices of the girls. We went quietly out the side door and saw the sun rise over Martha's Vineyard. And beneath the sun lay a broad avenue of silver shimmer across the water of Vineyard Sound. The clay colors of Gay Head were subdued, still in shadow. All the brilliance belonged to the sky and sea.

I followed the walkways to the bottom road, Waffles chose the grass along the side, and we went on down to the compass rose, and Charlie's house. Someone had stuck a lopsided wreath of goldenrod on the grille of the fire engine. The house had a sad, empty look.

When we climbed back to the top of the hill and breakfast, I saw Esther Veeder pegging out her sheets on the line outside her back door. Her front door leads directly into the post office, the "front room" of her small shingled house.

"Morning, Mrs. Veeder," I called.

"Morning." She was pleasant but wary, obviously puzzled that a stranger should know her name.

"I used to live here a long time ago, over on the point. Hugh Murray's my name. Sorry to hear about Charlie."

"Umm," replied Mrs. Veeder, nodding, her mouth full of clothespins.

"Any chance of my buying his house?"

She removed the two remaining clothespins and looked at me closely.

"Can't buy it. Don't want to sell. How about renting?"

"I think that'd be fine. How much?"

"Hafta let ya know. What d'ya want it for, anyway?

What did I want it for? I didn't know at all, I just wanted it.

"I'd like it as a kind of retreat," I said, vaguely.

"A what?"

"Oh, you know, a place to get away from it all."

"Well, it's that all right. Dinky little house, no hot water. Ya gonna *live* there?"

"Maybe. Off and on."

"Hafta think it over." Mrs. Veeder returned to her wash basket and I wrote down my name and address in Still River.

"When do you think you'll know? I can call you tomorrow from Gosnold's Bay, or you can get me at this address." I gave her the paper.

"Might know t'morra, why don'cha call anyhow?"

"I'll do that. Thank you." And I went down the walk to Bosworth House wondering what I had done.

Philip and I had a beautiful sail back. We had talked so much the night before that we hadn't much left to say, and I kept thinking of Charlie's house, wondering what it was like inside, and how Cuttyhunk looked in the snow. There must be heat of some sort, and plumbing. I didn't tell Philip about my intention to rent it. He would want to know why, and I couldn't have told him.

By three-thirty we were back at the mooring in Gosnold's Bay. The sails were bagged, the lines coiled and Philip and I had a last beer before going ashore.

"Last sail this summer, I guess," said Philip sadly. "We're leaving tomorrow."

"You'll be back Columbus Day weekend, won't you?" The long October weekend usually brought back most of the summer people, for Aunt Edith's annual oyster party and a last look at Indian summer.

"Not this year. We're off to Scotland. This is it. Always hate to have her hauled," and he patted the *Melande*'s gunwale.

"Thanks for taking me with you, and for that talk last night. You helped a lot, you know." I stopped, feeling guilt crawl in again for not having told him about the house.

"I'm glad I could. One thing I thought of that might help. You should try keeping a journal. Writing everything down can clear up a lot of confusion. Once you put something down, in words, on paper, you have it to see. Try it."

Back at the house, Aunt Edith was in a sulk.

"You're back," she said. "High time too, I should think. Consuela called last night. You might call her back and let her know how you are. She wondered when you were ever coming home, now that there's no reason for you to stay here. You and that dog."

So Aunt Edith had given me my walking papers, and Waffles, too. Well, well. I called Consuela. She sounded so far away, and preoccupied with children and cows. I told her I'd be home the next day, with all the rest of the Labor Day travelers, and went up to pack. There was no reason why Aunt Edith shouldn't kick me out, but I was miffed all the same. Waffles stayed with me. Was he avoiding her, too? He stayed upstairs on the bed during supper, not under the table by Aunt Edith's thick legs. Maybe the tide had turned.

Before I left in the morning I put through a call to Cuttyhunk. Mrs. Veeder still didn't know the terms, if any, of renting Charlie's house, but promised to let me know as soon as she had talked it over with her husband, who was "out fishing the bank." Most of the way home, I thought about the little house.

In my mind's eye, I was there already, with Waffles. Out of this world. I decided not to tell anyone at all. Which made me think of Consuela. Had she missed me? Had I missed her? Maybe I had always missed her? I had stayed relaxed and calm since talking to Philip, and I knew the urgency and compulsion to change my life and get out of my peculiar solitary state had dwindled. The irresponsible dream of retreat in Cuttyhunk was my private parachute to safety, more enticing by far than an analyst's couch. But I had vowed to be sensible, normal. No wonder I dreaded going home.

Still River

The Littleton Road was shady and empty, no roadside stands here to lure the suburban home canners or picklers. I passed the dead tree, and Solomon's pond, rattled over the trestle bridge ticking off the landmarks automatically. These were landmarks pointing home to my children, just as Hobbs Hill and Gilly's pigs had led the way for me in Tyringham. Still River wasn't home; too flat, for one thing, and too many cows.

West Meadow opened out beside me, and I saw the cows lying stupidly together under the big oak. The big cow barn boasted new red paint and stood squarely on the south side of the road, facing our house. The house looked shabbier than ever. Why didn't Consuela have it painted, not the barn? She had the barn rebuilt and painted twice since we moved in, but the house and little barn attached to it had been neglected. It occurred to me fleetingly as I drove in that Consuela might prefer cows to people, but I ditched that unhappy thought fast and got my stuff out of the car. Justin and Ward slammed noisily out of the house and ran to the car.

"Look!" Justin pointed a grimy finger in his mouth. "It fell out!"

"Let me see." I moved his hand away and inspected the very red gap in the even row of little baby teeth, speckled with Oreo crumbs.

"Rebecca just pulled it out with some thread. She says the tooth fairy will come tonight!"

"I go to First Grade on the Bus tomorrow!"

"Come on, Waffles. Come meet Alice." And we all went into the kitchen. Alice shuffled to her feet when I came in, and then lowered her large black head growling at Waffles as he pranced across the linoleum toward her blanket beside the coal stove.

"Maybe you dogs ought to get acquainted outside. Come,

Waffles, out. Alice, you too." But Alice wouldn't follow him. Her hackles were up and she clearly wanted nothing to do with this skinny, quick creature. "Don't be such a snob, Alice, out." I started to drag her out the door when she snapped at me. I think it was the first time in her life that she had ever snapped at anyone and it made me furious. I whacked her hindquarters hard and pushed her out the door. She approached Waffles slowly, threatening him with throaty growls and raised hackles. I watched as she forced him back from the house. He scurried under my car whimpering and wagging his tail every now and again, Alice advanced, and finally drove him backwards, past the bicycles in the driveway and into the dark barn, where Consuela's car stood. Alice hung around the barn door for a minute to make sure Waffles understood that he was to stay there, and then she walked stolidly back to the kitchen door and scratched to come in.

"That was horrid," I said as I let her in. Then to Justin, who was kneeling on the bathroom sink so he could look at his mouth, "Get down! Those pipes aren't strong enough to support you. Now, where's Mummy?"

"In the barn with the vet. Sweetwater Sybil has mastitis."

"Oh. What's for lunch?" I opened the refrigerator and looked for a beer. The refrigerator was cluttered and slightly smelly and I couldn't find any beer.

"Lunch?" repeated Justin, jumping off the bathroom sink and poking his cheerful dirty face around the doorway. "Peanut butter and honey? Want me to make it for you?"

"No, thanks. That's very nice of you to offer, though. I'm going to the barn to find Mummy." The kitchen was a mess and for the third time in ten minutes I regretted that Consuela was so careless with the house, and so meticulous with the damn cows.

"Why don't you guys clean up the kitchen?" I called as I went out. "At least rinse out your cups and put the food away."

Cam startled me when I walked into the barn to get Waffles. He plunged from the loft and screamed like Tarzan as he fell through the dusty dark. I didn't notice the rope hanging from the beam until he let go of it and touched the floor.

"Hi ya, Pa! See my rope? Kip gave me it."

"Gave it to me. Yeah, I see it now, but you really scared me at first. Where's Waffles?"

"He's here? I didn't see him."

"Well, find him, will you? I want to see Mummy." And I walked out and across the road to the other, the real barn.

I may not like cows, but I must admit that the smell of a good cow barn is unbeatable. The barn is as immaculate inside as Mabel's kitchen, and a lot friendlier. The floors had been hosed down, and the bedding was fresh and sweet, everything set for the afternoon milking. Consuela and Dr. Riley were in one of the box stalls in the back, binding Sweetwater Sybil's distended udder.

"I'm back. Hello, Dr. Riley."

"Hugh!" Consuela looked up, the roll of bandage in her hand, and smiled over the bony haunches of the cow. "I'll be done in a minute. You got back early!"

"Not much point in staying. What's for lunch?"

"Lunch?" Consuela said it as if she had never heard the word before. And again, "Lunch? I don't know. I'll be up as soon as I can. There are lots of tomatoes in the garden."

"Bacon?"

"I'm not sure. Just wait a few minutes. I'll do it."

"Finish with Dr. Riley. I'm going to get some beer, and then I'll put together something. See you in a little while."

It wasn't as if she didn't know I was coming back, for Christ's sake, I thought crossly as I drove to the liquor store. She might have left me a note or a sandwich or at least a cold beer, instead of that mess in the kitchen.

I opened a beer, and put the rest in the refrigerator, throwing out two rotten heads of lettuce and several squashy tomatoes first to make room. Shit. I took my beer with me to the vegetable garden behind the house, wondering where all the gardening baskets were. They were not on the shelf in the shed where I had left them the morning I closed the house to go to Gosnold's Bay. Why couldn't people put things back where they belonged? One of the baskets lay in the garden, with two soggy summer squash in the bottom. I picked up the basket to dump out the squashes and saw a huge fat slug in the damp imprint of the basket. My stomach turned. I stepped on it hard. It popped under my heel. Everything needed picking, and I spent longer than I meant to just getting tomatoes, lettuces and a few cucumbers. The last inch of beer was warm and I tossed it in the trash with the can as I came through the shed.

"Consuela?" She wasn't in the kitchen.

"She isn't back yet, Papa. How are you?" Rebecca called from the bathroom.

"Hi, sweetheart. I'm fine. Come give me a hand cleaning up this mess, will you?"

"Can't, Pa. I'm washing my hair."

"Well, when you're finished then, O.K.?"

"O.K."

I cleared out the sink and washed the vegetables. By the time Rebecca emerged, the kitchen was pretty clean, and I had made three sandwiches, and finished my second beer.

"I'm going to sit in the sun. Put a damp dish towel on those sandwiches, would you, so they don't dry out before your mother gets back, whenever that is." I took a fresh beer to the flagstone terrace outside the dining room.

The roses were doing fine, but needed pruning, and the chrysanthemums were full and still in bud. Except for an occasional weed or two poking through the thick mulch, my garden was in excellent shape. It was really the only carefully tended place on this side of the road, I thought, uprooting a stray burdock.

I waited almost an hour on the terrace for Consuela to come back for lunch. It was after two when she came out, wiping her hands on the seat of her pants.

"Sorry, love. Dr. Riley wanted to look at the Maternity Ward. The first twelve cows are due to calve within the month." She sat down on the foot of my chaise and took a sip of my beer. "How are you?" She gave me a scrutinizing look.

"What are you looking for, chicken pox? I'm fine. Except that I'm damn near starving. Let's eat." I got up. "You want a beer? Don't get up, I'll bring one out."

I brought the tray outside and set it on the table.

"It's like being at Aunt Edith's!" said Consuela. "A perfect little lunch. And thank you, by the way, for cleaning up the kitchen. I'm sorry it was such a mess."

I grunted.

"It's such a relief to be home again where I *can* leave a mess, and let the children run around dirty and fighting. You should have heard them the day we got back. They shrieked and punched each other all day. Obviously, they used up all their good manners in Gosnold's Bay."

"I think I did, too." I felt sluggish from the beer and the sun. Although I had planned to "talk" to Consuela at lunch, to tell her about my night with Philip, my plans to see doctors, to limit my drinking, the whole thing, it was suddenly too late to begin, and I was sleepy. Maybe I could do it after dinner.

"You want a nap? Just leave the tray out here, I'll take care of it later. Have a nap. I've got to go over the accounts with Will." Consuela got up.

"It is a holiday, you know. Why don't you have a nap with me? Don't you ever stop?"

"I'd like to, I really would, but there's so much to do. Doesn't the barn look nice?" She gave me a kiss on the cheek and went off, leaving the tray in the sun, smears of mayonnaise already yellow and rancid. I carried it inside and went upstairs to sleep, feeling depressed.

We had an early supper with the children, but I wasn't hungry. After all, it was only a few hours since I had eaten lunch. I drank the last beer with my spaghetti, and when the children went upstairs for their baths I was sober and ready to let Consuela know what was going on with me. I got as far as Charlie's funeral procession when Ward called her to rinse his hair.

"Stop for a minute," said Consuela. "After the shampoos, there are forty fingernails and forty toenails to clip, and I want to help the little boys lay out their school clothes. Wait until I'm finished, O.K.? I really do want to hear."

But by the time she came back down, I had found the Bourbon, and was in no mood to talk straight. Rebecca and

Cam wanted us to play dominoes with them, so we did, and I fell asleep thinking, I begin tomorrow already one day behind.

"You are going to work, aren't you?" asked Consuela in the morning, quickly zipping up her blue jeans.

"Mmmm. Why should I?"

"Vacation's over. Get up!" She shook my shoulder and I burrowed into the bedclothes. Work? Did I really have to face that today? I heard Consuela close the door and opened my eyes in private. Work. Philip, like Chekov, had seemed to think work would be good therapy. What a troublesome notion, maybe a foolish notion. But in the long run, it might be easier to deal with legal cases than to try to explain to Consuela why I stayed at home. Or to sit idle in the backwaters of her bustling industry. I got up.

Waffles slunk out of the empty silo and tried to get in the car with me. I fended him off with my briefcase.

"No, boy. Stay home. Wish I could too. Now, go on."

As I backed out of the driveway, Waffles stood in the door of the silo, his eyes burning out of the darkness. Behind me, in the rearview mirror, the children waited for the school bus. They stood by the mailbox in their new shoes, swinging lunch boxes under the sugar maple, whose leaves had already begun to turn. It was a September calendar picture, a classic.

Somewhere in the middle, between the bright children and the truculent dog were Consuela, standing by the door watching the children, and me, backing up and watching the children. Our positions and postures seemed relevant.

The school bus pulled in just in front of me. I waited for it to admit the children, one, two, three, four, and the doors snapped shut on the hostages to fortune. I followed the bus, returning the waves and funny faces from the jouncing bodies in the back seat, until we took our separate ways at the Still River fork. Without the bus ahead, I was on my own, with nothing to occupy my mind and distract it from inward probes and worries. Well, at least I was going to work. Philip would approve of that, his approval seemed important to me then. And if yesterday was a partial failure, too much booze for one, and not enough talk with Consuela for another, I could try to set that right tonight.

The Park Street Church bells began to chime nine o'clock as I entered the building. The outside office was empty, and from the faint buzz of voices coming from the ladies' room, I guessed the few prompt secretaries were "powdering their noses," an old, comfortable genteelism which I ruefully admitted had become an anachronism.

The glass door to my cubicle was ajar, curious, as I had closed it tightly when I left for my vacation. I pushed it open all the way and saw a young man sitting at my desk, poring over a brief. Had I been replaced?

"Good morning."

He looked up, startled. "Oh, hello. Are you Hugh Murray?" I nodded and before I could speak, he continued. "I'm so sorry. I didn't know you'd be in today. I'm Sam Marcus." We shook hands.

"Don't let me interrupt," I said. "I want to talk to the Chief, if he's in yet, and get some coffee."

"Please, I'd be glad to move. I would like to go over some things with you, too, when you have a minute. The Chief hired me to carry on for you while you were away, and now that you're back, you might like to know what I've done."

"Right. Finish what you were doing, and I'll be back in a few minutes." I left my briefcase in my/Sam Marcus's office and walked down the narrow hall to the Chief Counsel's corner room. His secretary sat at her desk outside, opposite the boss's door.

"Good morning, Ann. Is Mr. Hull in yet?"

"Mr. Murray! You're back! Yes, he's here. Shall I let him know you want to see him?"

"Please." I stood somewhat ill at ease while she announced me, thinking how much simpler it would have been to have stayed at home.

"Go right in, Mr. Murray." The door to Bill Hull's office opened as she spoke and he came out to greet me.

"Well, well. Back so soon? Come in, Hugh."

I followed him in and sat down facing the fumed oak desk.

159

Bill was a forthright, unemotional civil servant. He did his job precisely, and expected the same thorough efficiency from his staff. I sensed that he was disappointed with me, but that may have been simply my imagination.

"I assume your difficulties in Gosnold's Bay have passed? Jim Earl called after the hearing, he's a conscientious fellow." I inferred that I, by contrast, was not. "Since I really had no idea how long you'd be away, I hired a very good boy, Sam Marcus, to take over your clients."

"We just met," I said tersely, not bothering to add that not only had we met, but that he was sitting in my chair, drinking coffee out of my mug, a Christmas present from Rebecca.

"You did? Oh yes, you would have." He got up and looked out his dusty window to the street below. "Well, now that you're back, I guess we'll just have to put another desk in there for him. I'm due in court at ten." With this curt dismissal from the Chief, I returned to what was no longer "my" office. It was hard not to put my resentment on young Sam Marcus. I knew it wasn't his fault, but I still didn't feel especially friendly toward him. He, too, was appearing in court this week, so I would have command of my desk for most of the time. Before he left, he told me briefly what he had been doing, and asked me to follow up on a couple of cases. My attention was superficial and I waited impatiently for him to get out.

Once left alone, I did not get to work, but instead went through all my desk drawers to see if they were as I had left them, and, of course, they weren't. Oh, the desk was tidy enough, but it wasn't mine any more. Nothing was mine any more, nothing except Waffles. I took down the telephone book and called my doctor. He had had a cancellation and said he could examine me tomorrow morning. I would ask him to recommend a shrink as Philip had suggested, but I dreaded it. Then I thumbed through the cases Sam had left for me, something at least for me to do with my hands. I was incapable of reading them with any comprehension, incapable of doing anything outside of myself. At quarter of twelve, I decided to get out and have some lunch.

The Hare Krishnas were clinking away outside the subway

kiosk on the Common, saffron robes swirling as they bobbed up and down and around to the endless beat, over and over. Chi-Chi-CHING, Chi-Chi-CHING, Chi-Chi-CHING. The Doubleknits and Platform Shoes on their way shopping or to lunch slowed down near the kiosk to watch. Obviously, Hare Krishna served a real purpose to the Doubleknits. It was wonderful how all those "freaks" bolstered the morales of the swinging singles and the suburban shopgirls. Here at least they knew for sure they were better than those crazy people with the shaved heads and bare feet.

I looked at the scene, at the dancers on their way to Nirvana and the "normal" people, outside the pulse of Hare Krishna, on their way to lunch. For one intense extended moment, I envied the dancers. I envied their single-mindedness, their fervor, their bare feet, their Yul Brynner heads. When I forced myself to move on to lunch and a martini, I felt drained by that passing envy and pushed it from my mind.

Three martinis at lunch is usually too many, but I had to get through the day some way. From three to five I sat at my desk, trying hard to fight the gin and make some progress on the two cases Sam had left for me. It was difficult enough to sit there alone; how would I manage when Sam was there?

The Hare Krishna beat echoed in my ears all the way home to Still River. Waffles poked his head around the silo door when he heard the car and wagged his tail with delight in my return, yet he was still too terrified of Alice to leave his silo refuge. I went to him and by resuming this old absorption with a strange little dog, I silenced the Hare Krishna.

Although not entirely abstemious (after three drinks at lunch a few at dinner were a necessity, just to keep going), I didn't overdo it, and was able to talk with Consuela at last. She sewed while she listened to me, and I wondered if she was paying attention; I gave her every chance to understand me, and couldn't stop recounting even the smallest details, until I bored myself as well. If she couldn't, didn't understand now, it was not my fault.

". . . despite what Philip says, I'm not sure I *can* work.

Today was awful. Am I boring you? Why don't you *say* something?"

"Look," said Consuela, putting down her needle. "What can I say? I can see you're falling apart, I *know* you drink too much, I know you have some strange preoccupation with that dumb dog, and I have a feeling that all of us, the children, everything has become inconsequential to you. But what the hell can *I* do about it? If you drink too much, why don't you stop? If you think you're having a nervous breakdown, then *do* something about it. I guess that's just it. *Do* something. And stop talking." She got up, collected her sewing and started to leave. "I'm sorry. I didn't mean to sound so bitchy. I'm tired. And I think I'm . . ." She stopped short.

"You're what?"

"Oh, I don't know, never mind. Come on, come to bed."

She paused on the landing and said softly, "I'm worried too, about you. I'll help, if I can, I really will. It's just that help sometimes turns into coddling. And besides, I have so much to do."

She kissed me gently and went to bed. I turned off the lights and followed her, but when I reached the landing, I stopped, and went back down to the silo, never even questioning the impulse to do so. The night was light, much lighter than the shadowy silo. Waffles' food looked untouched in his bowl by the door. Had he eaten at all since we left Gosnold's Bay? When I picked him up in my arms he was undoubtedly thinner, frail even. Poor fellow. In my preoccupation with self I had neglected him. He ate the hamburg I took from the refrigerator and curled up on a little pile of hay I brought him from the pony's stall in the barn. I sat in the silo beside him on the cobbled floor breathing in the strange, slightly alcoholic smell of ancient silage. We were peaceful and I imagined I somehow gathered strength then, replenished a vacant storeroom tucked away in an unspecific corner of my soul, a reserve tank, an extra battery, stuff to get me through the next day, or week, or year.

The next morning, after my doctor's appointment, I resigned. Sam Marcus had already left for court when I got to the office. The note he had left on my desk was just patronizing enough to give me the initial momentum actually to quit, then and there. But I would have left eventually, no matter what. I had known it in Cuttyhunk when I mentioned working to Philip. It was a relief to cross it off my mental list of "pending." Now all I needed was a letter from Mrs. Veeder saying Charlie's house was mine. No, that wasn't all I needed, but it would help.

I fished in my pocket for the car keys, bringing up with them a crumpled scrap of paper ripped off the doctor's Rx pad with the name of a psychiatrist. My body was in adequate shape. The next item was to see to my mind. Soon, I would take care of that soon.

Back in Still River before noon, I was a truant in the empty quiet house. Consuela was probably across the street with the cows, the children were at school for three more hours and I was at liberty. I got a beer and called the psychiatrist's office for an appointment. An audience with Dr. Hale was like an audience with the Holy See. His secretary demanded so much information from me that I wondered what discoveries would be left for Dr. Hale himself to make, if indeed he elected to see me. I would receive a letter in a day or so with his decision. Dr. Hale remained on the pending list.

Emlyn, the Welsh pony I had mistakenly bought for Rebecca's sixth birthday, stood dejectedly in the little paddock by the barn. The flies were bad in the sun, and the barn and silo made no shadows at noon. The inside of the barn was a catchall for snow shovels, rusty tools, bicycle parts, empty paint cans and so many other components of our messy lives. Somewhere among all the rubbish I managed to find a bottle of fly repellent and a rag to wipe old Emlyn with.

My father had given me a pony for my sixth birthday. Next to Cousin Lucy, I had loved my pony beyond everything else. He had been put down just before Lucy's accident. That June, it seemed as though I lost everything.

When I brought Emlyn home for Rebecca I had been so pleased with myself, so excited for her. Her own pony! How happy she would be: Rebecca wasn't happy. In fact, she didn't even pretend to like him for my sake, the way I was taught to act when someone gave me something I didn't like.

"I hate it!" she had screamed. "It's ugly! I don't want to ride it. I don't want to touch it!" And she hadn't.

Sometimes Cam and Justin rode him around the fields, but mainly Emlyn stood in his scraggly paddock, looking sad. He was fat and slow and rather stupid, but I liked him, and I liked tending him. His rump was caked with dry mud, from rolling in the swampy bottom of the enclosure as a kind of protection from the bloodthirsty flies. He watched me brush him, blinking the flies away from his sorrowful eyes. The strong smell of the bug stuff cut through the air as I wiped him down.

"Have an apple, Emlyn." My act of charity completed, I walked around to the door of the silo.

The fieldstone tower had charmed me from the first trip we had made to Still River, before the papers were passed. It hadn't been used for silage for many years, not since the barn and modern metal silo across the road were built. Forty, fifty, sixty years empty perhaps, and yet the heady smell of fermented corn still clung, as if the stones were exhaling. I am sure it was the stones which attracted me; they were very like the stones at home in Tyringham. Grandpa's cellar holes were dug eight feet into the Berkshire hill, then lined with fieldstone, which went on right up to the sills of the windows. Both house and barn at home had always seemed enduring, permanent, and in contrast, the uneven clapboards of our settling farmhouse in Still River, although older in time, struck me as flimsy. But the silo stood impervious to weather and neglect.

I had wanted to make a "study" (if I were Cam's age, I would call it a hideout) on the top, under the pointed roof. Now that I was "at liberty" maybe I could begin to work on fixing up the silo. Physical labor might be salutary, especially if I could keep sight of the finished product. Yes, I would build a refuge here, for me and for Waffles. The inside of the silo was a mess and for a moment I lost heart. There was too much junk to think about clearing it out, and it was so dark in there that I could hardly see what the mess consisted of. Against one curved wall stood a wrought iron staircase about fifteen feet tall. Someone had left it there, free standing except for two frayed lengths of thick hemp which were tied to the top steps on one end, and to two large rusty hooks near the top of the silo at the other. An iron ladder was imbedded in the mortar of the wall beside the spiral steps, but unlike them, it ran from top to bottom. I squeezed behind the steps and began to climb the ladder, eager to reach the light at the top and look out over the world. A rickety wooden floor covered half of the top, a few feet below the windows. Two of the windowpanes were broken, where the light shot in, strong and brilliant, quite different from the milky glow coming in through the filmy glass. Here is where I would make my "study," "den" or hideout. My telephone closet. It would be a safe place, a lighthouse.

When Consuela came back to the house to usher in the children from school, she was appalled to see me, hauling an old harrow from the silo out to the sprawling mound of trash in the driveway.

"What in God's name are you doing? Are you crazy? This is awful! You can't leave it here." Consuela's voice had an unpleasant nagging quality, but I was enjoying myself so thoroughly that it didn't dampen my pleasure a bit. I only noted it in the back of my mind.

"I'm fixing up the silo. Come and see it. Oh, it's going to be fantastic! Let me show you." I left the harrow on the edge of the rubbish and took her arm. She resisted me and we stood facing one another, scraps of grain sacks and mildewed papers blowing past our feet.

"I thought you went to work?"

"I did. I went and I left. Quit."

"For good?"

"For good for now." I blew my nose, aware suddenly of the dust I had been breathing while I worked.

"Why? Why did you quit?" Consuela was not pleased, nor was she sympathetic. Not that I had really expected her to be.

"I couldn't work. I didn't think I'd be able to and I couldn't. Besides, Bill Hull had already hired that other fellow. He didn't need me too, and I couldn't do it anyway." I wiped my nose once more and stuffed my handkerchief in my pocket.

"It isn't a crime, you know, not to work. You know perfectly well we are not about to starve or go on welfare, and besides, I'm sick."

"You mean physically? Your stomach?"

"No. Not physically. My stomach problems are all from nerves. I am psychologically ill. 'Close to a breakdown' is how the doctor put it."

"Then I think you had better take care of it right away." There was no mistaking the hardness in Consuela's voice. "And I frankly can't see that making this mess is going to help you."

"Would you prefer that I stayed in bed, doing nothing but asking for trays, and beef tea?"

Consucla stared, her face set and impassive, almost, but for a trace of emotion. Was it scorn?

The yellow school bus shuddered to a stop. Consuela glanced at it quickly and said, "Please pull yourself together. See a doctor, anything, do *something.*"

She turned to the children before I could tell her that I *had* called Dr. Hale. Later. I would tell her later, after I had cleaned up the mess.

I went to the cow barn to find Kip, hoping he would help me load up the pickup truck and get the heap in the driveway off to the dump. But he was busy fixing up the stalls for the calving cows and had no time. He tossed me the keys to the pickup and I went back to the house to get the boys to help me.

We made three trips to the dump, and all that was left fit more or less in two trash cans and some busted-up bushel baskets. I left them just outside the silo. Next Monday, I'd leave them by the road with the household rubbish for the trash trucks to collect.

But by next Monday I had lost my drive for fixing up the silo. Consuela had drained me bit by bit with each silent accusation when she looked at me. She had drained me with her still, contained self in bed, with her busy obligations to the cows and the children (in that order) until I was certain that she was doing everything she could to make it plain to me that there could be no place in her life for a cripple. And there was no question in my mind that I had become, to Consuela anyway, a cripple. So the trash cans and baskets stayed by the silo, rained on, blown about, not carried to the side of the road on Monday morning.

Dr. Hale had generously agreed to see me. Consuela had been interested in that. In fact, she had pried the time and date of my first appointment out of me, which made me so cross that I didn't go at all. I called his secretary and said I couldn't make it after all and would she kindly reschedule my fifty minutes. So I kept Dr. Hale on pending for another week, and to make Consuela think I'd gone, I drove to Boston instead, and walked around the Common. A beaming girl in an orange sari had approached me, carrying a large cookie sheet.

"Hare Krishna!" She said it joyfully, looking me directly in the eye, peace, love, joy.

"Hare Krishna to *you!*" I replied, thinking, Or *Dalai Lama, Hari-Kari, Krishna Lama, how does it go?*

"Have some apple crisp?" she invited.

I looked on the tin, noticed that it was less than half full, and decided it must be non-poisonous.

"Thank you. I'd love some apple crisp." *Nice,* I thought. *How mean of me to think they only cared for the inner man.*

She handed me an inch cube of apple crisp, seemed uncertain where to put it, maybe because *I* was uncertain where she *would* put it, was I supposed to open my mouth and stick out my tongue, like at Mass? But I did put out my hand, and she did put it on my palm, still smiling as she said, "That will be a dollar."

So the "inner man" was an illusion after all.

When I resigned as Public Defender, I had asked the Chief to hold my check rather than to send it straight on to Consuela's and my joint account at the bank. Reminded by the Hare Krishna novice of the material world, I headed up the hill to School Street to collect my last earned money. I did not deposit it to our account in Still River. Instead, I went to the city bank next door and opened my own account, with my check from the state, and another, drawn on Consuela's and my bank. A little nest egg all my own, it didn't even seem like stealing from my wife. Perhaps that was because I chose to view it as a necessity. If, or when, I heard from Mrs. Veeder in Cuttyhunk, I might need to send her some rent, and I would feel so much easier knowing it was there, knowing that I would not have to ask Consuela to pay for my indulgence, nor to be forced to explain it to her.

Another week went by. The silo trash was wetter, and still stood next to the door. Waffles usually lurked behind the barrels just inside the silo, his uneaten dog food next to him. He was very thin and morose, not unlike me. Only in the mornings did I have hope. I focused on the mailman. Today he would bring me a letter from Cuttyhunk. I do not know what, if anything, Waffles waited for, but he must have been waiting for something or I truly think he would have died. I pretended he waited for me.

Again, I missed my appointment with Dr. Hale. I did manage to get all the way to his building in Cambridge, but my route was circuitous. The drugstore clock across from the doctor's building said ten to eleven, plenty of time, as I drove past, looking for a place to park. I didn't see any vacant meters and instead of trying the side streets, I just drove on, toward Boston. On the bridge over the Charles River with Dr. Hale's office well behind me I knew it was absurd, but I simply had to park in Boston, in the garage I always used when I went to work. My complusion embarrassed me.

As I stood on the subway platform at Park Street waiting for a Harvard train, I noticed how the other people looked at me. They were suspicious, scornful, and when I stared back at them, challenging them, they would look away, sneers on their lips. A bunch of boys, teen-agers, thundered down the stairs, bleating abusive monosyllables and laughing derisively as they shouldered each other. They seemed to take over the station and I watched them uneasily as they came down the platform, closer to me. They were so engrossed in themselves as to be unaware of the other people, but even so, they scared me. Would they single me out, laugh at me? Why did I suddenly feel so threatened? I tried not to look at them, to relax—the train would come soon now, I tried to soothe my nerves. I took a few steps forward, away from the jostling boys and toward the edge of the platform. It was worse with the boys behind my back, and I became almost hysterical with fear and a kind of claustrophobia.

I took a few careful baby steps to the edge, leaned over and spat. I watched the bitter spittle land close to the third rail and read the sign above it: CAUTION, LIVE RAIL. How about CAUTION, LIVE BOYS? Let me out. I was sweating, freezing, couldn't breathe, and then the train came and everything was fine. Saved. I read on the boys' purple and yellow satin jackets "St. Sebastian's High," so they were "good" boys after all, keeping the faith. Why had they scared me so?

It was eleven thirty-five when I reached the lobby of Dr. Hale's building. My appointment had been for eleven. I studied the directory, walked to the elevator and wondered what explanation I could possibly give for being so late. I might just ride the elevator up and then down. But I pushed "5" and got out in front of the open door to Dr. Hale's office. The woman at the desk smiled at me.

"Mr. Murray?" I nodded dumbly. "Oh, good. We were afraid something had happened to you." (If only she knew how close I had been!) "Your wife wants you to call her." Oh, Jesus! "There's some trouble at home. Why don't you use my phone?" She handed me the receiver.

Consuela answered on the first ring. "Where are you?"

"At the doctor's. I uh I had ah car trouble." My voice was false.

"Oh. Can you get home fast? Kip had a bad accident in the silo."

"What happened?"

"He was trying to fix up the top platform for you when he fell through one of those rotten boards. Jenny's driving him to the hospital now."

"Oh, my God! Is he badly hurt?"

"I don't know. He's conscious. He cut his leg. Luckily, he grabbed on to one of those ropes and slid most of the way down."

"I'll come right home."

"Thanks. Oh, the rotten plank hit Waffles."

"Waffles? Oh no! He's alive?" But I was sure he was alive.

"Barely. Dr. Riley wanted to put him away but I said no."

"Thank God! Where's Waffles?"

"At the animal hospital. Dr. Riley thinks his back is broken."

"I'm leaving now. I'll stop at the vet's on the way home."

My hand trembled as I gave the telephone back to the secretary. She nodded understandingly and handed me an appointment card for next week. I hurried to the street and took a cab to Boston and my car, no more subways today. I regretted my earlier blindness—the panic, the bad taste, portents again, and again unrecognized.

Just because I didn't know of anyone else whose mouth dripped with acid, whose gorge rose *before* a disaster took place, just because I didn't know of anyone else who shared telepathy with his dog, that didn't mean I was crazy, did it? No, it made perfect sense to me that adjusting to these new elements in one's life might take a little time, might upset old patterns.

Dr. Riley shook his head in disbelief when he met me at the operating room door.

"I wouldn't have believed it," he said.

"How do you mean?"

"Well, I could have sworn his back was broken. I wanted to put him away, but Consuela said to wait for you. I X-rayed him and though the picture was blurred, I was sure he had a compound fracture." Dr. Riley scratched his temple.

"And?" I prompted.

"I operated, prepared to do a spinal fusion, and when I opened him up, his spine looked fine, no break at all, nothing. I don't understand it."

"Can I take him home? Where is he?"

Dr. Riley pointed to the door beyond the operating room. "He's in there, in recovery. You better leave him here for a while."

"How long?"

"Oh, about a week. I want to keep an eye on him, and I

think he should be confined and sedated for a few days. He's also much too thin."

So I went home alone, to the children. About an hour later, Consuela got back with Kip and Jenny. Kip's leg was badly cut where he caught it on the metal staircase. He had a dozen stitches under the gauze and it would be a week or two before he could ditch his crutches and resume work in the barn. I agreed to do his chores while his leg mended.

That was also the day the letter came from Cuttyhunk. Twelve hundred dollars a year and the place was mine. It never occurred to me that it was a steep price for a shanty. I thought instead it was a cheap fee for my salvation, and put a check in the mailbox before I went to bed.

After the accident, my relationship with Consuela shifted again. Of course, with Waffles gone, I was bound to change a little, but it wasn't just Waffles' absence which caused the altered regard between Consuela and me. We each seemed to have a new and distant respect for one another, as between two co-workers. I was touched, too, that she had asked Kip to look at the silo and begin work on the top floor. She had done that for me, a surprise. I suspect that she had seen my interest in the silo flag, and felt in some way responsible for dampening my ardor. She may have guessed too, how much I wanted a private place of my own, safe and removed. Her very kindness to me made my own secrecy much, much harder, it made me feel like a cheat. Nonetheless, I still couldn't bring myself to tell her about Cuttyhunk. Not yet.

That was part of the change between us. The other part grew slowly as we worked together in the barn and the fields. Consuela's impulsiveness and efficiency were evident at once, and for the first time to me. I had thought of her always as steady and smooth. She had bought two houses on impulse, and yet to me her purchases had appeared planned and sensible. If someone had asked me to describe Consuela in motion earlier, I would probably have likened her to a puma, graceful and sure. But that was wrong, and my vision before was limited. In the cow barn, Consuela darted from stanchion to stanchion, never staying long, never letting her eyes rest on any one thing for more than a second. There was nothing catlike about her at all. Each motion was quick. Deft, confident and very quick. Almost impatient.

With me, she was not impatient. No, Consuela was a thorough teacher. Her instructions and explanations were careful and precise. She knew I wasn't fond of cows and didn't begrudge that at all. We both just accepted the necessity of doing the work as well as possible.

It was a busy time, as the cows began to calve in September. I thought it unnatural and wrong, this fall calving. The natural time for animals to have their babies is in the early spring. But dairy farming, as Consuela told me several times, is a business, and the farmers spend a considerable effort to change nature and bring the cows in season out of season.

"Milk is scarce in winter and we get a better price for it," lectured Consuela. "If you bring the cows in season early, like the end of January to March, then you get more fall and winter milk."

I learned a lot of things: it takes nine months to make a calf, just as it does a baby; hormones change the cows' cycles same as Enovid; artificial insemination is no picnic for the cow. This last I learned when Sweetwater Sal's first cycle went askew despite her hormone injections. She came into season while I was standing in for Kip.

"What do we do now?" I asked Consuela.

"Do? Why, call the inseminator and find out who's fresh. His number's on the wall by the phone."

I wrote down the names of the "fresh" bulls for Consuela to study: Maplecroft Marksman, Gallagher Galahad, Willowdale Blue William. I was all for William—we could name his offspring Sweetwater Blue Sweet William and put garlands on his neck. He would be born in May, just in time for my own garden's sweet william. To Consuela, the selection of bulls was no joke; she asked for Marksman.

The morning of the day he was to arrive, Consuela left early for the barn. I stayed behind in the quiet house with my last cup of coffee. This had become ritual over the last few days —I simply couldn't pull myself together in the morning the way

Consuela did—so I would have toast and coffee after the school bus left, after Consuela had put on her stable boots, in solitude. So that Consuela wouldn't object to my habits, I made it a point to clean up the kitchen, which she always left in a horrible mess, egg drying on the plates, peanut butter and jelly from the children's sandwiches on the counter with no caps, and not only that, but I also started running a load of wash after the first morning, when I heard Justin wailing the lack of clean underpants and then Cam instructing him to turn the dirty ones inside out.

Instead of the silo project (no longer necessary now that I had heard from Mrs. Veeder), I sought peace and a certain pleasure from ordering the house, or beginning to. I took the trash out. For three days the children had made their beds, put away their clean laundry (lots of underpants) and returned home from school to a clean kitchen, and I had done it all. The fourth morning I had the washing machine sloshing through the first load and was giving the oven a cursory wipe when I heard a knock on the back door.

"Who's there?" I called, not wanting to drop my sponge that minute.

"The bull."

"The bull?" Oh, my God, the bull! I looked out the window, expecting to see a van in the driveway, and saw instead an orange Volkswagen. I opened the back door on a nattily dressed gentleman about seventy. He smelled slightly sweet and familiar, of rose water, I think, as my grandfather had smelled, and he wore a panama hat. In his thin, well-manicured little hand he held a test tube.

"Better refrigerate him right away, or use him fast. Won't keep long in this weather."

He handed me the tube, tipped his hat and walked with a light jaunty step back to the Volkswagen, leaving me to stand in the doorway, amazed, the "bull" in my hand. Again I considered how unnatural farming is. I wondered how Consuela fit into such a contrived business. She had always seemed so honest and direct.

I took the "bull" to the cow barn immediately and stood

horrified while Consuela lifted up Sweetwater Sal's tail and shoved in the plastic tube filled with Marksman's seed. Sal stood chewing her cud, wholly unaware of this moment of creation. No pain, and no fun. A big nothing. Ah, sweet mystery of life.

Soon humans, too, will only breed this way, as Orwell and Huxley predicted. I walked back to the house, feeling sad—for the horny cow and the horny bull—and sad for men to come. It was only ten-thirty in the morning; the French clock in the living room chimed as I threw my head back and drank directly from the bottle, three good swigs. This was bad. I couldn't go on like this, drinking gin before noon in a muddled panic over desexed sex. My third appointment with the shrink was tomorrow and I would have to go. I drank to that.

The gin picked me up enough to carry on my chores in the barn and settle back into the inexorable schedules of cows and children.

The next afternoon I was composed and ready to meet Dr. Hale. I wasn't even late, not that either Dr. Hale or I cared much, but Consuela did. She desperately wanted me to get help, I could tell, and in fact she believed that I had already gone to Dr. Hale twice. I was tired of putting over lies. The unsaid lies, like the house on Cuttyhunk, were easier to live with. The spoken lies were nasty, and besides, Consuela was making a real effort to help me.

So I went. I parked the car in the Church Street Garage this time, right behind the building, and arrived in the waiting room at five minutes of one. I could have been at the dentist's, as I leafed through *Newsweek*. But I wasn't and knew it. Actually, it was more like going to confession. I sat with the magazine in my lap, my mind scurrying over cogent points (sins?). Where to begin? Would the good doctor help me get started? Was I supposed to cast back to my dreary childhood and pull goblins from closets?

"Sit down, Mr. Murray."

I sat.

"Now, let's see, ah, yes, Dr. ah Cross referred you." Dr. Hale leafed through an oak tag folder, several pages full.

How could he have assembled such a dossier before I had even come for an appointment?

He asked me some questions, personal history he called it, like where I worked (HA!), wife's name and age, children, etc. Throughout this inquisition he never once looked directly at me. His eyes were gray, and slightly hooded like a reptile's. Because he wouldn't look at me, I, in turn, became visually locked on him, on those cold gray eyes. I would *make* him look at me, dammit, the same way one can reliably make an animal look away.

But it didn't work with Dr. Hale. He was totally impervious to my compulsion. This annoyed me, among other things, such as the long pauses for which I was paying roughly a dollar a minute.

When he had finished with his questions, or seemed to, I looked around for a clock, wondering whether there was enough time to start fishing. The clock was on his desk, facing him. I couldn't read it. Nor could I manage to pull out my own without embarrassment. I turned my head and looked at the "couch," only it wasn't a couch at all but one of those enormous leather reclining chairs. It was in the corner of the room, opposite the desk, as if someone had tried to tuck it away, out of sight. But instead, it loomed, dominated the corner. Would Dr. Hale invite me to sit there? I hoped not.

He sat across from me at his desk, looking slightly over my left shoulder.

"Well?" I asked.

"Yes?" replied Dr. Hale.

Say something, must say something, hurry, do it, and I was consumed with panic. I opened my mouth.

"Drink," I said.

"Drink?" repeated Dr. Hale.

"Drink. I drink too much. That must have been on my record?" Dr. Hale wasn't telling. He continued to stare unblinking over my left shoulder. The silence which I found so unnerving had no effect on him whatever. Finally I spoke again. Well, somebody had to. I was sure that anything, anything I said would be easier to endure than no talk at all.

"I've been trying to cut down, but it's no good. I need help."
Obviously, none was forthcoming from Dr. Hale, and the uncomfortable silence made me literally gasp for breath. I
couldn't look at his lizard's eyes any longer and lowered my
head on my hand, my eyes closed against the dizziness. And as
I sat there, stoop-shouldered, mute and blind in the doctor's
office, a glorious inspiration burst in on me, and with it every
psychological term I'd ever met. A tumult of corny phrases,
and catchwords poured out of my mouth. I was delighted, for it
seemed to me that I was dressing the bare office with a clutter
of jargon. Aha! I would furnish it to *my* taste.

"Anxiety. I have terrible anxiety, Doctor. Drinking makes
it go away, or at least recede, so I drink." Pause. "That makes
me angry with myself, hostile. I have a frightening hostility,
which eventually turns into a deep depression. That of course
works into the old anxiety and there we are, back at the beginning." Are you deaf, Dr. Hale? I wanted to shake him 'til his
teeth rattled. Or pull down his pants and humiliate him. But I
just went right on with my monologue.

"I suppose you'll say I'm repressing something." He didn't.
"Well, I am!" That came out with an unexpected vehemence.
"I know it. It's guilt. That's what I'm repressing." No reaction.
I sighed, took out a cigarette defiantly and glanced at him to
see if he had noticed. His eyes remained over my shoulder.

"What am I so guilty about? That's what *I'm* supposed to
figure out, I guess. . . . Aren't I supposed to work on that
one? . . . Aren't I , Dr. Hale?" Sez who? Sez you, Dr. Hale?

"Drink. That's what I'm guilty about. It's sort of a circle!"
Help me, Dr. Hale! I are guilty. I are drunk, I are repressed,
depressed, hostile. How can you just sit there, looking over my
left shoulder, unmoved by my sad story? But of course, I
haven't told you my real story, have I? I never will, either.
You wouldn't care, you have no right to know. I was quite
proud of myself.

Dr. Hale got up and walked to the door. I followed
obediently.

He opened the door and I escaped through it, feeling that

176

I had popped out of a vacuum seal. The secretary handed me a card for next week. Maybe I would drop dead before then.

Cameron met me on the road astride Emlyn. The pony's back was so broad that even Cam could hardly straddle him comfortably. I was pleased to see them, shuffling down the road under the yellow maple leaves, and I stopped the car just in front of them.

"Hi, Cam. That pony is certainly fat!"

"Yeah. He's nice, though."

"Ought to be ridden more. Tell you what, that's what we'll do, we'll see if we can get old Emlyn in shape. Time Justin and Ward learned to ride, too. We'll work out a program, O.K.? Maybe even build a few jumps in the woods."

"Super. Thanks, Pa."

"See you at home. Don't forget to look at his feet and brush him off when you're finished."

Working with Emlyn and the boys would be a good project to start when Kip was well enough to take over his old chores in the barn. What the hell, if I wasn't going to work, I might as well enjoy myself, my children, and my animals. Oh, and my wife.

It was only quarter of three by the kitchen clock when I got in. I took a beer out of the refrigerator, almost opened it, then put it back, dropped ice cubes in a glass and poured in some Bourbon. Into the closet with you, Dr. Hale! I banished him with booze and called the vet to see if Waffles could come home.

Consuela came into the kitchen just as I hung up.

"I'm going to get Waffles," I told her. "I wish you'd clean up this house today. It's so filthy it's unlivable."

Consuela looked startled as she ran her long thin fingers back and forth over the dribbles and circles of dried lemonade on the table.

"Me clean it up? How can you ask me to clean the house when you know I'm shorthanded in the barn? You have more time than I do. Why don't you clean it up?"

"I already told you, I'm going to pick up Waffles. Besides, the housework really isn't my department even if I have tried to help with it lately. If you can't keep the house and the cows going, maybe you better get a cleaning lady."

"And pay her? You don't even have a job. And how much is your dog going to cost?" Consuela was being mean and miserly. I couldn't believe it. Never before had she been anything but generous, yet without warning her money, formerly touted as "ours," reverted to single ownership.

"*My* dog is going to cost one hundred and fifteen dollars. One hundred and fifteen of your dollars. Are you intentionally trying to make me feel lousy because I don't have a job? What's wrong?"

"Oh shit, Hugh. It is my money and if I didn't have it you wouldn't be able to quit work like this and sit around the house."

"I'm not sitting around the house, God dammit, I've been helping you in the barn, remember?"

"I know, I know, you have helped in the barn. But that's not the same as having a real job and taking the responsibility for it. I feel like all the responsibility for everything is on me now, which I suppose is O.K., but I don't think it's fair of you to start bitching about the house not being immaculate. It's never been immaculate."

"No, it never has." I said the words caustically. "And I have never been in the house so much either, so the cobwebs and the flaking paint, and the dried splatters in the sinks and toilets are more obvious and thus more irritating to me now. At the same time, I'm grateful to you for your money." A tinge of sarcasm here. "I wish it were my own. Not only is it more blessed to give than to receive but it's a damn sight easier, too."

Consuela listened to me with a superior, steely glaze on her face. I tried to make her look like Aunt Edith, but that was stretching it a bit. Still, Consuela did not look like herself.

"It's not my fault my father was rich and yours wasn't. You may help yourself to my money, no strings. Spend it all on liquor if you want, I don't care. You're drunk most of the time as it is, or else sober and contentious. But please stop running me down. I do triple what you do and you're in no position to criticize me. Christ, I wish you were, I wish you would be so

178

busy, so committed that you had practically no time for me. Or for drink. I wish you were so strong I didn't dare to fight with you."

"Do you dare to fight with me now?" I asked her.

"No, I don't. I'm afraid I'll wipe you out." She burst into tears and ran outside.

I noticed Rebecca in the bathroom doorway, her face white and scared. We listened to the car peel out of the driveway.

"Don't worry, baby. It's all right. You know grown-ups fight sometimes too. Mummy and I really do love each other, we're just going through a strange time right now. You know, you keep on growing up, and that means 'growing pains' too, until the day you are dead." I hugged her and patted her head. "Please cheer up. We can't have everyone sad or angry. I'm going to get Waffles. I'll be right back."

"Can I come?"

Poor Rebecca, desperate for reassurance, attention, security. Did she feel that there was nothing she could count on to stay the same, from her body to her parents' marriage? I would have taken her with me anywhere, anywhere, except to get Waffles. That, the reunion, was private to me, almost holy. I did not want her to be there. And I felt rotten saying no.

"I don't think you better. Stay here and wait for Mummy. I don't know where she went or when she'll be back, but she may want you when she does get home. You can come another time, O.K.? Maybe I'll take you to Tyringham to see Grandma."

Rebecca nodded, still looking downcast. "When are you going to Tyringham?"

"I'm not sure, sometime soon, before the leaves fall. Think you can miss a few days of school?"

She brightened up a little, not much, but a little. "Oh, sure, Pa." I gave her cheek a kiss.

About Consuela's outburst I was confused, not sure whether I had provoked it or whether she had made it happen. I had thought things were much better between us, until she exploded like that. She hadn't said a word about my drinking before—I had thought she hadn't noticed. But now it was as if she had known that I had deliberately put on a sham performance for Dr. Hale. As if she had known how unwilling I was to let him help me.

There was a magnetism, an energy, a preternatural connection between the dog and me, I knew that. Anything so strange and unexplained might certainly make anyone drink more. I didn't need a shrink to tell me. Anyway, he wouldn't tell me that. He would most likely try to tell me there was no connection, no dynamism and I did not want to hear or be forced to hear that. I knew the dynamism was there between us. What terrified me was I often thought that its force was evil, deadly, of the devil. I could not deny the force. My heart pounded as I turned into the dirt road leading to the Harvard Animal Hospital. The jumble of Waffles-connected thoughts plus his imminent release made my adrenaline race. I hoped Consuela would get home safely from wherever she had fled to and not crash in the car, my final thought or prayer as I waited for someone to open the door to the kennel.

Waffles shook with pleasure when I took him out of the cage. The colorless hair had begun to grow back where the doctor had shaved it to operate. It was good to have him beside me on the seat again, his thin nose in my lap, as we headed for home.

I stopped on the way back; once at an apple stand for cider and a bushel of Stamen Winesaps, and once at the liquor store. My spirits lifted with Waffles back again, and I felt ashamed that I had let Consuela go on the way she had earlier. I paid for the liquor, and then went back to the shelves and picked up a bottle of nice Rhine wine for supper. Supper, I would make supper for just Consuela and me. The children could have McDonald's hamburgers early, and Consuela and I could have a night together, maybe set things right.

I drove to Groton for fresh Cape scallops, french bread, cheese and watercress, and for the children's soy flour "hamburgers" and "non-dairy shakes."

Consuela was not at home when I got back.

I cleaned off the table and distributed the junk food, then

went out to the silo with some horsemeat for Waffles and a couple of old blankets.

While the children wolfed their hamburgers, I ran the vacuum cleaner around the living room, dining room and library, and swept the clutter of toys, tattered comic books and odd socks into a shopping bag for the children to sort out. Cam finished supper first and turned on the TV in the library, bellyflopping on the couch whose cushions I had just plumped. For his sins, I made him help me and stuffed an old undershirt saturated with furniture polish into his hand. He wrinkled his nose at the sweet cloying smell but then went right to work, and rubbed every dusty surface with an almost manic zeal.

In less than an hour I had the children fed and the downstairs picked up and fairly shining. It was after six and still no sign of Consuela. She had been gone for over three hours, and I began to worry that something had happened to her. Suddenly, I remembered all the little "accidents" that had happened since George Livingston's momentous one. This time, this time I would be alert and ready. I tasted my spit carefully, sucked it to my tongue from the recesses behind my molars and swished it in my mouth before I finally swallowed it. There was no bitter taste, no taste at all except for maybe a hint of old whiskey. I was concerned about her, but the strange panic that had swept over me before, the panic which went with the bitter taste was not there. I read to the little boys and tucked them in and still Consuela wasn't back. Cam and Rebecca had finished their homework and were watching the television when I decided to call Kip and Jenny.

Jenny was surprised, too, when I told her Consuela was not home.

"I know she had that doctor's appointment at three-thirty because she asked Kip if he felt well enough to give Will a hand bringing in the cows for the milking. But I thought she'd come right back afterwards."

"Doctor's appointment?" I asked Jenny. "She didn't tell me about that. Is she sick?"

There was a long pause. At last Jenny said in a stiff, embarrassed kind of voice. "No. I think it was just a checkup. Or something."

I thought about calling the police, but felt ridiculous asking them if they had seen my wife, who left four hours ago for an appointment with the doctor. Surely if there had been an accident they would have called me. I also hesitated calling them because I didn't want to tell them that Consuela and I had had a fight. I didn't want to consider the possibility of her running away, even for a few hours, or a few days. Maybe I thought, maybe if she isn't back by eight I will call the police.

At seven-twenty Consuela came in. Her hair was tousled as if it had been blown by the wind, her face was pale and sharp, and her eyes looked darker and larger. She had a wild haunted look to her which scared me.

"Where have you been? Are you all right? I thought you had had an accident."

"No, no accident, at least not the kind you're thinking of."

"Well, what happened?"

"I'm freezing cold, Hugh. Let me have a bath first. Then we'll talk."

"You want a drink? A hot toddy or a whiskey sour?"

"In a minute. I'll have a whiskey sour after my bath."

Twenty minutes later Consuela came downstairs looking more like herself, although there was a new gauntness to her face, and an uncertain fluttering to her motions. Consuela uncertain? Afraid, like me? What a horrifying thought.

She sat down opposite me, next to the fire, and started talking with no hesitation or introduction.

"I went to the doctor this afternoon."

"I know."

"I'm pregnant. I've suspected it for a while. I'm six weeks pregnant—it was that night in Gosnold's Bay, the night you came down. I counted wrong."

What could I say? "What did the doctor say? Is he worried about you?"

"He said I could have an abortion. That's why I didn't come back. I wanted to think about it alone, before I told you. I wanted to decide by myself."

"Without telling me? You wanted to make the decision alone?"

"Yes. All alone, like so many other decisions I make. I don't want another baby, I don't want to go through with that operation a fifth time, I don't want to go backwards in time and return to diapers and feedings all day and night. I really don't want to give up myself again for another person, not after I've gone back to me again."

"What are you saying? I can understand how another pregnancy and section would be dangerous. It scares me too, you know, to think of you going through all that again. But what is this about giving yourself up for another person? And going backwards in time?"

"It's brazen selfishness, that's what. The idea of having a baby, one more totally dependent creature, dependent on *me,* is repulsive, much more repulsive than being cut up again, or than lumbering about for the last three months with the threat of a ruptured womb. I just don't want my wings clipped."

Consuela had stared right at me since she began speaking, as if she were watching me closely to see what effect her tired candor had. If she wanted a reaction, I didn't disappoint her.

"You mean you would commit murder—that's what the Church still considers it, in case you've forgotten, murder—you'd do that just because you are tired of children? Because you want your 'freedom'? And you wouldn't even ask me?"

"That's right. That is exactly right." Her voice was flat and hard.

"Who *are* you? I thought you were for life, for Christ?"

"Did you indeed? Maybe you had better sober up and rethink, then. You might have lost touch with me, Hugh. Have you ever thought of that? You're so preoccupied with yourself, and how you've changed in the past month or so, while all the while I believe you truly think that I am the same old Consuela you married. Can you admit that I have changed? Look at me!"

She faced me sitting straight in her chair and I looked at her for a few minutes, astounded and I guess saddened, too, by what I saw. I had to force myself to look at her. There was clearly less of Consuela than there used to be. She occupied less space, less of *my* space. What sat so erect in the chair was not the supple, silky girl of my dreams, but a too thin, worn-out woman. Woman? No, that is not quite true, for at the edges of the stiffness and the tense exhaustion of her body I could still trace the dusky outline of my old Consuela, the one I always see in my mind, the one who slipped into this new shell in front of me, although I never noticed. I was sad for a few minutes as I sat there, looking at her, until regret gave way to irritation that she could have tricked me so.

"I can't believe that you could disappoint me!" I said with bitterness. "You can't have changed so fast. I know how you fccl about abortion, unless all you said before was just lies."

"Not lies." There was a pleading note in her voice now, which I hadn't heard before. "I've just had a private little trip, all alone, to hell. I wish I could make you understand what it was like, but I can't. I'm only making you cross and impatient and that's not my intention. Listen to me, please." She was urgent now, and pleaded harder. "I was so shocked and horrified by *myself,* don't you see, by what I had become behind my own back. That's what I wanted you to see. I didn't know what I was at all, and I was scared of myself. And I'm sure you didn't know what I was, either."

"First me, then you." Hop scotch, hop scotch, we all fall down. I wasn't sure whether Consuela meant that she was falling apart like me (had she caught my germ? was it my fault?), or just that I wasn't alone in my changes, or whether she was pointing out in a peculiar way that she had been neglected, by me and by herself. "But we wander, don't we? What about this baby? This abortion?"

"After I left the doctor's I was kind of crazy, this new me suddenly crept out and took over. I drove too fast, never thinking about where I was until I saw the turnoff for Manchester, hit the brake and swerved down the exit ramp. I drove until I came to the beach. No one was on it. I walked and cried and ran. I prayed too. The old joy I had always felt before whenever I was pregnant was replaced by a kind of hideous nausea at being consumed by an evil growth within me that I couldn't control. A cancer inside my body which would ultimately rule me. It wasn't life but rather a kind of death I was nurturing. Can you understand any of this?"

"I'm trying."

"To make it short—and I might as well, because I don't think I can make you see anyway—when I decided to have the abortion, and I did decide to, it was an abortion of death I was planning, not life, not the murder of a baby. I just knew that whatever was growing in my womb was deadly, like slavery. That it would make a part of me die.

"But which part? It took me a while to figure it out, though the answer is so simple. A baby will kill my independence. My monstrous selfishness. So now I have to get used to the egotist I've become. Maybe you do know me better than I know myself?" She looked at me questioningly.

I said nothing.

"But you don't." She said it flatly. "I shall not have the abortion. In a way, I already had it, on the beach. You don't follow me at all, do you?"

"I don't think so. You mean you *are* going to have this baby?"

"But of course."

"Then why are you so upset?"

"What scared me was *myself,* don't you see? That was the hell, seeing what I really was."

I shook my head. What was she saying?

"Skip it," said Consuela. "Let's eat."

There was a trace of resignation in her voice and I felt as though I had let her down. Consuela had confused me, and I was not just disappointed but angry as well that I couldn't understand what was so important to her. One thing only was clear as a bell—that neither of us could understand the other and it was no use trying. Philip was wrong about the so-called "moments of truth." All they did was to confuse and confound and I determined to have no more of them.

For all the well-intentioned talk, I was alone. It came as a brilliant revelation. Here in the house I called Home, with Consuela and the children packed in with me, I was quite by myself. My mind skipped at this thought, skipped over any consideration of Consuela and *her* probable aloneness, to the silo and Waffles. Waffles was the exception. If you counted him, I was not alone, far from it. All the complicated confessions to Consuela, even to Philip, had partially failed. No matter how I tried, I couldn't really get through to anyone. Yet wordless Waffles knew it all, he was like an extension of myself. How could I consider myself alone? And how could I have been so stupid as to have kept on trying to make other people aware of what was clearly Waffles' and my business?

Our business, and I had wasted so much time. We would get right to it, whatever it was. I knew as I cooked the scallops and tossed the salad, I knew as I lighted the candles and poured the wine that some day soon Waffles and I must go away to Cuttyhunk together. Just the two of us, no explanations. (There really weren't any plausible explanations.) In a way, Waffles and I reminded me of how Lucy and I had once been. Again, it was an exclusive relationship. This time, however, there was a new spice to it, namely violence. For it had become quite plain that Waffles was bloodthirsty, and he knew just where to suck it from his victims. On Cuttyhunk, I would devote myself to our dangerous symbiosis. I would try to discover all I could about our bond, especially why I thought of Waffles' victims as my own. I would devote myself to this entirely, until one or both of us gave up, or until I knew how to snap the energy between us. More important, until I *wanted* to snap it.

My long-range plan was clear but there were some immediate snags to take care of before I could leave. I began by canceling my next and all other appointments with Dr. Hale. Then I phoned my mother in Tyringham. She sounded perplexed when I told her I had quit my job, and downright disapproving when I said I wanted to see Lucy.

"I really don't understand you, Hugh. Are you well?"

"Physically? Yes. I'll probably be up in a couple of weeks, if it's all right."

"Fine. You know I always like to see you."

186

"I might bring Rebecca, too."

"Wonderful. Omar and Miles are arriving next week. I think they'll stay until Christmas for the hunting. Take care of yourself, dear. You sound quite tense. But then, you always have."

Omar and Miles. Well, it would be an interesting visit at any rate.

Consuela would have to be told, but there was time, I planned to move slowly, and she still needed me in the barn.

One "snag" I couldn't clear up at home was my drinking. When I got to Cuttyhunk, I would stop cold, and hope to be spared the D.T.'s. Another bit of unresolved business was the Church. Since my return to Still River I had tried to switch off religion but I couldn't do it. Religion remained the one force which matched the intensity and power between Waffles and me. The two seemed to be in balance. I went to church with everyone else and was pretty successful in maintaining a certain distraction through the Mass each Sunday, until the consecration, when week after week I would automatically raise my eyes (and more) to the wafer of unleavened bread as it became for me, my Lord. I just couldn't help it. But there was no way of reconciling myself and Waffles with Christ, no way at all, so I did not receive Holy Communion. Not with my mouth. I stayed in the pew while everyone else ate His Body. Perhaps that denial in itself was a stauncher recognition of my Lord and Savior than if I had followed the crowd to the altar with open mouth and smarting soul. What I am saying is that my faith, somehow, remained intact and, in a sense, uncorrupted. So religion could not be dismissed before I left for my hermit's life, nothing I could do but bundle my faith with the rest of my personal effects and take it with me.

The days passed comfortably. Consuela and I were companionable co-workers, in the house and in the barn, but we seemed to be detached from each other. She hired a high school girl to come two afternoons a week to help with the cleaning and general housework, which pleased me as I knew that I would be leaving soon and I wanted Consuela to be looked after, especially when pregnancy and childbirth would restrict her. I helped the boys work out on Emlyn, kept up with the tomato and squash harvest with an eye out for black frost at night, and spent many scattered minutes each day in the dark silo with Waffles, quietly breathing the fermented dusty air. Soon. We would go soon.

Consuela turned her back on my few attempts at lovemaking. Granted, I myself was not caught by passion but by a sense of duty to her, a sort of "last chance" screw. Unfair of me, too, as Consuela still did not know of my plans to leave.

"You're drunk, Hugh, and I don't like to make love when you're like this. It has no meaning at all. Besides, you know you never *have* one when you drink too much."

"I'm sorry. I just wanted to give you a good time." Feeling her up and down.

She removed my hand and sat up, leaning on her elbow. "I wish you'd understand that the only way I have 'a good time,' as you put it, is when you do."

"That's not what the books say. They say you can have an orgasm—"

"Fuck the damn books!" Consuela interrupted. "I am not just an animal. I can't lie here as if spread out on the doctor's table and enjoy it while you work me over, your little penis bobbing like a baby's between your legs. What you're doing is just one step beyond masturbation and it makes me sick."

So we would sleep, back to back.

I knew the time to leave was growing near. The long Columbus Day weekend was late this year, and on the seventeenth of October we loaded the car and left for Gosnold's Bay and Aunt Edith's oyster party. The weather was beautiful all weekend. Warm for October and beautifully clear. Lucky for Waffles, too, as Aunt Edith was not happy to see him back in her house. He obligingly slept under the back steps and stayed out of her way. His moods matched mine so often it was uncanny. I am positive he knew of my Cuttyhunk plan at least as soon as I did, and maybe sooner. So he, like me, was biding his time until we left.

On Sunday after church I took the children and Waffles to the beach while Aunt Edith and Consuela helped Mabel put up a picnic before we left. A wooden mooring buoy glistened where the *Melande* should have been, and the inner harbor was empty, no spars moving back and forth on the waves. The three older children were busy building a complicated fortified town on the hard sand near the edge of the water. Ward was excluded from their project for being too young and clumsy. He stood apart from the huddle of their hunched backs and put his hands over his ears to shut out the noise of their busy city-planning.

"Cheer up, Ward." I knelt on the damp sand and gently removed his fine little hands from his ears. "Let them build their old city; we'll build a lake and put dribble castles all around the edges. Come on."

His downtrodden face lifted as he dropped to his knees beside me and began to dig. Handful after handful of cold wet sand was brought up and our well, though narrow still, grew dark and deep.

I sat back on my heels and lighted a cigarette. "Stop a minute, Ward. Remember that poem 'When I go down beside the sea'?"

He shook his head.

"Listen then, and watch what happens to the hole.

"When I was down beside the sea
A little spade they gave to me
To dig the sandy shore.

"My holes were empty like a cup,
In every hole the sea came up,
Til it could come no more."

We watched the water seep into our hole, full attention on the water as it carved an ever widening rim around the edge of the well, until, grain by grain, the side would slide to the bottom. And while the side slid down, the sandy bottom seemed to rise up, with the water.

"Why does it, Pa?"

"Why does what?"

"Why does the sea come up, why?"

"It just does, it wants to fill up the emptiness. I think really it has something to do with Bernoulli's theorem." A dumb answer but it satisfied Ward. We worked silently side by side as we enlarged the lake and embellished it with secondary waterways, landscaping and grim gothic towers of dribbled ooze. Each new hole I dug for another canal or connecting pond held me for that second when the water came up. It was familiar, reminded me of something but I couldn't follow the thought through. When it was time to go I left reluctantly, my puzzle unsolved as the tide came in and swiftly erased the morning's labors.

The car was peaceful on the way home. The little children and Consuela dozed, Rebecca sat beside me in front and lisned to rock and roll, and I was free to let my mind wander as I followed the broken white line of the highway home.

That theorem, Bernoulli's or whoever's, reminded me of what had happened recently to myself. Perhaps I had been full of holes, or empty places. My father, his mother, Lucy, all of us may have been riddled with holes, and, like the water rushing into the wells on the beach, something had rushed into our empty places, too. A kind of craziness; alcoholism, anorexia nervosa, depression and whatever I had, I couldn't stick a label on my brand of lunacy, although I lingered on possession and tried to ignore hallucination. I was sure this was some kind of a key to the whole situation, and grew light-headed, my mind less and less on driving the car and more on myself. Until the howling blast from a tractor-trailer screamed in my ears and I came to, swerving as I touched the brakes and the speedometer dropped from over eighty to seventy. I fishtailed, out of control for a second, and then pulled into the right-hand lane.

"Jesus God, what are you doing?" Consuela was wide awake.

"I don't know. I really don't know." I pulled into a rest area and stopped.

"You don't even have your lights on and it's almost pitch dark! What *is* the matter with you, anyway?" Consuela got out of the car and marched around to my door. "I'm driving. You get in back."

We exchanged places and although she didn't say any more, I could feel Consuela's scorn smolder behind the wheel. Why, I couldn't be trusted, even to drive a car! I leaned against the back seat, my heart still pounding. Christ, we had been close to hitting that truck. It was the horn that had scared me and so caused all the trouble. If I hadn't braked, we would have been fine.

Cameron moved closer to me and pressed his cheek into my arm. "Are you mad?" he asked, his voice muffled by my sweater.

"No. I was scared, though."

"Yeah, me too. I won't do it again, I promise. Not without telling you first."

"Do what?"

"You know, pump your fist up and down to make the truck drivers toot their horns at you. Usually they don't beep anyway, and I never thought it was dangerous, honest." The children were wide awake now, and squirming all around me.

"My bottom itches," piped Justin.

"So scratch it, dummy," retorted Cam.

"Mine does too. It's like a tickle and an itch together," added Ward.

"Maybe you sat in poison ivy with no pants on," I said.

"It's just worms," stated Consuela. "I was going to worm everybody anyway. "We'll do it tomorrow."

When we got back home and the children were in bed, I asked Consuela what she meant about the worms.

"Pinworms. We all have them."

"What do you mean? I don't have worms!"

"You want to bet? If the children have them, you have them. Come with me, I'll show you." She took a flashlight from the cupboard and we went upstairs to Ward's room. Consuela carefully pulled back first the covers and then his pajama bottom. She turned on the flashlight so it lighted his flat white rump and told me to "spread his cheeks." It seemed a rude thing to do to a sleeping child, but I did it, for an ugly second, just long enough to see the writhing nest around his puckered rectum. They were vile, these colorless internal parasites, which would never see the sun, just the intestinal wall of my baby. At night, Consuela told me, they ventured forth to lay their eggs. And as if that in itself wasn't disgusting enough, she continued to tell me that the eggs were air-borne. For the life cycle to continue, the eggs must then be ingested, until they hatched two weeks later in our intestines again. It revolted me, and I could not believe that I was harboring these creatures in my bowel.

It may have been the worms that finally pushed me to leave Still River. The next day was a holiday, and we slept a little later than usual, Kip having offered to do the barn chores alone, now that his leg had healed.

When I came downstairs, Consuela was pouring what looked to me like blood from an apothecary bottle into two shot glasses, while Ward and Justin looked on unhappily.

"What is that?" I asked her.

"Blood," said Ward. "She says it's medicine."

"It is *not* blood, Ward," said Consuela a bit crossly. "It's stuff for your worms. Now drink it up and then you can have some juice."

"Blood," said Ward, but he drank it, made a face, and guzzled his juice.

"You're next, Justin."

"S'not fair, Cam and Rebecca don't have to have it." Then Justin pointed to me and glared. "HE's not having any."

"We get these huge pills instead. Look at them—they're much too big for you to swallow. And we have to take a whole lot of them, not just one," consoled Consuela.

"How many?" demanded Justin. "How many does Pa take?"

"Eight."

"Eight? All at once?"

"Eight all at once. He'll show you." Consuela shook out eight throat-blocker pills on the table in front of me. I had been revolted by the blood stuff that Ward had taken, but these pellets of dried blood were no better. Consuela put a glass of orange juice in front of me.

"Before I have my coffee?"

"Now." Consuela and Justin and Ward waited, their eyes on me.

"Four at a blow!" and I threw half of them into my mouth. Two rushed down my throat with the juice, while the other two went aground on the shallows of my tonsils. More juice and the rest of the blood pellets finally were washed down where they could begin their mission.

I poured my coffee and took it into the living room, unable to watch Justin choke down his vampire's drink. Ward followed me in.

"I'm having my coffee in here alone, Ward. Why are you following me?"

"Tell you something. Mummy says tomorrow if we look at our poops in the toilet we can see all the dead worms!" He laughed in happy expectation and darted out. I poured a large slug of Bourbon into my coffee, my hand shaking so badly I could hardly get the top back on the bottle.

Rebecca was still in bed when I went upstairs to dress. I knocked on her door.

"It's Pa. Do you want to go see Grandma today?"

"Oh, yes! When?"

"I'd like to leave before lunch. Think you can miss four days of school? I might want to stay through the week."

"Sure!"

Consuela wasn't as enthusiastic as Rebecca when I told her our plan; she didn't seem to care one way or another. She made it plain that my presence or absence really didn't make much difference to her.

"Do drive carefully and bring Rebecca back safely," were her chief concerns, and "my love to your mother." She kissed us both good-by and off we went.

Tyringham

Waffles kept his head out the window almost all the way to Springfield, where we stopped on the turnpike for lunch at Howard Johnson's. Rebecca went to the ladies' room and I walked Waffles for a minute. He was cheerful and excited, very like me.

Rebecca and I had a nice lunch. She was very chatty and bombarded me with questions about growing up in Tyringham. Back in the car, I continued to tell her about the house, the places and the people who had made up my youth. Most of what I said was guarded. I tried not to inflict my biases and judgments on the people and places she was about to see.

"You remember the house, don't you?" I asked her. "It was built by my grandpa, your great-grandfather, as a hunting lodge."

"He was pretty rich, wasn't he?"

"I guess so, at least for a while. But he lost a lot of his money in the stock market crash. He kept it a secret, which was too bad, because my father and mother thought there was plenty of money left, and they kept on spending it until my grandfather died and they found out there was nothing much except the house and land. That was when we moved into the house."

"Was your grandmother living there, too?"

"Well, not exactly. She was still alive, but she was sick and lived in a hospital nearby."

"What did she have? Cancer or something?"

"No. She had something wrong with her mind. People used to call it crazy. Now they say mentally ill."

"I know what you mean. Did you ever see her when she was sick?"

"Oh yes, all the time. Why?"

194

"I just wondered what crazy people were like. I've never known any."

Indeed?

"They aren't much different from other people. My mother used to say that everybody was a little bit crazy. Some people just can't live very easily outside a hospital. Granny was like that. She was happier at Ewell-Lowe, the hospital, and everyone at home was happier too, because sometimes she could be awfully unpleasant when she didn't feel well."

"Your father went to that hospital, too, didn't he?"

I had no idea where Rebecca had learned that, but she would have found out sometime. "Yes, Rebecca, my father died there."

"Did he have what your granny had?"

"Uh, sort of."

"Was it catching?"

"Inherited is more like it."

"Inherited. That means you might get it. Or me."

"It's possible. But don't worry about it, love. I doubt that'll happen." This topic made me most uncomfortable and so I changed it. "I wonder where Grandma will put us this time?"

"Before, when I've come with the boys, she's always put us all in the nursery wing. Maybe this time she'll let me sleep in one of the guest rooms," said Rebecca wistfully.

"Maybe," I agreed. "But beware of the 'new' guest bathrooms. They aren't as private as you might think."

"You mean because of the hole in the ceiling? Why is it there anyway?"

"Grandfather added the bathrooms long after he built the house. He converted two storage closets, one into a john and one into a tub and shower room. But he couldn't figure out any easy way to ventilate them, so he decided just to cut a hole."

"What's up there?" asked Rebecca. "The attic?"

"Yup."

"Can you get up there?"

"Of course. Why do you think I said the bathrooms weren't private? There's a trap door and a ladder in the closet of my old bedroom." I laughed. "When I was Cam's age, no guest was safe."

"Pa! You didn't!"

"Horrid, wasn't I?"

"Did you ever get caught?" Rebecca was both shocked and impressed.

"Caught? Not by the guests."

"Whew." Rebecca looked out the window, speechless at my undetected wickedness.

But I had been caught, once. And what a price I had paid.

I had just graduated from Exeter, while my brother Omar and his friend Miles were lofty juniors at Williams College. They had been more patronizing than usual, particularly Miles, and I was annoyed with them. Miles was spending the summer with us, something he had done almost every year since he and Omar had been roommates at Exeter. Miles is English, rich and slimy. I have never liked or trusted him, although he is a favorite with most people and especially with my mother.

That day twenty years ago I was mad at Miles for teasing me again about Lucy. Lucy and I had planned an elaborate picnic that night on Bald Top. It was supposed to be a secret, only Miles had found out, and then told everyone—". . . isn't it sweet, Hugh and Lucy," etc.

I remember going past the shower room and hearing Omar's and Miles's voices above the sound of the water. What are they doing in there? I wondered. I was too old to spy on people, I knew that, as I climbed the ladder and crawled across the attic, under the eaves to the hole. Someone had just turned the shower off; the steam was still rising as I put my head over the edge.

Miles was kneeling on the bathmat, his skin pink and wet. Omar stood facing Miles on the mat, his dark wet curls very close to my face. He was breathing hard and rhythmically as Miles knelt there, his blond head pumping back and forth.

"Queers!" I spat on them. Two measly globs of bubbly spit —how I wished it had been a gallon of lye instead.

Miles looked up at me and smiled his angel's smile, flirting.

"Feeling left out?" he cooed.

But Omar had looked unmistakably guilty and ashamed. "Get out of here, you little sneak."

"I am, you fairies. Fags!" I climbed back down and locked my door, suddenly terrified, particularly of Miles. The lock released with a loud click and I heard Miles's resonant laugh right outside in the hall.

"Scared? Oh, don't be. Join us, if you like. We won't tell." He laughed again and went away.

An hour later, Lucy and I left the car on the old logging road which cuts through the sugar bush, and walked the rest of the way to the rocky summit of Bald Top. The view of the hills and, below us, the valley, bisected by the brownish-green streak of the Housatonic, was spectacular. Lucy spread out the picnic and opened me a beer. I cleared my throat and told her what I had seen from the attic.

"I always knew Miles was no good, and now I've proved it. He's corrupted Omar. Christ, I'd like to kill him," I said, throwing stones down the mountain for emphasis.

"Would you indeed?"

The sound of Miles's smooth English behind me made me turn around abruptly, and there he was, with Omar, above us, smiling down benevolently.

Lucy and I ate our supper in silence, nearly choking on the food. Omar and Miles sat down beside us with two flasks of whiskey. They were already tight and noisily mocked us while we pretended not to hear.

"Hugh here doesn't think we're very virile, do you, Hugo?" Miles pronounced it virīle. I ground my teeth together in an effort not to say anything. "No," continued Miles, batting his pretty eyelashes first at Lucy, then at me. "Hugo doesn't think we're a bit manly, do you, my little 'man'?" Miles got to his feet with difficulty and stood next to me, emphasizing his lanky six and a half feet as contrasted to my mere five eight. "Have a drink, Hugh, I see your beer's finished." Miles thrust the flask in my face in a most threatening way.

"No tha—"

"Drink it!" He banged the silver mouth of the flask against my teeth, and I opened my mouth and drank, nearly but not quite choking, my eyes watery. "Well done, little man. Now have some more." Miles went on bullying me until I finished the flask. Lucy stared at me but said nothing.

Both flasks empty, Omar, Miles and I staggered to our feet and stumbled down to the car, while Lucy, surefooted, sober Lucy went ahead with all the baskets.

"Now," said Miles as we reached the car, "can my sober little manling with the hollow leg take us all safely home?"

"Get in the car, you fucking bastard," I howled at him. "You'll see how well 'the little manling' can drive. Get in!" I sat down in the driver's seat and slammed my door, when I felt Lucy's hand on my knee.

"They're crazy, Hugh. Don't pay any attention." Her voice was soft and scared.

"Oh-oh, Lucy my love, no helping. Let the homunculus do it himself. You're coming in back with us." Miles reached in the door and began to pull Lucy out of the car.

"You leave her alone, Miles, or I'll kill you." I meant it. They mustn't touch Lucy, my Lucy.

Omar stuck his face in my open window, his breath warm on my cheek. "It's our turn, now, Hugh. My turn for a piece of cunt." I swung at Omar and missed, shattering the side vent instead. Omar laughed and got in back behind me. He held his arm around my throat, pinning me against the seat.

"Now drive, you stud. We'll see who's the big stud!" He and Miles laughed very loud, and stopped laughing very suddenly. "Omar said, 'Drive,' manling, what's the matter with you?" said Miles. I felt Omar's arm pull harder.

"I will choke you, Hugh, I really will," growled Omar, increasing the pressure on my neck. I remember thinking, "I've got to get down this mountain fast, before they do anything to Lucy. I've got to get down fast."

The car jerked forward and we twisted down. I couldn't see clearly because of the whiskey to begin with, and the logging road was hardly the easiest road to navigate after dark under any condition. I have no idea how fast I was going, but by the time we were halfway down and in the sugar bush, I know I had my foot to the floor. Lucy was screaming "stop it," Omar

198

and Miles were laughing, and I was convinced that Lucy was yelling at them, that they were violating her. My neck ached through all the noise and speed as Omar kept his rough grasp on it.

Near the bottom there is a straight stretch and I relaxed my grip on the wheel, forgetting that the incline increases here, although the road is temporarily straight. I remembered about the sharp curve too late, we flew off the road and rolled over the steep bank. Nothing was very clear after that, but somehow Omar and Miles managed to get Lucy and me out of the car, and to get help from the main road. I remember being put in the ambulance next to Lucy, but nothing in between.

"Pa, look!" Rebecca tapped my arm and pointed out the car window. "It's beautiful, isn't it?"

We had climbed quite high in the Berkshires and were getting close to Tyringham. I looked across the valley, gaudy with foliage.

"Over there, Rebecca, that's Gray Face with the rocky slab." The slopes and shears were recognizable now. I felt the land pressing in.

"Are these real mountains?"

Real enough to make me claustrophobic, I thought, and then replied, "In my old geography book they were painted washed-out beige on the maps and called 'old, worn-down mountains.'"

"I wish we had mountains at home," said Rebecca.

"Do you? Personally, I prefer the ocean." I looked nervously out the window for an horizon. The hills began to stifle me. They always do that.

"The ocean's O.K. but I feel safer in the mountains."

"Not me." I knew what Rebecca meant, there is a sheltered safety about mountain bosoms which some people find comforting. I had trouble breathing. Just over that next hill, maybe I will find the sea, that's what I long for, a wide ocean, instead of these rings upon rings of mountains.

It was a relief to leave the turnpike and the long vistas for the narrow back road to Tyringham. Unlike its fashionable neighbor, Stockbridge, Tyringham has retained its terse, tough

New England character. Except for my grandfather's house and my Uncle John and Aunt Deborah's, where Lucy grew up, the rest of the houses are poor. I saw as we passed several of them that each yard had at least one and sometimes a fleet of snowmobiles under plastic shrouds. I veered right at the fork, over Ten Mile Creek dam, and up Stony Ridge Road to the house.

My mother was on all fours in her flower garden, tucking in her flowers for the night with old camp blankets. She sat back on her heels for a minute when we drove up the dirt driveway, waved to us and went back to her task. By the time Rebecca and I got to the front door, Mother had finished and came to greet us, tugging off her old canvas gloves as she walked up the terrace steps.

"Grandma!" Rebecca ran to her and seemed to be about to throw her arms around Mother's neck when she stopped short and extended a prim hand instead. My mother took it in both of hers and then performed that peculiar well-bred ritual of offering a cheek. I can still see them frozen in this ridiculous posture in my mind, cheek to cheek, one nose pointing east, the other west. Rebecca was thus initiated to my mother's gentle, impractical, vague and old-fashioned world of landed gentry.

I guess she was glad to see us, although Mother never registers much emotion. Everything is taken for granted, from birth to death, her two favorite exclamations being Oh Dear and How Nice. When my father was at his most drunk and contentious, Mother behaved exactly as she had when he was charming and sober. I used to think she was blessed with endless patience, but gradually I began to think that it was obstinacy instead, that she simply refused quite consciously to admit to my father's condition. Occasionally, I would wonder whether she really noticed him, or noticed anything she didn't want to notice. She never seemed to be much affected by anything, so of course she was never very happy, or unhappy.

"Miles and Omar here yet?" I asked her.

"Yes, they came yesterday. I believe they've gone over to have tea with Lucy. Now," said Mother to Rebecca, "I have put you in the old nursery as Omar and Miles have the two new guest rooms. Hugh, dear, you are in your old room and my,

you look worn. You and your father never were very strong."
She sighed and put her gardening basket on the back porch
table. The house was cold inside as it usually was in the fall.
Beginning in September, the nights are freezing in the
Berkshires, but we always postponed starting up the furnace as
long as we could, not wanting to surrender to winter. There
was plenty of work outdoors in the sun, where it was warm,
and at night, we would sit close to the fire in the library. Although the house was chilly, at least it was not dark like Aunt
Edith's, but light and open. The house is protected on the north
by the hill. To the south, the land falls away steeply and affords
an open view down across the valley to the perimeter of solid
hills several miles beyond. Once inside the house, the hills no
longer suffocate me, perhaps because their proportions are reduced when seen through the comfortable scale of windowpanes.

"It still smells the same," I said to Mother, sniffing.

"What do you mean?" She sounded very slightly offended,
as if I meant old garbage or sweat, instead of the fragrant mix-
tures of wood, oiled and seasoned, or burned, left over from
last night. Half stone on the outside, the house inside is all
wood, even the ceilings. It would be darker even than Aunt
Edith's caverns if my grandfather had not insisted on great windows all over the southern side. Most of the curtains, rugs and
slipcovers had not been touched except for cleaning and mending since my grandparents' time. They were shabby now, but
old friends, and I would have been horrified if Mother had
changed them.

I sat down on my bed next to the suitcase and rested for a
minute, wondering why I had been driven to come back home
like this. Waffles distracted me by barking at the door, already
bored by our sleeping quarters. I let him out and went downstairs with him, glancing in as I passed the guest rooms, where
Miles and Omar had staked out claims of shoes and jackets and
bottles of bay rum.

In the living room, a healthy looking girl not much older
than Rebecca set down a tea tray in front of my mother.

"Hugh, you probably don't know Annie Bradley from Lee.

Her father is Keith Bradley, you know, Bradley's grain?" My mother smiled a little, Annie blushed, and I bowed, or rather lowered my head, more so I wouldn't have to look at Annie's pink face than out of deference. "Her sister Karen is helping Lucy," continued Mother. "I don't know how we would manage without them every afternoon." She nodded to Annie, who seemed relieved to be excused.

Rebecca finished her tea quickly and left us to look around outside. We had only brought the children to Tyringham a few times, principally because of my reluctance to see either Lucy or Miles. It was easy to avoid Lucy, as she rarely left the gardener's cottage on her parents' estate, where she had lived ever since she got back from Ewell-Lowe ten years ago.

Miles was a different case altogether. Everyone except me considered him a member of the family. My mother and father enjoyed Miles's easy outgoing manner, and from his days at Exeter felt more at home with him, I think, than they ever had with me. His British courtesy charmed them; I found it oily and overdone. His devotion to Omar touched them because they didn't suspect, or didn't want to know the truth. And Miles made a great hit with my parents' friends, particularly with those who had the best connections. He made it a point to remember their quirky interests and would delight even mere acquaintances by sending them pertinent clippings, books or whatever. No dinner party or weekend went unthanked, no letter unanswered.

Omar and Miles were side by side through school and college. Miles's parents both died before he graduated from Williams, leaving him with an enormous inheritance. Omar does not share my neurosis about money; he has, in effect, been kept by Miles for the past twenty years. First Miles started the boat school—with Omar as one of the faculty, naturally. When they grew bored with that, they came back to Tyringham. Mother was a recent widow and was delighted with their company.

Miles decided to spend some more money and bought several hundred acres of land on the coast of Maine, not far from the land my family had once owned. He and Omar founded an elite survival camp for boys there, a kind of Outward Bound for blue bloods only. As titular directors, Miles, Omar and sometimes Mother, too, would spend a great deal of time in Maine. I gather they did not kill themselves with work, as Miles had hired someone else to run the camp. Winters were spent in Tyringham or traveling.

Omar was praised for being such a dutiful son, but no one thought to notice that he, unlike me, could easily afford to be dutiful, with no job, no wife, no children. Not just Omar, but to a degree Mother too, was kept by Miles. He was generous in helping with the upkeep of the house, as well as in paying for Mother's expenses when she joined them in Maine or on a trip. I knew Miles would look after Mother in her dotage, if necessary.

Yes, Miles and Omar were the heroes, munificent and amusing. How I would love to drag them through the mud, shout from the hills, "Cocksuckers! Perverts!" But who would believe me?"

"So Miles and Omar are having tea with Lucy," I said to Mother.

"They often do. They've become quite close, you know. It's nice for Lucy. She really hasn't anyone except her parents and the Bradley girl."

"How is Lucy?" It was hard to ask.

"She's well enough, Hugh, very well. I told her you were coming, and she seemed pleased. I said you would probably call her."

"Why? Why did you say that? I wasn't planning to call her." I wished that I had never said anything to Mother about seeing Lucy. It infuriated me when she spilled private information in her brainless pleasant way.

"Not call? But, my dear, you can't just go over without calling first! It's very rude, dropping in like that, especially on a cripple."

There. Mother had finally said it. Someone had called her that at last. Not even to myself had I allowed right out that Lucy was a cripple. Oh, there were many ways of getting around it—". . . not since the accident . . ." or ". . . her illness keeps her from . . ." Mother's words were like a branding iron; cripple, freak, what's the difference? Perhaps she was only trying to prepare me for the next day, when I would go to the side show in person.

I went out to the pantry, ostensibly to take the tea tray to the kitchen, but I only did it so I could sneak a drink. Two fingers of whiskey and I could feel the blood returning to my extremities, and that included my head. I was just screwing the cap on the bottle when I heard Miles and Omar come in the back door. I pushed the bottle in the cupboard and slammed the door, too late. Before I could stand up again they were in the pantry, suddenly silent as they watched me for that monstrous second when I straightened too quickly, and greeted them too brightly.

But no one mentioned it, or asked what I had been doing stooped over the liquor cabinet. We shook hands and mouthed all the standard jokes about how good it was to see each other, and how long it had been. I devoutly wished it had been longer. Rebecca came in and we all went upstairs to bathe and dress for dinner.

I looked at my face in the mirror, aghast that I looked so old. Omar and Miles now appeared younger than I, and both of them handsomer than I would have believed possible, the healthy, solid kind of good looks you might expect to find in the ideal counselors at the ideal Bible Camp. In contrast, I looked old, shaky and slightly degenerate, *me,* not them. My skin seemed bloated under the yellow remnants of my Gosnold's Bay tan. How unfair of life to mix things up so. Twenty years ago I had been the handsome one. I wasn't as tall as Omar and Miles, but in those days people had fussed more over my fair hair and skin and blue eyes than they ever had over Omar and Miles's rather boring good looks.

Drinks were friendly and low-keyed. Omar sat mending his moccasin with an awl, sipping sherry from time to time, while Miles made light chatter with Rebecca and Mother, to their obvious enjoyment. I sat, wedded in almost total silence to my successive martinis and, under the couch, to Waffles, who lay

204

out of sight but never out of touch as he pressed against the back of my ankles.

"You're very saturnine tonight, Hugh," observed Miles. "Is something wrong?" There was nothing in his voice to suggest sarcasm, but I couldn't believe his question was an honest one.

"Sorry," I said. "Just tired. I drove back from Gosnold's Bay yesterday, and then up here today."

"We almost had an accident yesterday," volunteered Rebecca. Mother gave me a skeptical glance which made me think she wasn't as vague as I had thought. It was plain to see that she knew something was wrong with me.

After dinner, Omar announced that he was going to a meeting of the Hunt Committee. Miles offered to teach Rebecca how to play bumper pool in the playroom, while I pleaded fatigue and stayed with Mother next to the library fire.

"You look more like your father every day, Hugh, I can't get over it. But you don't look well, you know. You haven't thought of going off for a little 'rest,' have you?" Mother is the only one I know who can speak quotation marks.

"What do you mean? I'm having a 'little rest' now. At least from work." I was uncomfortable.

"Yes, well, that's not quite what I had in mind. I meant a rest from, ah, from drink, yes, and away."

"You don't mean rest, you mean dry out. Why don't you say it?" I got up and poured myself some more brandy, to spite her.

"It was only a suggestion, dear. You needn't get so cross." She changed the subject to Rebecca and the boys, knowing I was in no mood to admit to drinking too much.

"Consuela must be glad to have you at home to help her. How she does all she does, I will never know."

"As a matter of fact, she wasn't especially glad to have me at home."

"No?" said Mother, holding a clump of embroidery floss to the light and carefully selecting the right strands. We might have been discussing the weather.

"No. I think she was delighted to see me go. I've been in her way, you see. And I'm going through a bad time, now.

That's why I stopped working. Consuela doesn't want to know about my difficulties. I don't think she's capable of knowing about them anyway, and if she were capable of understanding, she would die of boredom. I am planning to go away, incidentally. Not to a dry-out tank, but away." I said this very casually.

"Oh? Where?"

"Well, I thought I'd go to Cuttyhunk. I've rented a little house there for the winter."

"Cuttyhunk? I can't imagine why you would choose to go there, but never mind. When are you leaving?"

"I'm not sure exactly, pretty soon. A lot of things are bothering me, and I need some time alone, to think. But I wanted to see you and Lucy before I went."

"And Miles and Omar—how long has it been since you saw them?"

"Who knows? I didn't come to see them." I knew I was being unnecessarily mean to her but didn't really give a damn. And for once I got a little reaction out of her.

"I don't know why you have to be so nasty to Miles and Omar. I really think you're jealous of them." She put down her sewing and looked at me, sadly disapproving.

"Jealous? Of what?" I sniped.

"Oh, don't be silly, Hugh. You've always been jealous." She sighed. "You and your father, like two peas in a pod!"

"Why do you keep saying endlessly, how alike we are? Then you stop, and never say just *how* we're alike. It's getting tiresome." Petulance crept into my voice and standing in front of the fire, I could almost imagine this all taking place thirty years before, save for the wasted image of myself in the mirror before dinner, which I could not dismiss from my mind.

"From the day you were born, you were restless, fidgety, starved for attention. I remember your father standing over your carriage one Sunday in Central Park, furious because you began to scream while he was telling me something and I was distracted from him. He pounded on the carriage hood and raised his voice over yours, out-shouted you. Already, there was competition."

206

"What else? How else are we alike?"

"He used to go to any lengths to be noticed. If your father was not the life of the party, which he often was before he got too drunk, then he would get completely intoxicated and be noticed for being drunk, if for nothing else. You started off doing that when you deliberately cut your leg with the razor in the middle of Omar's eighth birthday party, and came shrieking into the dining room, dripping blood. You would do almost anything for attention, until you and Lucy found each other. It was a great relief to us when you discovered her, because you stopped your unreasonable demands on us, I guess you transferred them to Lucy."

"Never mind that. Tell me about these demands, Father's and mine."

"Both of you had the same need for affection, really quite out of proportion. Both of you would hug and kiss me, stand so close to me I always felt crowded, with no thought at all as to whether or not I wanted to be petted like that. And as if that weren't enough, you would go on to demand the same affection back that you had given me, both of you. Neither one of you could ever seem to understand that Omar and I just aren't particularly demonstrative, in fact, it rather repels me. It was too bad that you and your father couldn't have exchanged your affections between yourselves, but no, I always had to be in the middle."

"What about Omar?" I asked, biting on his name.

"He kept his distance better than you did." She picked up her embroidery but didn't start to sew again, she just sat holding the hoop in her hand, looking into the fire. "Sometimes," she said in a tired voice, "I feel very sorry for Omar and me. Your father used to flood us with himself, drench us with his egoism. I wondered sometimes if he could only exist through other people, and if that was why he would bully us all into watching, listening, reacting to him. He couldn't seem to live outside other people. Oh dear, I've put it badly."

"Not at all," I assured her, thinking, it's sort of like pinworms. Aloud, I said, "He was a parasite, is that what you meant?"

207

"I guess it is." She began to sew.

"And you think I'm like that, too?"

"I'm not sure. I guess I used to, especially when you were so dependent on Lucy. I admit that when I've seen you with Consuela you have been delightful, and I never thought to compare you with your father until now. Funny, isn't it? It could be because you're drinking more."

"Could be." I wondered idly, without feeling, what that speech cost her. I stared hard at her, but she stared equally hard at the fire, her embroidery forgotten in her lap.

"C'mon, Waffles. Bedtime." I let Waffles out, took the coffee tray and my brandy snifter out to the kitchen, hesitated a moment, poured some Bourbon, downed it and returned to the fire. Mother had taken up her embroidery again. I couldn't sit there very long, my stomach fluttered nervously despite its load of supposed pain-killer, and I felt some of the old dread coming back. "Good night, Mother."

"Good night, Hugh." Sew, sew.

I let Waffles in, comforting myself with the thought that anyone would be a little tense under the circumstances.

"Nothing's going to happen, is it, Waffles? I worry too much." Waffles wagged so hard he looked for a moment like a snake undulating across the spread. I popped a couple of Valium and fell asleep with the light on, *The Thirty-Nine Steps* on my chest.

My room was freezing when I woke up the next morning, and the sound of the wind and rain outside made it seem even colder. I was sad to see the hills, so colorful the day before, stripped of leaves and bleakly ready for winter. The blankets my mother had tucked around her chrysanthemums were heavy with water, breaking the stems underneath; the season was over. The rain turned to sleet, and then snow, as the cold front came in across the Hudson Valley.

After breakfast, I called Lucy. I dreaded it, and added just a little brandy to my coffee to steady my dialing finger. It also made my mouth taste better. Lucy's voice was just as I remembered it, only now it made me feel uncomfortable. But she

208

seemed very pleased that I was coming to see her. I brought along Waffles and Rebecca, too, as chaperones.

"It looks like the Gingerbread House!" said Rebecca as we drove under the arch of frosted trees to the bungalow. The roof hung almost to the ground on the sides, and the fieldstone face of the house was glacéed with sleet and trimmed with pink window boxes and a pink door. Rebecca was right, it looked thoroughly edible.

A long-haired yellow cat lay asleep on the windowsill, but woke up as we came up the walk. It stretched, yawned, and blinked at Waffles, and jumped down from the sill. We rang the bell and a few seconds later the door opened.

But no one had prepared me. Lucy's small face had disappeared in the immense rolls of flab and fat which dimpled and fluttered around the shiny wheelchair. Rebecca picked out Lucy's tiny outstretched hand and held it gingerly. I watched, horrified, as Lucy put it back in her lap next to its mate, two bloated little gloves, skin stretched so taut and shiny it reminded me of glass.

Oh, my God, a kiss for this stranger, I would have to do it, and I did, by sheer force of will, drop an assembly line kiss somewhere in the folds of flesh near where I guessed her cheek was tucked.

"You can say it, Hugh, I've changed. It's all right, you mustn't worry, or pretend not to notice." Lucy smiled, her teeth twinkling in the distance behind all that skin. The teeth were the same, and the eyes, but they looked so small compared to the rest of her. I saw hanging out below the plaid blanket covering her legs, one skinny stick of an ankle with a thin lifeless foot stuck on the end.

"Come into the sun-room," said Lucy, aware of my awkwardness. "Rebecca might enjoy my music boxes and dolls. I collect them now, you know. And I have some candies, too!" She spun her wheelchair around with an amazing, to me, abruptness and expertise. Welcome to the fun house! A laugh a minute!

We followed the silent track of the wheelchair through the living room and down the ramp to a glass room facing a walled garden. Some of the plants outside had kept their green leaves, the chrysanthemum blossoms and snapdragons looked like bonbons, and the Chinese lantern pods were even more brilliant than usual against the early snow.

The glass room was warm and humid for the many tropical plants growing in the low bay window facing the garden. Shelves and a long desk lined the other two walls, with more windows and plants, and the fourth wall, divided by the door and ramp, had two astrological charts, with columns of small type at the bottom. In the corner was a very large globe with pieces of string pinned all over it. The heads of the pins were of different colors. It looked like something out of a war room.

The shelves were filled with old dolls, as limp as Lucy's legs, and some manual music boxes. Lucy pointed to them as she said to Rebecca, "Help yourself. The music boxes on the bottom shelf are broken, but please play with any of the others, and with the dolls if you want to."

"They're lovely, Cousin Lucy. Thank you."

"Have some candy, too!" Lucy popped a chocolate into her small pink O of a mouth before handing the silver bonbon dish to Rebecca. Then Lucy turned to me, staring with her bright china eyes. Her chins rested on her collarbone like a pink jabot.

"Let me look at you, Hugh. Hmm. I see you're not immune after all."

"What do you mean, 'immune'?"

"But you must have an idea, surely?" Lucy was quizzical for a second, and then she selected a nougat.

I watched her chew it and swallow, truly grieving for Lucy then, for her fatness, for her dead legs. I remember thinking how hard just breathing must be for her.

"Oh, Hugh, you're not listening!" said Lucy. Rebecca finished winding up one of the music boxes and "Silver Threads Among the Gold" tinkled over the tile floor. Lucy repeated almost peevishly, "Hugh!"

"I am, I am listening. You said I wasn't immune, whatever that means."

"Isn't it sad we have to talk like everyone else now?" I

could hardly hear her, she spoke so softly. "I know you remember how it was before, when we could understand without words. But that takes a concentration no longer possible for us, doesn't it? Why, we both have other obsessions now, not just each other."

How did she know? I looked at her sharply, prickling with attentiveness. "Obsessions?"

"Food!" chirped Lucy. "That's one of mine." Her sweet soft laugh mingled with the halting notes of the music box and sent a chill right through me. "I've also been studying about ley lines, magnetic variances and power points."

"Why? I don't know what you're talking about."

"Ley lines, magnetic power. I'm very interested in power. I won't explain it to you, Hugh, because I think you are quite capable of finding out exactly what I mean." Then she turned to Waffles and giggled again. "Why, look at your dog! He's listening to every word!" Lucy tittered once more and gracefully arched her inflated hand into the candy dish.

I had to leave and got up.

"Come on, Rebecca, we'd better go. It's stopped snowing and I promised to take Grandma to the store." I walked over to the door which led to the garden.

"Would you put away the dolls and music boxes, Rebecca?" asked Lucy. "I can't reach. No rush. We'll be outside in the garden." She opened the door and I stepped out into the fresh air and melting snow. On the flagstones, she did that astounding maneuver with her wheelchair and fixed me with her blue eyes, still familiar to me even in the gross folds of her new body.

"Listen, Hugh," she said. "Listen to me carefully, because maybe I can help. That's why you came, isn't it, for help? Once we had each other. That was the first obsession. Go back a generation, your father's was booze, probably more, too, that we don't know. Your grandmother, my great-aunt, smoked opium. You didn't know that? Oh yes, her depressions came when she didn't have any, that's when they sent her off to Ewell-Lowe. She also claimed she had divine powers but nobody seems to know what they were. Never mind about that. I know what you and I had once, and I know that when it was taken away, we were both left with a great emptiness. First, I made my hole bigger by not eating, at least that's what I thought I was doing. Actually, I was filling it up with an obsession about food. I have other obsessions, too, and they all have to do with power. What have you filled up your hole with? I can see you drink, but what else? I know there is something else." Lucy's voice toward the end had gotten urgent, even desperate. Welcome to the freak show.

"Shit, Lucy . . ." I burst out. Then, relenting, "Oh hell, sure. I drink. Lots of people do."

"What else?" she asked again. "I hoped you'd escape it. I hoped you'd be a sport, in the botanical sense, that is. Tell me what else you do?"

"What else, what else, is that all you can say?"

"Then I'll say it right out, Hugh, who are you killing?"

"Killing? Lucy what are you saying?"

"Your father, Omar, me, we all committed a kind of murder. Your father's was suicide, with a few lives lost along the way, like your mother's. He pretty well annihilated her. Omar is anti-life. He and Miles (and sometimes me) perform their sexual rites against life."

"Shut up!"

"You shut up." Her eyes paralyzed me. "Omar and Miles go even farther when they solicit new recruits by corrupting the boys at camp. Homosexuality is an obsession with Omar, whereas with Miles it's perfectly acceptable and normal." She looked at her lap. "Me, I have destroyed my body, anyone can tell, first by starving and then by eating. Now I dabble in what used to be called black magic, too. What is your sacrifice?" Suddenly, the tension left her and gravity reclaimed her fat. She wriggled obscenely in her cushions. "Please, won't you tell me what it is?"

I glanced inside to see if Rebecca was within earshot. She wasn't. "You're right," I said to Lucy, "something is wrong, although I don't know what you mean about a sacrifice. That reminds me of what I wanted to ask you, though. Do you still go to church?"

"That's an unexpected question! Yes, I still go, must keep up appearances and all that, but it doesn't mean much. My God is quite different now. Darkness instead of light. And you?"

"I'm a Catholic. Now and still. But something's working against it, and I think it has to do with that dog."

Lucy held out her hand for Waffles to sniff, then spread each finger like a pudgy fan. She stared at her hand and finally spoke. "There is a power with that dog. I felt it when you came. Now I can almost see it around my hand."

"Lucy, that's *crazy!*"

"Is it? What are halos then? What makes them glow, the goodness, or the *power* of goodness? I know that power in itself is visible, especially if you train yourself to see properly." Again the obscene wriggle. "And I know you can feel it. I can feel power in the dog, I can dimly see it, and it is what *you* would call an evil power."

"I know that. It scares me, and I seem to have no control over it." Lucy looked at me queerly.

"But you *do,* Hugh. At least as much control as the dog. Your strengths are equal. But you've always been such an idealistic ass, you wouldn't know *how* to use it."

"How do you know so much?"

"Never mind. Here comes Rebecca."

"May I come back tomorrow?"

"Of course you may. But you won't."

"Don't be a nit, I'll be back. Say good-by to Lucy, Rebecca."

Lucy picked a sprig of green from among the cracks in the lichen-covered wall around her garden and gave it to Rebecca. "It's rosemary. Please come back and see me, Rebecca." Lucy unlatched the wooden gate and we left her in the garden, pulling up herbs here and there from the wall where they grew within reach of her wheelchair. I was shaken.

I went upstairs to take a nap after lunch, and lay on my bed, daring to hope that perhaps Lucy might know something that could help. The vocabulary was the same, that much I

knew. It was possible that Lucy still knew me, even if I had
forfeited my end of the relationship by the reckless plummet
down Bald Top. I was finally sure that I shouldn't feel guilty
about the accident. It was Miles's fault, Miles, not even Omar
and Miles. I gave up the notion of sleeping, put on my shoes
and went downstairs, pretending I was not going to have a
drink. Omar had taken Rebecca to Pittsfield with him, Mother
was resting, and the house seemed empty. I stumbled on the
stairs in surprise when Miles walked out of the living room to
the front hall below me. He looked up when he heard my feet
on the stairs.

"Hullo, I thought you were having a 'layme-down.'
Couldn't sleep?" Good old solicitous Miles.

"Didn't want to, really. Too nice a day." Rhymes with
"go away." Waffles was one stair ahead of me, and I noticed
that his hackles were just perceptibly raised, the difference in
color and texture you might get from rubbing velveteen
against the nap.

"A good day for a ride," said Miles. "Want to come?
Omar just picked up a new horse, a beautiful headstrong son of
a bitch that he hopes to make into a hunter. I thought I'd try
him out."

"Thanks, I'd love to." I hardly knew I'd said the words, but
they did send Miles upstairs for his riding clothes. Waffles and I
went to the storeroom off the back hall, stopping on the way in
the pantry for a quick shot of Bourbon, which I gargled, and
chased with another shot. In the storeroom I found some old
boots of my father's which fit me, and a patched hacking
jacket, and went outside to sit on the railing in the sun to wait
for Miles. He came down in a few minutes, looking as if he
stepped out of Abercrombie and Fitch's catalogue. Waffles'
hackles ruffled again as Miles approached him, and I kept my
hand on his neck until Miles got in front.

Miles kindly offered to let me "have a go" at the new
horse, but the horse had an ugly look to him and I declined. I
wanted a pleasant ride, something to help me unwind, not a
wild gallop. Instead, I tacked up Challenger, a nice enough
fellow whom Omar had hunted for several years.

"Are you really taking him out?" I asked Miles as he fought to get Viceroy, the new one, to take the bit.

"Yes, the bastard. You know, I never liked to ride until Omar got me going a few years ago. He's a marvelous teacher. Stop that." Poor Miles struggled with the girth as Viceroy tried alternately to kick him, and to squash him against the side of the stall. Miles was obviously the kind of person who controls animals by hate, not love. He seemed to loathe the horse, and to be terrified of him as well. It became a battle of wills, and I watched with a gruesome fascination. This would be some ride, I thought to myself, leading steady Challenger out into the paddock.

"Need any help?" I called to Miles.

"No, God dammit. I'll be right out." His voice truculent, and I rejoiced that my question offended him.

He came out in a few minutes, very red in the face but mounted at last, his jacket hitched up on one side, and the polish on his boots dimmed by dust and manure. Waffles led us down the cart road. Miles tried with difficulty to keep beside me. When we reached the edge of Long Meadow I suggested a little trot and canter, to settle Viceroy down. Miles agreed and off we went, with Waffles alongside us now.

Miles looked as though he had learned to ride from a book. He posted dutifully but without any reference to the horse. Miles Equitatis, I thought, malicious. I kicked Challenger into a canter, deciding that Miles had suffered the trot long enough. Waffles ran in front, enjoying the fast pace. I began to turn so we could go back across the field the way we'd come, and avoid the old sugar bush ahead of us. With Miles and Viceroy, I wanted to stay out in the open. Over my shoulder I saw Miles yank the reins rudely, while at the same time he dug his boot heels into Viceroy's glistening flank.

Viceroy was confused by Miles's demands and then enraged. He fought to get the bit in his teeth. Miles began to yell incoherently, continuing to bully the horse. Old hatred and new welled up as I watched the prancing pretender. I found myself wishing the horse would throw him, trample him, kill him.

Just then, Waffles saw something in the trees and veered into the sugar bush. What the fucking hell, I thought, why not give Miles a little lesson? I kicked Challenger into a gallop and we followed Waffles through the rustle of leaves beneath the naked maple branches. Uncle Gilly used to tell me there were evil spirits in the sugar bush except when the sap was running, or when the leaves turned in the fall. These were the only times it was safe to go in a bush, said Gilly, and I had always believed him.

Without either leaves or sap buckets I felt the sugar bush was truly haunted as we sped through it. Miles was alongside me now, and out of control. He shouted to me, I'm sure it was "Stop!" but I just laughed and gave him a cavalier wave as we galloped together, splitting every now and then as a tree came between us. Every hell-bent second was a pleasure for me and I'm sure for Waffles, too. I could have gone on forever, watching Miles as he bounced in the saddle, white-faced with terror. The reins flapped against Viceroy's neck—Miles clutched the mane instead, and put his face down on the horse's neck away from the branches which snapped past.

There seemed to be no end to the sugar bush. We were rushing through it so fast that it ceased to be familiar, and I was aghast when the trees thinned out with no warning to make way for Route 102. I reined in fast, but Waffles ran across the road before I could stop him. Fortunately, there was no traffic and he made it safely to the other side.

I was so worried about Waffles that I forgot about Miles and Viceroy. The horse galloped blindly past me, in hot pursuit of Waffles. He had his head completely by now, and Miles was merely an unwilling passenger. There was nothing either one of us could do to stop the horse, or to warn the pickup truck coming down Route 102. Miles jumped off just before the truck hit. Everything stopped in that long second which followed impact —all noise and motion and fear and excitement stopped dead. In the hiatus I saw only Waffles' face grinning triumphantly at me from the other side of the highway. Then Viceroy's shriek pierced the air, and motion resumed. He kicked against the side of the truck a few times, and then lay still. Cars stopped, the police came, and then the ambulances. I sat on my horse, not moving, not helping, dumb. I spat a lot at first, trying to get rid of the poison in my mouth. When the police asked me questions, I answered in monosyllables. Both Miles and the truck driver were injured. Once again, I rode from the sugar bush to the Pittsfield Hospital, only this time it was Miles, not Lucy, who was next to me in the ambulance.

Miles cracked a couple of ribs and broke his arm. He also bruised his handsome face, but he was, on the whole, lucky to have escaped with so little damage. The only thing he said to me as we waited together in the emergency cubicle was, "Why? Why did you do it?"

And you know what I answered him? I said, "But, Miles, I thought you were enjoying it!"

Omar and Mother came in some time later. Omar said he'd stay with Miles and Mother took me home, to supper and Rebecca and Waffles. I was unable to speak, a condition Mother attributed falsely to fatigue and shock. But I was far from being tired; Waffles and I were wound up tight. We hummed with our own vibrations, and stuck so close together that I could feel him quiver through my trousers. Speaking would have been an impossible distraction. I was high, zapped up, frantic. My heart pounded, my mouth tasted sour. Gradually, hunger and cold trespassed to the extent that I was at least aware of some discomfort, but not enough to sever the tension which seemed to shackle me to Waffles. Even as I took care of my bodily needs before the fire with a tumbler of straight brandy and a supper tray in front of me, I was really only conscious of racing, galloping on with Waffles.

Mother made a few attempts to talk to me, gave up, and spoke instead to Rebecca, in a low voice. I was not aware of either of them. When there was no more food left on my tray and the heat from the fire had died I shook myself and said thickly that I was going to bed.

I was in my pajamas on the bed with Waffles when Omar knocked on my door.

"What do you want?" I asked him brusquely as I continued to stroke Waffles' thin coat.

"I have a note for you, that's all. From Lucy. She says it's important."

I put Waffles on the floor and opened the door. Omar gave me a black look and handed me an envelope.

"Thanks, Omar." I closed the door and went back to the bed. Waffles watched me, his eyes ruby red in the shadow of the tensor lamp, and I stared back at him, not opening the note. I let the tension between us build again. With a moan of effort, I forced myself to look away, to look at the envelope in my hand. I opened it and read:

Hugh, dear—

Liquor only obscures the power. If you stop drinking, you will be more able to understand and use it. I know.

Love,
Lucy

I crumpled the paper in my hand and threw it in the wastebasket. Waffles jumped off the bed, close at my heels, but I slipped out of the room, shutting the door before he could follow me, and tiptoed down the back stairs alone to the pantry. In defiance of Lucy's mysterious note about temperance and power, I poured three fingers of Bourbon in a jelly jar and tiptoed back to bed, shuddering with cold.

That night, when the Bourbon finally put me to sleep, I dreamed the dream again, but the sponge was Lucy, not Aunt Edith, and the leering faces in the holes were Miles's and Omar's. I tried to take the sponge away from Waffles this time, but the sponge got bigger and heavier. It grew like leavened bread until I was dwarfed beside it, but I still struggled to pull it away from Waffles. Waffles grinned at me once, and then jumped into one of the empty holes. In that instant, I hated him. When his face reappeared looking out of the hole, I struck it, over and over, until it was only a bloody smear. I could feel the warm, sticky blood on my arm, I could feel it and even smell it in my sleep.

When I woke up, Mother was at the door, her hand still on the light switch, while Waffles lay in a bloody, battered tangle at my side on the floor, licking his own blood from my arm, where it had run in streams from my clenched fist.

"Hugh! What are you doing?" Mother's careful diction pierced my clumsy brain.

"Oh, my God, my God, I don't know." I shivered and cried.

The anguished look of reproach in Waffles' protruding eyes ripped me apart as I left him.

"I can't leave him, can't leave him like this," I pleaded.

"Don't worry about the dog, for Christ's sake!" said Omar, impatiently propelling me out of the room and down the stairs. "I'll take him to the vet's, don't worry. But we've got to get help for you, first."

I don't remember anything else about that awful night, except the deadening loneliness and cold.

Drinking was the easiest of my ills to spot and to cure. Mother and Omar whisked me off to Ewell-Lowe in my pajamas, without even washing off Waffles' blood. I know Mother was relieved to have me finally committed—she must have known all along that I, too, would do time there, sooner or later, like most of my relatives.

I say drinking was the easiest to cure, but all the same, the first two weeks at Ewell-Lowe were hell. I couldn't get out of bed, I had no will at all. Some of this extreme lassitude can be attributed to sedation, I know, even though I often tucked the pills under my tongue and then spat them out after the nurse had left. I was not in pain, I was not anything, that was the problem. Omar had a bug collection when he was a boy, and I was like the beetle with his soft new shell—*instar* I believe it is called. And like the weary vulnerable beetle, I, too, had changed, had molted. I am not just alluding to my restored liver—in the end, my liver was incidental to the discoveries I made.

While I lay stupidly in my bed at Ewell-Lowe those first weeks, Waffles was in much worse condition at the vet's. No one told me until later how badly I had beaten him up, or how close he was to death. His recovery was nothing short of a miracle. But for a while we were, both of us, helplessly weak.

As my strength returned, I felt more healthy but somehow incomplete. Without Waffles, I was only half, a useless electrical circuit with only a negative charge, the positive missing, broken, wires dangling. Week after week, I went to psychotherapy like a good alcoholic boy, and I never once mentioned Waffles to the doctor. Like *not* receiving Holy Communion to preserve my religion, by *not* telling anyone about Waffles, I protected him, kept him safe in my mind. Two trusts which I had not violated. I became aware of how much Waffles was with me.

The dream I had when I beat Waffles bothered me still. I was relieved at first that the tremendous power between us seemed, for the time being, to be dormant. But gradually, as I became stronger, I missed Waffles and the energy between us. Meanwhile, Waffles had recovered his strength too. Toward the end of my sentence at Ewell-Lowe, I grew so impatient that I wondered if perhaps Waffles and I could connect with each other long distance.

Two questions bothered me. Was it Waffles I missed or the power we generated together? And, an even harder question to answer, was it love or hate which bound us?

I was released on Valentine's Day. Mother picked me up in the teeth of a bad snowstorm. Consuela called from Still River during lunch to say she'd come tomorrow, when the roads were clear. Talking to her was pleasant but ordinary. When I hung up I realized that I hadn't really missed her much, or the children. They had been eclipsed again by Waffles. And now I would have to wait another day to see him.

At least I had seen Consuela and the children at Christmas. I was let out on trial for two days then, and blew it after midnight Mass with a tumbler of brandy. There were too many people all at once, not just Mother, Consuela and the children, but Omar, Miles and Lucy, too. On top of that, Consuela had left Waffles behind in Still River. I was miserable, and delivered what Consuela described as an enraged, incoherent speech,

220

none of which I remember, which pretty well cast a pall over Christmas.

But this time, the house was empty, with just Mother and me. Miles and Omar were off cruising in the Caribbean, and although Lucy was nearby, I didn't want to see her again. At least, not now. She had left a package for me, of books, all of them having to do with demonology. I looked at one of them quickly. It was a collection of essays by well-known Roman Catholic theologians on satanism and the Church. I was astonished to find myself reading, not just flipping through as I had meant to do. I wrapped the books up again and put them with my big suitcase by the front door. Something to take to Cuttyhunk, I thought, and then, Cuttyhunk! Cuttyhunk had been totally blocked out while I was in Ewell-Lowe, maybe because Ewell-Lowe was a kind of Cuttyhunk in itself, but a Cuttyhunk without Waffles.

Mother and I brought our dinner in to the library and sat in front of the fire. The snow had stopped, and I knew that tomorrow Consuela would come and take me back to Waffles. That thought made a contented kind of thrill pass through me, not frenetic in any way, just a nice peaceful tingle of expectancy.

Mother interrupted my thoughts. "Hugh, dear, I am so glad that you've done it now, gone through Ewell-Lowe and out the door again. If your father had faced his problem earlier, think what might have been spared us all." She sighed and smiled at me.

"I wonder why we all end up there, sooner or later," I said.

"There's that crazy Cameron gene, you know. I'm sure that must be it."

"What gene?" I demanded, suddenly very wide awake.

"I guess it came from Mary Cameron and her husband, Hugh. They were your great-grandparents, and also first cousins, Camerons both of them."

Oh, sweet Christ, spare me another inbred family tree. It could have been Consuela talking, not my mother, and my wing chair could just as easily have been the thwart of the *Melande*. The story was the same.

"Your grandmother Murray was Mary and Hugh Cameron's daughter. And Uncle Hugh, Lucy's grandfather, was their son. That's why they were so peculiar, because their parents were first cousins."

"Why didn't anyone ever say anything before?"

Mother looked at me apologetically and said in a weak, old lady's voice, "I'm sorry. I guess I should have. Your father wouldn't allow anyone to mention it when he was alive. The very idea of any of his flesh being different, mentally or physically handicapped, was abhorrent to him. He once told me when I was pregnant, that if there was anything wrong with the baby he would expose it on the mountain. I tried to pretend he was joking, but he wasn't."

"You mean we've all inherited the same crazy strain?" Shit, I thought, and then added aloud, "What about Omar? Does he know?"

"Omar must have guessed. That's why he never married, he didn't want to continue it."

"Omar," I said in a nasty tone, "is married. He's married to Miles."

"Hugh!" Mother was outraged. "That is an ugly thing to say."

"And I suppose that I have no business saying it, since I have 'continued the strain,' as you put it, whereas Omar has made a great sacrifice and has not had a family."

"Well, at least you didn't marry Lucy, dear. That would have been disastrous."

"So that's why!"

"That's why. And a good thing too you married Consuela with her new, strong blood. You have lovely children, Hugh, nothing to worry about now."

But I switched off my attention as the image of Consuela undressing on Christmas Eve came to my mind. I had forgotten then that she was pregnant, until she took off her loose dinner dress and stood in her bra and panties beside the mirror, the white elastic on her pants rode just below the curve of her gently swelling belly. This baby she carried must be the one who carried the gene. It would be a defective baby. I knew there was something wrong with it, a harelip, a clubfoot, a club soul, maybe. If only Consuela had had an abortion after all. Of course, there was still time for a miscarriage, or I could expose it on the mountain as my father had threatened. These thoughts flew through my mind, with blinding intensity and clarity, despite the speed in passing.

I got up and shook my shoulders. I tried in vain to dismiss all thoughts of babies, and finally just excused myself, pleading exhaustion, and went to bed. I brushed my teeth furiously, in an attempt to get rid of the bitter dregs of fear which once again had seeped into my mouth. I heard the telephone ring and was sure it was for me.

It was Jenny. I shivered almost convulsively when I heard her voice. I was icy cold all over and knew before she told me that Consuela had had an accident.

"She was in the cow barn with a cow who was down with milk fever. That dog—"

"What dog?" I broke in. "Waffles?"

"Yes, he raced into the stall and scared the cow. The cow pinned Consuela against the side of the stall. By the time Kip moved the cow, Consuela was bleeding. She's in the hospital now. They don't know if they can save the baby."

I took Mother's car and started home to Still River immediately. The two-hour trip seemed only minutes long, the dark drive home was so crowded with prayers for Consuela, for our baby, and for me. This time, I knew for sure that I had caused the accident, just as I had been afraid that I had had something to do with all the other "accidents." But how? "Oh, God, you've got to help me," I begged.

The baby was dead when I got there, and Consuela looked dead, although the doctor said she would in time be all right. Still partially anesthetized, Consuela needed rest more than she needed this husband in name only whom she couldn't even recognize, so I went home.

Waffles materialized from nowhere in the snowy driveway, his ecstasy poorly concealed by his appropriately servile greeting. Like a violent reflex action I kicked him with all the strength I had, again and again, until I had him pinned against the side of the silo. Something about the sound his body made as I kicked it against the stones made me stop. It was the same dull thud that George Livingston's polo stick had made in the Magic Circle. I turned away from Waffles, my face in my hands. Waffles crawled close to me, and as I felt him shaking next to my leg, I knew that he would have to stay beside me, that we must be together, that we must be isolated. No distant dream of peace and quiet led me to lease Charlie's house, no, it was instead the need to remove myself, all of me, from the so-called "real world." I would go away with Waffles. On Cutty-hunk, I would devote all my thoughts, energy and time to our awful power. Consuela and the children, Omar, Lucy, Aunt Edith, they would all be barred from my thoughts. There would be no distractions, nothing to break my concentration. If I could be unremittingly single-minded and vigilant, especially vigilant, perhaps I could prevent more "accidents." It was important that there be no more bloodshed from here. I couldn't go back to Ewell-Lowe, not without Waffles.

Jenny met me at the kitchen door. I saw her only as a distraction. My intentions would have to stay on the shelf until Consuela was back to normal. Until then, I would stay in the household harness, good old paterfamilias Hugh.

"What should I tell them to do with it?" she was saying when I started to listen to her.

"Do with what, Jenny?"

"With . . . with the baby."

"The baby's dead."

"I know. It's the body. The hospital wants to know what to do with it."

Now there *was* a chore: rescue the baby from the garbage. Once I finally crunched the gears into overdrive, everything went along all right. The baby was buried, I even bought a cemetery plot in town; the children had Hostess Twinkies in their lunch boxes; Consuela's nightgowns got washed and re-turned to the hospital for her to wear; Mother came from

Tyringham to "help out," and also to retrieve her car, and the guest room was ready for her an hour before she arrived.

I didn't bring up the subject of the baby, but the day he was buried Consuela said out of the blue, "I know you think it's your fault, the accident and everything." I just looked at her, not saying anything, while I wondered how on earth she knew.

"It wasn't your fault, Hugh," she went on, "and besides, the baby was deformed. They said he wouldn't have lived anyway."

Consuela stayed in the hospital ten days, and when she came home she was still weak. I was glad to wait on her, glad to fuss around inside the house with her and the children while winter raged outside. We went from day to day; no one spoke about the future, but every day as I saw Consuela grow stronger I knew I was just that much closer to Cuttyhunk.

There was a bad ice storm on the twenty-eighth of February. The next morning when I got up, I looked across the field behind the house and saw the big willow tree, suddenly yellow in the sunshine against the glare of ice and snow. It was March, almost spring, the willows were always the first to know. I would have to leave soon, and have to tell Consuela even sooner. I did not look forward to that.

When I brought her her breakfast tray, I put an extra cup on it for me. The bedroom was sunny and warm, and seemed to have an extra brightness from the icy trees shining outside. Consuela sat in a chair at the card table, instead of eating in bed, and I sat across from her, wishing I could think of how to tell her.

"The willows are turning yellow," I said.

"I guess you'll be leaving soon, then, won't you? For Cuttyhunk, I mean." Consuela was matter-of-fact and continued her breakfast while she said this.

"But how did you—?"

"Mrs. Veeder," broke in Consuela. "She called while you were away. I asked your mother if she knew anything about it, and then put it together. I also talked to Lucy."

"Lucy? What for?"

"I wanted to. There is so much I didn't, don't know. While you were in Ewell-Lowe I tried to find out as much as I could. About the drinking, about your great-grandparents, about Lucy, and Omar."

"Well?" I was stunned and relieved at the same time.

"Although you haven't actually said it, I know you think there is something strange between you and the dog. There was probably something strange between George Livingston and the dog, too, don't you think? Then there's this business with the intermarriages. When I talked to Lucy, whom, incidentally, I liked—"

"You did?" I was astonished. "I think she has gotten very peculiar. In fact, she scared me."

"I liked her. She seems to think that Waffles and maybe even you are in league with the devil, but that's a little far-fetched. Your mother and Philip Potter—oh yes, I talked to him, too—they believe your troubles are more psychological and hereditary."

"And you?" I asked Consuela. "What do *you* think?"

"I think you're probably right to go away, or at least try it. You're so changed—removed and frightened on the one hand, contentious on the other—that I don't know what to think. You seem to be outside everything. I don't feel that the children or I really reach you any more anyway. I'm tired." She stood up, and I helped her back to bed. "Maybe next week you could go. Don't tell the children, though. Let me do it after you've gone."

And so at quarter of six on St. Patrick's Day morning, I bade a still good-by to the sleeping household. The silver cups and porringers hung dingy with tarnish on their hooks over the sink. In an hour they would overflow with orange juice and Cheerios. I glanced at my garden as I went out to the car, where Kip waited, engine running, to drive me to Fairhaven and the eight o'clock boat to Cuttyhunk. The snow had melted partially and in the light from the kitchen I could just see the thick blanket of old manure protecting my plants. The roses needed pruning, but I put that thought away with all mainland responsibility and turned inward to myself.

part 3

END

Cuttyhunk Island

Thursday, September 26

Dearest Consuela,

Perhaps it is still too early to tell you, but I think it is safe. I refer, of course, to the title of this notebook, I will type it again: E N D. This is what happened.

Saturday, the day before the hurricane hit, I mailed the notebooks off to you, you must have them by now. That night, the air was ominously still and heavy, and even though I was exhausted, once again I couldn't sleep. Waffles was restless, too. It seemed that every time I would doze off, he would wake me up again, either by jumping off or on the bed, or merely by prowling around with his scratchy toenails on the linoleum. For several months I wondered if he wasn't deliberately trying to keep me from sleeping. Anyway, Sunday morning I was more wrung-out than usual. I hadn't slept for days, and couldn't be bothered to eat. I lay on my bed, only dimly aware of the hurricane preparations going on around me. Cuttyhunk, as you know, is always hard-hit in these storms, the water damage great along the shore, and the wind destruction great up on the hill. But none of it mattered to me. Several well-meaning islanders came to the door to offer me refuge on higher land, but I turned them down or scared them away with my snaggle-toothed smile. As I said, the hurricane didn't matter, all I wanted was peace.

Waffles was horrible and wouldn't leave me alone. I wanted to sleep in the morning as the hurricane moved in, but Waffles tried to play with me and then lovingly tried to make amends for disturbing me, first one then the other, until I thought I would go mad. Out of desperation I began to weep. He stared at me, for a few minutes mildly interested in my discomfort, and then sauntered to the door to be let out. I got out of bed and released him into the gray wet wind. He looked so thin and frail as he headed down the steps that I immediately felt guilty, sending him out in an incipient hurricane.

229

"Hey, Waffles," I called. He stopped but did not turn around. "Be careful, will you? Don't stay out too long, boy." He walked away from me without acknowledging my admonition. I guessed with all that wind he hadn't heard me, but at the same time, I felt hurt, neglected in a way. Lately, Waffles had been restless, had made me feel inadequate, or superannuated. Was I disappointing him in some way? Was he looking for another, more devoted master? What rot, I thought, and closed the door.

In spite of the wind and the rain and the rattling windows, the house had a calmness which soothed me. I went to the table and looked at my books: The Book of Common Prayer, St. Andrew's Missal, and the King James Red Letter Edition Holy Bible were in one pile, and next to them, the four books on demonology from Lucy. I picked up the top devil book and brought it to the bed, stretched out and began to read. I had no interruptions, Waffles was outside. I read the first few pages, about a French girl in the fifteenth century who was possessed by a devil, and I fell asleep thinking, *poor child,* and then I sighed with relief as I slept at last.

I don't know whether it was Waffles scratching to come in or the storm which woke me up. I know that I was conscious of both as I slept through the last seconds of my bold daylight dream. Yes, again it was the sponge, but this time must have been the grand finale. I watched Waffles drag a succession of sponge corpses past me to an open mass grave. First George, whose eyes somehow remained alive though the rest of him was cellulose. He winked at me as Waffles pulled him in front of me, and into the trench. Then came Polly, Aunt Edith, Miles, and then a very little sponge with stunted limbs, each one twisted at the end like a pretzel. When Waffles dragged the baby sponge to the grave, Consuela, Rebecca, Cam, Justin, and Ward followed him, dressed in black all singing the *Dies Irae.* Ward held a sea gull sponge, which he dropped in the grave on top of the other sponges. Lucy, all cured, and Omar appeared with shovels. They were laughing, and slapping each other's backs. Then everyone lined up beside the open earth and waited. Waffles grinned as he trotted past me on his way to get another trophy, and his head became, for an instant, a leering death's head. The last sponge was very fresh, so fresh that the metamorphosis wasn't yet complete. The last sponge was me.

The horror of the dream remained after I woke up and went to the door to let in Waffles. I was shaking so hard and had so little strength left that I could barely push the door open against the wind. It opened with a rush and whammed out of my hand, banging flat against the outside of the house. I stood shivering face to face with Waffles. Fully awake now, I could still trace the death's head and the sneer on his pointed face. We stared at each other while the door slammed again and again against the house. He finally blinked his large protuberant eyes and tried to nuzzle my hand.

"No, it won't work any more. I know you now. Legion. Legion's curse, that's what George said as he died. You can't come in." I stepped outside to grab the door handle, intending to shut Waffles out, once and for all, but of course, it couldn't be that easy. While I struggled to pull the door against the wind, Waffles managed to get between me and the threshold. He lunged at my throat just as the wind got behind the door. The door slapped me into Waffles as it slammed shut, throwing him and his deadly bite askew, momentarily.

Once inside the house, the fight took on a tense carefulness. Waffles' advantage lay in his lightning speed and in his cunning. My intelligence and strength were supposedly superior, but I had gone to seed and couldn't count on anything except my consuming hatred. My fishing rod stood next to the door. I grabbed it and managed to give Waffles a few savage licks before he jumped for my throat again. And so we went, around and around the room, first the whirr of my fishing rod as it sliced the air and then a smack! as it sliced him. Followed by an ugly guttural rattle from Waffles and a fast strike, like a snake. The storm lashed outside; inside we stalked and panted, and every now and then broke our thick silence with a fleeting skirmish. I had no idea how long Waffles and I had been at it, only that I began to feel my hatred suffocate under the weight of tiredness, when the noise of the hurricane dropped. I was next to the porch windows, facing Waffles, who crouched against the adjacent wall. I slid my eyes quickly to the windows and back to Waffles, and felt his muscles tighten for a lunge even in that split second that I did not watch only him. But I had seen through a clearing in the salt-caked window that it was lighter outside, and I thought I saw a bright edge of blue in the southwest sky. Maybe the eye of the hurricane would pass over us. Yesterday someone had said something about that, what was it? Cuttyhunk attracted eyes of storms, something to do with magnetic variance? But I was too tired to reconstruct it.

Waffles' eyes burned red as he waited in the shadows. They reminded me of something but I didn't know what. I was too tired now to care. But the half-formed memory nagged and pinched. Waffles was bleeding from the welts on his back, but he was still vigilant. I couldn't let go now, no, I must stay alert. What was it in his eyes, must remember, something about an army—Napoleon? Hannibal? Washington? Genghis Khan? While I tried to figure it out, I stole closer to Waffles. He backed up, moved down the wall to the other corner.

Then I remembered. Attacking with the sun at his back, and thereby blinding his enemy. It seemed then like divine revelation. I lashed out with the pole again, thinking, *that's about it, no more strength,* but at least I maneuvered him so that he was facing me and the windows. I only had to wait a few seconds. The sun flashed in his eyes and in that first second of blindness, I wrung his neck. It only took a few wrings to kill him, I felt him go limp, but I couldn't stop twisting. A new energy and power surged through me. I stood in the hurricane sun and disfigured, abused, violated what had been so sickeningly sacred. I don't exactly know what made me stop, but when I did, I saw how dark it had grown, and heard the windows resume their rattling.

I opened the door, again the wind blew it out and against the house. Then I went to the dead dog and kicked and dragged what was left of him out to the porch and down the steps. The water was rising fast and was only a few yards from the house. The sky was gray again, the blue eye moving off up the Sound. I felt rain on my face. The water felt good, so I stood there for a few minutes, letting it sprinkle me while I tried to rub away some of the blood, mine and Waffles', which seemed to cover me.

It would be high tide in another hour or so, I thought automatically, high tide and the backlash would hit together. I turned away from Waffles and the rising tide and let the wind blow me up the hill to the church. The sumac trees bowed to the ground in the howling wind, the rain stung as it whipped me, and yet for the first time in many months I was quiet inside.

The church was full of evacuees, like myself. They welcomed me with coffee and dry blankets, and praise. "Mr. Murray! Oh, thank God you're all right!" How could they lavish so much care, so much feeling on me, when I had seldom even returned their terse hellos? I rejoiced in the wind, rain and humanity. Like my neighbors, I, too, thanked God, two words, thank you, lay down on the hard pew and slept like a baby.

The next morning, I woke to a clean world. Oh, there was debris everywhere scattered about, but it didn't matter, everything was purged. At least, that's how I saw it. Charlie's little house had taken a beating; the door had blown completely off its hinges and the water had rushed in. I looked for Waffles near the steps, where I had kicked him, but there was no trace.

The flood tide had trickled out the channel of Cuttyhunk Pond to Vineyard Sound and Buzzards Bay, where it had come from. Today the pond was September blue and flat. I walked down to the shore, careful to avoid the litter in my path. I knew I was looking for Waffles but I looked for him reluctantly, he was no longer important to me. His death, however, was.

I finally found his body quite far out on the point, where it was abandoned by the water sucking out of the Pond. There were a few drowned water rats, too, and a lot of other junk washed up. A lot to clean up.

We've been busy since then, Consuela, but I think everything's in order now. In a few days, after you've gotten this letter, I'm coming home.

Love,
Hugh